4

D1707206

The Little STOREHOUSE in the Middle of the Block

Bruce Rolfe

BRUCE ROLFE

δ
Dingbat Publishing
Humble, Texas

THE LITTLE STOREHOUSE IN THE MIDDLE OF THE BLOCK

All Rights Reserved
Copyright © 2024 BRUCE ROLFE

Primary print ISBN 9-798-329296891

Published in the United States of America
Dingbat Publishing
Humble, Texas

All rights reserved. No part of this book may be reproduced in any form or by any means without written consent, excepting brief quotes used in reviews.

This book is licensed to the original purchaser only. Duplication or distribution via any means is illegal and a violation of International Copyright Law, subject to criminal prosecution and upon conviction, fines and/or imprisonment. No part of this book can be reproduced or sold by any person or business without the express permission of the publisher.

Thank you for respecting the hard work of this author.

This is a work of fiction. Names, places, characters, and events are entirely the product of the author's imagination or are used fictiously, and any resemblance to persons living or dead, actual locations, events, or organizations is coincidental.

FOR CORA,
Grace, beauty, style, & love.
You will forever be my always.

PROLOGUE

My name is Harry Morgan Hamilton and I'm an alcoholic. Other than my penchant for writing, a life well lubricated with alcohol is the only thing I have in common with William Faulkner, F. Scott Fitzgerald, Ernest Hemingway, Raymond Chandler, Ian Fleming, and Truman Capote et al. After dealing with pushy retail customers and inept salesclerks on a daily basis for the past 17 years at the Fashion Valley Nordstrom in San Diego, California, I can truly relate with why these great writers sought solace at the bottom of a bottle. Not that sobriety is any consolation for writing pulp fiction or remaining unpublished.

It's been ten years — seems longer — since I awoke and stumbled into the bathroom with head pounding and mouth tasting like a circus had just moved out. I didn't like myself much as I gazed into the mirror through bleary, bloodshot eyes and recalled a meaningless acquaintance's voice on the phone from the night before. "You really should stop drinking, Morgan," she'd said. And in one lucid moment of revelation I pushed myself away from the sink, turned and stumbled out into the kitchen, and began pouring the contents of every liquor, wine, and beer bottle down the drain. Still, it takes a hell of a lot of willpower to quit cold turkey, and if there's one thing that hadn't been pickled beyond salvation during those sodden years it was that. Unfortunately, I'd never employed it sooner. Otherwise, my son Bobby wouldn't be in prison and my novels might already be in print.

I have always loved to read and, ever since I can remember, my mom encouraged me to write, constantly reminding me how great I could become if only I applied myself. However, it wasn't until I sobered up and began staring down retirement that I took her advice seriously. With a retail career maxed out and at least half my life gone, my youthful dreams of becoming a big-time writer like Upton Sinclair, Norman Mailer, John Updike, or Gore Vidal returned. I set my goal to win a Pulitzer with my first novel because Mom always said it was the best way to jumpstart a writing career. With file drawers filled with half a dozen finished and unpublished manuscripts that have been turned down with hundreds of rejection letters, I believe she may have a point.

Norman Mailer supposedly said that "In America, a writer can make a killing, but not a living," which is why I've been supporting my family by working retail and writing in my spare time. I'd be kidding myself if I said I wrote for the money. In the past few years I'd made less than $100 selling one short story and two humorous anecdotes to periodicals. Nothing Mom would have been proud of but, to be honest, it was euphoric seeing my name in print. Having a publication pay for my writing seemed not only to validate it, but also temporarily assuage the nagging self-worth doubt of a budding mid-life crisis.

Nevertheless, in a publishing industry that spends millions on sensational true crime stories, autobiographies by scandalous politicians, and memoirs of neophyte and has-been celebrities, there seems to be little or no money left over for purchasing quality fiction. Marketability appears to have trumped writing ability and it's extremely frustrating reading book reviews every weekend by critics who pan the latest popular releases, while I'm collecting rejection letters for what I consider much better stories.

Meanwhile, Bobby is doing 10 to 25 for second-degree murder while under the influence, which is truly heartbreaking and, except for the guilt I feel, certainly nothing to write about — least ways not an entire narrative that anyone besides family members or close friends would be interested in reading — even for the cathartic release. However, when the telephone jangled on the bedstand beside my head early one morning a little more than three years ago, it began a sequence of events that would make a compelling memoir with definite marketability. All I had to do was write it.

ONE

Putting it down on paper was more difficult than I imagined as I recalled the strange male voice on the phone.

"Mr. Hamilton?"

"Yeah," I'd said, trying to read the digital clock on my wife's side of the bed. "Who wants to know?"

"Mr. Hamilton, this is Detective Meadows from the Sedona, Arizona Police Department." His gravelly voice vibrated the earpiece. "I apologize about the early hour, but I'm afraid I have some bad news. A neighbor found your mother's body last night and—"

"W-what?" I interrupted, thinking I must be having a bad dream. "Found where? What are you talking about?"

"We're still investigating, sir. However, I wanted to notify you as soon as possible."

The red numbers came into focus: 6:15 a.m. I didn't know what to say as I tried to clear the cobwebs out of my head and wrap my mind around what he'd just said: my mother was dead! I couldn't believe it, but told the detective my wife and I would drive over and be there sometime later that day.

Nobody expects their parents to live forever and I'm certainly no exception, because deep down we all know that someday we'll have to say goodbye. Although Mom was 71, she appeared to be in good health and was always on the go. Every time Gloria and I tried to schedule a visit she would make a big deal about having to cancel or reschedule some social activity or club meeting. Then it was almost embarrassing the way she fawned over me in front of her friends in the Chamber of Commerce or at Friday night Bunco when we did get over there. I thought she had at least another ten years before we'd have to consider any changes to her lifestyle.

It seems that no one ever picks a convenient time to die and my mother certainly was no exception. Right before Memorial Day, with sales promotions and extended shopping hours already in the works. I turned things over to my young assistant, Justin Forsyth, giving him his chance to shine. Then Gloria and I set out for Sedona, amid the crush of holiday weekend drivers clogging the highways, to make funeral arrangements and do whatever else we had to do.

The afternoon sun glared off the windshields of approaching cars, causing me to squint as we arrived at the intersection of Highways 179 and 89A in "Red Rock Country," which is what Sedona residents called Arizona's premier resort, recreation, and retirement center. Driving through the canyon, I often wondered what the first settlers must have thought about the magnificent geological creations as their covered wagons creaked and groaned across the desert hardpan. Descriptive names of formations such as Chimney Rock, Coffee Pot Rock, and Steamboat Rock offered a clue. The rugged terracotta landscape provided an unbelievable backdrop to cottonwood and sycamore trees surrounding my mother's adobe brown, Del Sol townhouse complex. I couldn't begin to imagine a world without Mom as Gloria and I walked up the sidewalk where bright yellow tape with **CRIME SCENE, DO NOT CROSS** in bold black letters was tacked across her doorway. I hadn't had a drink in ten years but, at that moment, one sure sounded good.

TWO

The door opened and man about my height, built like a bull-dog, said, "Mr. Hamilton?" I immediately recognized the gruff voice. He was wearing a dark brown suit, light blue Oxford shirt with a burgundy tie, and blue protective shoe covers over what appeared to be brown penny loafers. A silver shield with Sedona Police highlighted in turquoise enamel hung from a lanyard around his neck and white latex gloves covered his hands.

I nodded, unable to speak.

"I'm Detective Meadows," he said, pulling the glove off his right hand and extending it past the crime scene tape barring the door. "I'm sorry about your loss."

Gloria grabbed my other hand and squeezed as I stared at the tape.

"W-what's going on?" I stammered, reaching for his hand.

"We're not exactly sure, but we're just about to wrap up here. As soon as my investigators leave I'd like you to take a look around and tell us if you notice anything of your mother's that might be missing."

I saw two men behind him, dressed in black cargo pants and black polo shirts with Sedona CSI embroidered on the left front in turquoise and their names on the right. They wore highly polished black boots and tool belts with radios, flashlights, and various other items clipped around their waists, looking nothing like any of the investigators I'd seen on TV crime shows as they stepped around a large brown stain and shards of glass on the carpet in front of Mom's sofa.

Detective Meadows ducked beneath the tape as he stepped out and closed the door behind him. "Why don't we wait in the car," he said.

Gloria held my hand as we followed him to his unmarked patrol car and took a seat in the back with the doors open. The afternoon sun burned down from a cloudless sky and it was probably twenty degrees hotter than when we'd left balmy San Diego. Meadows sat behind the wheel and started the car before turning sideways and draping his arm over the back of the passenger's seat. Even his eyes appeared turquoise as he glanced between my wife and me.

"What happened to Morgan's mother?" Gloria asked.

He took a deep breath and let it out as he turned on the air conditioner. "It looks like she fell and hit her head on the corner of the coffee table, lost consciousness, and bled out. But we're not ruling it an accident until the medical examiner has had a chance to perform an autopsy."

"Is that really necessary?" I asked, feeling my shirt sticking to my back against the plastic seat cover.

"I'm afraid so; he's already taken her body. Because your mother didn't die naturally and didn't die witnessed, it moves her death into the category of unexpected or unexplained, which is somewhat suspicious. Do you happen to know if she had a medical condition that might have affected her balance or caused her to pass out?"

It had never crossed my mind that my mother could possibly have been murdered.

"No," Gloria said, "she was healthy as a horse."

"How about an excessive use of alcohol?" he asked as the first blast of cool air whooshed from the vents.

"My mother doesn't drink," I said, a bit too defensively, "never has."

His eyes narrowed as he looked at me. "How about enemies? Was there anyone you know who might want to harm her?"

"Everyone loved Jenny," Gloria said, placing a warm hand on the top of my thigh and gently patting. "She would give anyone who needed it the shirt off her back. We couldn't go anywhere that she wouldn't drop a few dollars into some homeless person's hand or offer to buy them a meal."

I looked at her askance.

Meadows closed his door and indicated for us to do likewise. "Did she ever offer to bring them home? Pay them to work around the house?"

"She may have been charitable, Detective," I said as Gloria and I simultaneously closed our doors, "but she wasn't foolish. What makes you ask?"

"Even though there was no sign of a break-in, and nothing seems out of place except for the broken coffee table, we still have to ask. Nevertheless, we'd like you to get back to us after you've had time to look things over."

"That may take a while," Gloria said. "We don't get over here as often as we should. Jenny may have gotten rid of some of her things and I'm sure she wouldn't have checked with us first."

"I'm more concerned with items that could be easily pawned or sold; jewelry, electronics, coin collections, things like that," he said, as the door to Mom's townhouse opened and the two investigators walked out carrying toolboxes and several brown paper bags stapled at the top. The car was just beginning to cool off.

THREE

Over the years many of my friends have lost parents to heart failure or cancer, while others watched the ravages of Alzheimer's slowly steal them away. I suppose I was lucky because Mom was vibrant and healthy. Although she sometimes kidded about living long enough to gracefully don the mantle of eccentricity, others thought her a curmudgeonly old woman with no sense of humor. But her mind never faltered. I loved the way she'd raise eyebrows with comments such as "The First Amendment was ratified to protect us from Republicans and the Second to protect us from the Democrats." It was an endearing trait that brought us closer together, even throughout my teenage years. I'm sure she would have injected just the right amount of cynicism into the present situation to distance us all from the pain of her death.

Mom's place was just as I remembered when we stepped through the doorway; I half expected her to waltz out of the kitchen and greet us with a tray of fresh-baked cookies and tall glasses of ice-cold milk. I swallowed hard and asked Gloria where she thought we should begin.

She stepped by my side, pulled a tissue from her purse, and handed it to me. "Detective Meadows said the medical examiner will be releasing her body within seventy-two hours. Now would probably be a good time to make the necessary funeral arrangements and call Barbara and the kids."

My sister didn't have the capacity or wherewithal to get herself to Sedona before then anyway. So, after wiping my eyes and blowing my nose, I contacted a travel agent, made reservations, and paid for her ticket. I then called St. Andrew's Episcopal Church and talked to Mom's priest before calling Barbara, hoping that maybe at 4:30 in the afternoon I'd catch her sober. However, my sister lived in Brunswick, Maine, and my mistake was not taking the different time zones into account. At 7:30 p.m. her cocktail hour was well underway.

Ice clinked against glass as she answered the phone, slurping at whatever was in the tumbler and stumbling over her words. A mournful, guttural sound emanated through the telephone after I told her Mom was dead.

"Noooo." She wailed. "No. No. No!"

I tried to make her understand that all she had to do was get to the airport in Portland by 10 o'clock the day after tomorrow and I would pick her up in Phoenix. It was difficult to know for certain whether or not I'd gotten through and resigned myself to the fact that I wouldn't know until the plane arrived. Undoubtedly Barbara would drink herself to sleep the next two nights and I could only hope that she would wake in time to catch the mid-morning flight on Tuesday. Even hungover she should be able to call a cab and it was the one arrangement I'd left up to her.

I couldn't get through to Bobby, who'd told me that he was planning on going camping over the long weekend in Hole-in-the-Wall Campground near Essex, California, which was in the Mojave Desert about 230 miles east of Los Angeles. So I doubted that he had cellphone service. My daughter, Debby, and her family lived in Palm Springs where, according to the Zagat Guide for Southern California, they owned one of the ten best restaurants. My timing wasn't much better when I reached her as they were busy prepping for the evening meal.

"Hello, kitten," I said, after one of the waitresses who'd answered the phone found her and told her who was calling.

"What's the matter, Dad?"

"I've got some bad news. How could you tell?"

"By your voice and... you also never call at this time of day. What's wrong?"

There was no sense beating around the bush so I just came out and said, "Your grandmother Jenny has passed away."

"Oh, no; where are you?"

"At her place; your mother and I drove over this afternoon. The police were here and have taken her body in for an autopsy."

"Oh, good heavens; did someone kill her?"

"They don't really know, but I don't think so. It looks like she fell and hit her head on the coffee table and bled to death before she regained consciousness."

"That's horrible. What can I do?"

"I'd like you to be able to come over for the funeral on Wednesday, if you can."

"Certainly. I'll bring little Morgan with me, but I doubt that Bud will be able to make it."

"That's fine," I said. I couldn't remember if they'd ever met anyway. "See if you can get hold of your brother. He said he was going camping in the Mojave Desert this weekend and I've been unable to contact him."

"Probably doesn't have cell service, but I'll keep trying."

✖ ✖

By the time I'd finished with my phone calls I felt wrung out and didn't feel like doing one more thing. Detective Meadows would just have to wait for us to inventory Mom's things over the weekend. I handed Gloria the keys and she drove us to Poco Diablo Resort where we regularly stayed when visiting Mom. After checking in we went to the local bar & grill for dinner. Gloria had a Cobb salad. I ordered pan-seared salmon and a bottle of beer. Gloria glanced at me with disapproval, which wasn't necessary. I felt guilty enough stepping off the wagon after ten years.

When we returned to our room the message light was blinking on the resort phone. I called the desk and was informed my daughter had phoned with an emergency and needed me to return her call.

The background noise in the restaurant kitchen was annoying as I listened to Debby explain how Bobby had totaled his car early that morning and was in the Needles City jail after being arrested for driving under the influence.

"He called me after I talked to you; didn't want you to know."

"Is he okay?"

"Of course he's not okay, Dad, he's in jail."

"I mean, was he injured in the accident?"

"He said he got a few stitches in his hand and bumped his head, but couldn't tell if it hurt from the accident or beating it against the wall withdrawing from the heroin."

"Heroin! What the hell, Debby, what the hell?"

"I know, Dad. I'm sorry to be the one to tell you, but somebody had to. He's been using for a few months now — nothing serious, just chipping — but had it under control. He just hadn't worked up the courage to ask you for help."

"Did you tell him about Mom?"

"His five-minute call ended before I got the chance."

I couldn't breathe and handed the phone to Gloria. This was my fault; I should have noticed that he was developing a substance abuse disorder along with his increased drinking. I'd been there myself. But heroin; there's no way I could ever have imagined that.

"We'll go see him tomorrow," Gloria said, just before hanging up. She turned to me; her eyes filled with tears.

"What about Mom?" I asked.

"Jenny's dead, Morgan. Bobby isn't. We need to see if we can help him and let him know about his grandmother. They were very close and he doesn't deserve to find out about it over the phone or, worse yet, in a letter. We can always reschedule the funeral."

✖ ✖

Gloria had gone online and looked up inmate visitation requirements for the Needles City jail, while I went for a run to relieve the stress. Inmates were allowed visitors from 1:00 p.m. to 3:30 p.m. and we dressed accordingly before heading out the next morning. Needles was close to a four-hour drive from Sedona; 30 miles up I-17 N to Flagstaff, which was a few miles more than taking 89A, but five minutes faster, and then 210 miles on I-40 W. We got an early start, stopping for breakfast at the Roadkill Café & OK Saloon in Seligman about two hours later. Unless the next town was more than half an hour down the road, or there was nothing else around, Gloria and I rarely ate in chain restaurants or fast-food diners and were seldom disappointed. I gave the Roadkill Café four out of five stars.

Arriving in Needles we got off the Interstate at the J Street exit, which was part of historic US 66. Three blocks later I pulled into the San Bernardino County Sheriff's Department parking lot at quarter to one. *Perfect timing*, I thought, as I locked all our personal belongings in the interior trunk. The entryway was far more inviting than what I feared awaited us inside as we approached the double glass doors.

The desk sergeant checked our photo IDs and told us that our son had been involved in a motor vehicle accident going the wrong way on the Interstate while high on alcohol and drugs. He hadn't been badly hurt but, unfortunately, the occupant of the other car hadn't fared as well. The driver had been pinned inside her vehicle and had to wait two hours before emergency responders could free her using the Jaws of Life. She'd experienced a lot of blood loss from internal organ damage and was still in critical condition at the Colorado River Medical Center down the block.

"The arresting officer gave your son a field sobriety check at the scene, which he failed, and then a breath test, which he also failed. After that he took him into custody and brought him to have his hand stitched up and a blood sample drawn; it'll take a few days to get the results back. Meanwhile, the prosecutor is deciding whether to charge him with a misdemeanor or felony DUI based on the victim's condition."

"Oh, good grief," Gloria said. "When can we see him?"

FOUR

Bobby looked like hell when we finally got into the visiting booth and found him already seated on the other side of the glass. His nose dripped as he grabbed both of his elbows and trembled at the sight of us. Although he'd been taken to the medical center and checked out the morning before, and then incarcerated, he still had blood and vomit on his sweat-stained clothes.

Gloria collapsed in the chair and burst into tears. "Oh, Bobby," she said. "Bobby, Bobby, Bobby. What are we going to do with you?"

His shoulders slumped as he reached for the phone receiver hanging beside the window.

More tears trickled down my wife's face as I stood beside her and picked up the receiver on our side. I tried to hand it to her.

She closed her eyes and shook her head as she wept.

"We only have thirty minutes," I said.

She sniffled and nodded and fumbled for a tissue in her pocket.

I waited while she blew her nose and dried her eyes as much as possible before taking the receiver. I leaned in close to share it with her. "You want to tell us what happened, Bobby?" she asked.

"I don't know, Mom," he said with a catch in his throat. "I— I don't remember."

He was visibly shaking, whether from withdrawal or from anxiety I didn't know. But just the way he answered gave me pause. It wasn't always easy to tell when he was lying, but I suspected that he was.

"They're not going to release you until next Thursday at

the earliest, son," I said, leaning over my wife's shoulder.

"What do you mean!" he said, raising his voice enough for me to hear two feet away. "They can't hold me more than 48 hours without charging me."

"The desk sergeant said they actually have 72," I said, "which doesn't include weekends and holidays. So, is there anything you need that we can get for you before then?"

Bobby glanced around, shaking his head in disbelief. "No, that's wrong."

"Afraid not, Bobby; they're going to keep you until the prosecuting attorney makes up his mind about what to charge you with, and that will depend on what happens with the woman you smashed into. I'm sure she doesn't want to be where she is either."

Gloria shivered beside me.

"You've got to get me out of here, Dad."

"Oh, Bobby," Gloria said, "we'll do what we can, but we've got our hands full at the moment. Your grandmother died last Friday and your father and I—"

"Oh, my gosh!" he interrupted. "W-where, h-how? What happened?"

"We think she had a stroke," Gloria said.

"Actually," I said, "she bled to death after falling and hitting her head on the coffee table in her living room. A stroke wouldn't have killed her by itself." I glanced down at Gloria. "And, if she'd been living with us as I wanted, she'd still be alive."

Gloria lowered the receiver and looked at me. "You don't know that, Morgan. You're not a doctor and we've talked about having Jenny move in with us several times. But she didn't want to be a burden. Besides, if she had moved in with us, it could have just as easily happened while we were both out. She could have bled to death in our living room. Think how you'd feel about coming home from work and finding her that way. As it was, the medical examiner said she didn't suffer."

"What would he know? It could have taken hours for her to bleed out. Lying there helpless on the floor knowing she would eventually die if she didn't get help. Don't tell me she didn't suffer."

"Stop it," Bobby yelled, raising his injured fist and pounding it against the glass, immediately attracting a guard's attention on the other side.

"You got a problem, Hamilton?" The guard's voice came through the receiver loud and clear.

"My parents just told me my grandmother died," Bobby said.

"One more outburst, Hamilton," the guard said, stepping up behind my son and placing his right hand on the nightstick hanging from a wide, black-leather belt, "and this visiting session is over."

Bobby dropped his hand and clutched his stomach. "Yes, sir," he said in a low guttural voice. "It won't happen again."

"It better not," the guard said, removing his hand from the club.

Bobby's eyes looked teary but I knew he wasn't going to cry where other inmates could see him. Maybe later in his cell when the lights were out — if he was lucky enough to have a cell of his own in such a small facility — but not there and then. He and Jenny had been close — even closer than she and I, if such a thing was possible.

Before heading back to Sedona, we drove up to the Wal-Mart in Ft. Mohave and picked up a change of clothes and some personal hygiene items for our son.

✖ ✖

Barbara's flight arrived at Sky Harbor International on schedule Tuesday morning, and I waited as all the passengers deplaned and several crewmembers, including the pilots, exited the waiting area pulling their carry-on luggage behind. However, when a new crew headed out the gate, I asked an attendant standing behind the check-in counter if my sister's name was on the previous manifest. As she was checking, I heard Barbara's voice and looked up in time to see her ricochet off the doorjamb left of the boarding ramp and stumble into the waiting area, cursing at the flight attendant who was trying to keep her from falling. The young man appeared exceedingly glad to see me as I slipped my arm through Barbara's. After expressing an apology and my appreciation to both attendants, I led her down the concourse. Barbara ranted about the male *stewardess* who'd refused to sell her any more than two little drinkies long after we'd retrieved her luggage and exited the airport.

It was about 110 miles to Sedona, most of them straight up I-17 past or through a plethora of interesting-sounding places such as Montezuma's Castle, Dead Man Wash, Horse Thief Basin, Bloody Basin Road, and Big Bug Creek. I stopped at Sunset Point, a rest area about halfway, because Barbara had to go to the bathroom. She staggered to the flagstone restroom embarrassingly drunk, trying to hold onto her shoulder bag, which kept sliding off her arm every time she lurched. Her gait seemed a bit steadier as she returned to the car and dropped heavily into the bucket seat, her purse sloshing as she set it on the floor between her feet.

Although she chewed noisily on a stick of Wrigley's Doublemint Gum, her breath still reeked of alcohol.

"Who do you think you're kidding?" I said, looking away and cranking the engine, trying to lose myself in the powerful rumble emanating from twin glass packs as I backed out of the parking space.

"How much farther is it?" she asked, ignoring the question.

"Not far enough for you to sober up," I said.

"I don' know what ch're talkin' 'bout."

They say it takes an alcoholic to know an alcoholic, but I don't know if that's true. After Dad died and Barbara went off the deep end, no one seemed to recognize or even care about her excessive drinking. Not even me. And everyone knew I was a drunk — everyone, that is, except me.

"I didn't think so," I said, mashing the accelerator to the floor and squealing the tires. The back end of my '86 Corvette fishtailed ever so slightly, leaving twin black tread marks on the asphalt behind us, and I wondered if I'd made a mistake insisting she come out. Instead of helping me cope with Mom's death, would my sister ultimately drag me back into the very bottle I'd crawled out of three years after she crawled in? As I reentered the highway, Barbara's head lolled back and her mouth gaped open.

FIVE

The day of Mom's funeral rain drummed on dozens of colorful golf umbrellas with a dull, thudding monotony. It was unusual for it to rain in Sedona during the month of May, but somehow it just seemed fitting. Father John stood behind Mom's casket delivering the eulogy. Graveyard plots, each separately surrounded with foot-high adobe brick walls terraced up the gently sloping hillside of Sedona Community Cemetery, blended seamlessly with the natural desert ecosystem of prickly pear cacti and yucca plants under a canopy of pinyon pines. Cold, steel-gray clouds pressed down, obscuring a normally magnificent vista that surrounded the memorial park. I cleared my throat and buried my nose in a handkerchief after the priest finished the eulogy and a choral group began the a cappella finale of "Amazing Grace."

After the funeral we went to work sorting through Mom's personal belongings so we could notify Detective Meadows if we thought anything was missing. The only thing I really cared about was Mom's Seth Thomas eight-day clock with Westminster chimes. It had been in the family three generations, originally a wedding present given to my great-grandmother by her parents, and had been passed down to her son when she died. I remember my grandfather would open the glass face-cover every Sunday after church and wind the clock, using a large brass key that lay on the mantle beside it, before setting the time to coincide with his shiny gold pocket watch. When he died, my father became the keeper of the clock until leaving it for Mom. I'm not sure what happened to his pocket watch, but I felt powerfully drawn to the old timepiece even though, at the moment, it stood eerily silently. The stopped hands were another sad reminder of my mother's untimely death. I just hoped Barbara wouldn't want it, too.

"Let's begin in the kitchen," Gloria said, explaining that there were fewer personal items in the cupboards and it might be less painful for Barbara and me to sort through them first. My sister readily agreed and excused herself, returning from the bathroom just as I finished winding the clock and setting the key down beside it.

I glanced warily at her and carefully tilted the clock to one side before easing it down again, setting the pendulum in motion. Almost immediately the resonant tick-tocking soothed my jangled nerves and the syncopated rhythm slowly began to regulate my breathing. Not having the pocket watch, I checked the quartz Seiko on my wrist and advanced the frilly black minute hand around the old clock's tattered white face, stopping at fifteen-minute intervals to delight in the familiar melodic chimes. After setting the correct time and closing the face-cover, I noticed Barbara chewing ferociously on a piece of gum and nodded to Gloria that we should get started. My sister wouldn't be much help for very long.

One of the first nostalgic items we came across was our boot-shaped Roy Rogers and Dale Evans drinking mugs. Barbara's was molded from pink plastic and mine from blue. As I turned the forgotten mug over in my hand, a folded fifty-dollar bill fell out onto the kitchen floor. Barbara quickly turned her mug over and shook out two more, which she thought was only fair. Then Gloria produced a cashbox she found in the back of Mom's pantry with a little more than two hundred silver dollars in it, to which we added our new-found booty.

In the silverware drawer there was a hundred-dollar bill wedged under the Rubbermaid tray, between the partitioned recesses created to separate knives from forks and forks from spoons, which refocused our attention. We found money in the oddest places: a Ziploc freezer bag full of Mercury head dimes buried inside a Tupperware container holding two pounds of flour. A roll of twenties bound with rubber bands tucked inside a false-bottomed can of Del Monte corn, a folded fifty under a potted silk geranium on the windowsill, and another hundred frozen to the bottom of an ice tray in the freezer. Mom had stashed another $150 in tens between the pages of her cookbooks, and a wad of one dollar silver certificates inside a half-eaten box of Wheaties. I wondered if she'd ever thrown money out after finishing a box of cereal and was sure that we might have if Gloria hadn't insisted we look in, behind, and under everything imaginable. If there was any more rat-holed cash in the kitchen we didn't find it. But it wasn't for lack of looking, or because someone had stolen it.

Mom had lived through the Depression, which obviously was the reason she avoided keeping her money in the bank, but the more we found scattered throughout the house the more ambivalent I began to feel. A sense of sorrow was understandable, but the morbid sort of thankfulness eluded me until I realized Barbara was more interested in finding the money than drinking. By nightfall her hands were shaking so badly she wasn't able to hold a half-filled glass of water without sloshing some over the side. It didn't take a rocket scientist to know that any rehabilitation program she might undertake, either now or in the future, would have to include medical help.

There was a feeling of aloneness in the realization that with both our parents gone my younger sister could possibly predecease me if she didn't change her lifestyle. Of course, it was foolish to feel that way with Gloria and Debby and her family giving me all the love and support I could possibly want. But with my son in jail facing felony DUI charges I did, and I couldn't expect my wife to understand since both her parents and siblings were very much alive and sober. So, I said nothing.

Gloria wanted to drive back to Needles and bail our son out of jail but I was torn. Bobby was 23, a full-grown man who needed to take responsibility for his actions. But would someone using heroin actually be capable of taking responsibility? Even though the bloodwork wasn't back from the lab, Debby had said her brother admitted that he'd been using heroin. If we were going to bail him out, we also needed to get him into a rehab center. That night we scoured the Internet looking for a facility close to us where we'd be able to support him with regular visits. Until we finished taking care of Mom's affairs, he was where he needed to be.

After the first day I began to feel somewhat detached from the process and started seeing many of Mom's things as worthless junk, wondering whatever possessed her to waste money on them in the first place. Then one of us would find another something she'd squirreled away and I'd refocus. Finding Mom's diamond ring in the medicine cabinet above the bathroom sink reminded me of the time she dropped it down the drain and Dad had to take the pipes underneath the basin apart. Fortunately, it hadn't washed through the P-trap and he was able to retrieve it. For a minute I thought about giving it to Debby because of how close she and her grandmother were, but instead took it to my sister in the living room.

Barbara began to cry when she recognized the ring and collapsed on Mom's old sofa, which had belonged to her mother before her and had been re-upholstered at least twice since I was born. Barbara slipped the ring over her finger and held her hand out to admire the flawless half-carat stone in the brilliant midmorning sunlight. A kaleidoscope of jiggling rainbows speckled the walls and ceiling in harmony with her quivering hand.

"Time to get back to it," I said, patting her softly on the shoulder and hoping that now she wouldn't argue with me over the clock.

"Where's her jewelry box?" Barbara asked.

"Normally," Gloria said, looking at the ring on Barbara's finger, "I would say it was in the bedroom, but after finding that in the medicine cabinet, I'm not so sure."

I recalled one of our visits when my father was still alive, seeing Mom pull an exquisite Victorian cameo pendant circled with diamonds on a 14K gold chain from a wooden cigar box that was filled with art deco, antique, and estate jewelry she'd collected from pawn shops and thrift stores over the years. Some of it was quite valuable. When I mentioned this to my wife and sister, we all proceeded into Mom's bedroom to begin the search. Unfortunately, the cigar box was nowhere to be found.

"Maybe that's something we should tell the detective about," Gloria said.

"I don't think so," I said. "Someone would have had to know just where to look. If a burglar had broken in and was looking for something like that, he would have trashed the place after finding some of the money we did looking for more."

"Good point, but if we don't find that cigar box, or if we

find it empty, I think we should tell the detective anyway," Gloria said.

Barbara nodded, wiped her eyes once more, and suggested we look through the cedar chest at the foot of Mom's bed. I agreed and minutes later felt my own hands begin to tremble as a knot formed in my throat, when I knelt in front of the large wooden chest filled with Mom's most treasured items. Gloria sat beside my sister on Mom's bed as I opened the lid and pulled out a plain brown quilt, hand-tied with beige yarn at six-inch intervals. The aromatic scent of red cedar permeated the heavy blanket and Barbara immediately recognized it as one our grandmother had made.

"Oh, can I have it?" she asked.

"Sure," I said. It was more utilitarian than decorative; however, it had sentimental value, and I was glad to see Barbara so enthusiastic. As I handed it over, our eyes met with a flickering understanding I hadn't felt between us for a long time. It was a strange feeling knowing that with both our parents dead we had just become orphans.

Next, I pulled out Mom's wedding dress, packaged in a once-clear plastic pouch that had yellowed and cracked with age.

"I want that, too, Harry," Barbara said.

Again, I didn't object; surrounding myself with the trappings of someone else's life, even Mom's, somehow felt stifling. Her old mantle clock would be more than enough connection to the past for me. The cedar chest was filled with vestiges of our mother's entire life and I wondered whether she ever took them out to look at or just kept packing them away. I could only imagine as I lifted a stack of numbered blue envelopes tied with a faded red ribbon, the top one addressed to her in Dad's distinctive scrawl with a green three-cent Nevada Centennial commemorative stamp in the upper right-hand corner. The August 14, 1951, USS *Thomas H. Mitchell* postmark was a good indication he'd sent it while en route to Korea. Another stack tied in yellow was addressed to him in Mom's clear, looping style and triggered the memory of her trying to teach me the art of penmanship, using the Palmer method, after I entered school and learned my ABCs.

Barbara wanted to stop what we were doing and read the letters immediately, but I reminded her that they weren't written to us. "How would you like it if your kids opened the love letters you and Brice wrote to one another?"

"Can't," Barbara said with a short snort, "I burned them. Besides... they weren't all that mushy anyway."

"Maybe these aren't either," I said, clutching them tighter. "But it doesn't matter because they weren't written to you."

"Well, too bad because I want to know more about Mom."

"You had years to learn but couldn't seem to sober up long enough. You still haven't. We're going to burn these, too."

Barbara jumped off the bed and snatched the bundles from my hands. "The hell we are. The letters are mine. You can have everything else, but I want these."

"Gloria?" I said, imploring my wife with a look to back me up. "What do you think?"

"I'm afraid that's something each of you is going to have to find your own comfort level with," she said, diplomatically avoiding a decision. "I can understand why you feel the way you do, sweetheart, and I know what I'd do. But—"

"Just going through this stuff is making me uncomfortable," I interrupted. I knew that I'd never be able to read those letters and thought Barbara shouldn't either. However, Gloria had a point. I turned back to the chest and found plaster casts of our handprints from kindergarten carefully wrapped in tissue, and just about every picture we'd ever drawn in primary school with the teacher's grades and comments written across the tops in red pencil. Each drawing was sandwiched by tissue paper to keep it from smudging the next. Crayon drawings that were nothing more than scribbling, to a pencil sketch of an underground city with war planes bombing the gun turrets and tanks defending it. Obviously, Barbara and I had been the artists, but only the underground city looked familiar, and I'd probably drawn it in the third or fourth grade.

While other kids my age were collecting baseball cards, I was building a personal library filled with autographed books, something I've done ever since Mom took me to have Dr. Seuss sign *How the Grinch Stole Christmas* when I was seven. The old shirt box with a signed first edition of *The Old Man and the Sea* caught my attention right away. Stuck between the pages in the middle of the book was a folded sheet of onionskin paper with a cryptic typewritten note dated March 15, 1960:

Jenny,
Please see that Harry gets this on his birthday.
Rosa

I refolded the note and stuck it back in the book before handing it to Gloria, wondering who Rosa was and why Mom had never given it to me. The chronology of her keepsakes became more apparent as I continued to dig through them. Next I unfolded a small square of tissue with my name printed across in pencil. Inside were two locks of hair, one cut off and dated the year I was born and another from my first haircut. Two little plastic vials, which sounded like miniature maracas when I lifted them from their resting place near the bottom, were filled with baby teeth the tooth fairy had taken from beneath Barbara's and my pillows leaving, as I recall, a dime in their place for each one. Even taking inflation into account, my kids made more money on a single tooth than Barbara and I did on both vials combined. I looked to Gloria, wondering if she'd saved our children's teeth. My throat suddenly began to tighten as I realized I didn't know. So much time had gone by since their births and it alarmed me just how quickly it had.

The relics Mom buried in her cedar chest were grim reminders that my life was probably more than half over and I couldn't remember much of it by anything she'd saved — until pulling out a story I'd written in the ninth grade. The big red C at the top wasn't familiar but the hazy central character whose mother was overly protective, totally unlike mine who always stood back and let me make my own mistakes, triggered a faint recollection. I recalled also that, try as I might, Mom was never satisfied with my stories. While raving about plot or dialogue, she picked apart their weak narratives and I eventually gave up, turning my interest to more boyish things than writing, such as football and girls.

Why I began writing again after years of abstinence is still a mystery, but I remember the idea for a story gnawing at me and it wouldn't let go until I put it down on paper: a short story about two teenage boys who got away with the perfect murder and how it changed their lives. Since short stories were far less intimidating than a novel, I wrote a dozen or more before finally selling one about a pet psychiatrist for a whopping $30. However, if Mom saved a copy, it wasn't in the chest among her other treasured memories, which I suppose was a testimonial in itself and much more painful than all the rejection letters I'd ever received. Nevertheless, the confidence garnered from that meager sale had pushed me into writing my first novella, about a faux murder and the attaching legal jeopardy, which still hasn't sold and probably never will. But it was the next step toward writing a full-length novel, now complete, and good practice to boot.

A pair of white baby shoes with laces, a pressed corsage from Barbara's first prom, and other such trivia that I retrieved from the chest were divided into two piles on the bed by Barbara and Gloria. However, the cigar box wasn't among them. The last item on the bottom of Mom's cedar chest was a cracked leather folder with a picture of Dad in uniform, a copy of my parents' marriage license, and a sealed manila envelope from the Miami-Dade Circuit Courthouse postmarked April 4th, 1951. It was addressed to Mr. & Mrs. Leon R. Hamilton, on N.E. 99th Street, in Miami Shores, Florida, and the address took me by surprise because I never knew my parents had lived anywhere but California. Yet that didn't bother me nearly as much as the documents inside. Those changed my life forever.

SIX

I felt like someone had kicked me in the chest, knocking the wind out of me, and more devastated than when I'd entered Mom's townhouse last Friday afternoon, if such a thing was possible. Hyperventilating to keep from passing out, I stared at a space somewhere between Barbara and Gloria, trying to avoid eye contact with either. The thought of the woman I'd called Mom and loved so dearly lying to me for the past 47 years was more weight than I could bear. I ran for the bathroom, unsure of everything except where the commode was. Great rolling heaves racked my stomach and I doubted if I'd make it, but couldn't have cared less.

I hunched over the porcelain bowl, but nothing came up. The paperwork rustled as it slipped from my hand and fell to the floor. Somewhere behind me I recognized Gloria's worried voice coming through the stifling haze. "What's wrong, Morgan? Honey, what's wrong?"

I kicked the door closed and curled up next to the toilet, staring at the documents scattered around me. Husband, father, department store manager, student, son, none of them seemed important any more and none of them defined who I was as my eyes focused on the Final Decree of Adoption. The petitioners, Mr. & Mrs. Leon Randall Hamilton, had been named my adoptive parents one year to the day after my birth.

How could it be true? My birth certificate was from California. No one had ever questioned it, not USC, not the IRS, not even Social Security. Regardless that I had been legally adopted in Florida, California wouldn't have issued a birth certificate unless I had been born in California. As far as I knew, they weren't reissued like automobile titles with each state residency change. A person only got one — and that from

29

the state in which he or she was born. It made no sense to me as I slowly sat up and gathered the papers. A Florida birth certificate listed me as a healthy baby boy, born April 4, 1950 in Miami, Florida. Was the California certificate I'd been using all these years a fake, or had Kaiser Foundation Hospital in Los Angeles really issued it? Each time I had been required to produce it, it appeared real. If not, it was a darned good counterfeit.

Fragments of a thousand questions raced through my mind making me crazy, because I didn't begin to know the answer to one when another would take its place. Was Barbara also adopted? Or had we grown up together totally unrelated? Did I or we have other brothers and sisters somewhere in this world we didn't know about? Were my birth parents still alive? Out of the blue, there was a whole other side of me I never knew existed and didn't know anything about — a frightening, disturbing feeling if ever there was one.

A Miami Shores attorney had handled the adoption for $6,200, most of which I imagine went to my real parents. I'd been bought for $6,200, a lot of money in 1950, which was more than the people who'd raised me ever had back then. So, the big dollars raised even more questions. Where had the money come from? Or had Jenny and Leon Hamilton struggled for years to pay off my real parents and their lawyers while we lived in a National City tract house that probably cost just about as much?

I pounded my fist against the floor and closed my eyes. How could my parents not tell me that I'd been adopted? And why had Mom left this stack of papers for me to find without any explanation? She had to know that eventually I would — not to mention how much it would hurt. In the aftermath of her death, with Bobby in jail facing hard time if convicted of a felony DUI, the adoption papers had me teetering on the edge of an emotional cliff.

Gloria rapped gently on the door and opened it despite my having slammed it in her face. I felt that I might just slip over the edge into oblivion if I didn't reach out and hold onto someone real, and my wife was as real as they came. She had always been able to see beyond the social veneer of cool that college jocks wore to cover feelings of insecurity and, on rare occasions, sensitivity.

I'd gone to USC on a baseball scholarship with an uncharacteristic nervousness around beautiful girls because, like my narratives, Mom never approved of them. She thought beautiful girls were self-centered and shallow and would ultimately break my heart, which struck me as odd considering how beautiful Mom was. Yet somehow Gloria was different and knew I wasn't behaving normally when we first met and I'd tripped over a chair and cut my hand on a broken beer bottle. She'd wrapped gauze around the deep gash across my palm and drove me to the emergency room for a dozen stitches that benched me for three weeks. Of course, Mom fawned over my injured hand, blamed Gloria, and totally ignored her when she brought me home from the hospital. I wound up jogging a lot of miles those three weeks.

Now my hand shook with anger and fear as I reached up to Gloria, aware that if anyone could see us they would certainly question why a petite, middle-aged woman needed to help an able-bodied man a foot taller than her to his feet. Nevertheless, I allowed Gloria to be strong because at that moment I didn't know what else to do. I clung to her, too afraid to speak as she pulled me off the floor.

Gloria held me and waited patiently, putting no pressure on me to speak, yet I didn't know where to begin. Although in excellent shape with the girlish figure of her youth, which she maintained by lifting weights and jogging around an indoor track at the gym every day, Gloria could only support me for so long. After an indeterminable amount of time she gently disentangled herself from my feeble grasp, pried the wad of papers from my hand, and began leafing through them.

"Oh, Morgan," she said, pursing her lips at a loss for words. But there was nothing she could say or do to fix it and comfort me, and she knew it. When she reached over and took my hand I wanted to cry, but couldn't — not for myself. Even though I suddenly no longer knew who I was, somewhere way down deep inside I knew my strength. Shedding tears for Mom seemed natural, in retrospect; however, the tears had been more a response to the way she died than for my own personal sense of loss. At least that was what I told myself as I stood beside Gloria examining my Florida birth certificate and adoption papers.

Did I want to find my real parents? And, if so, the big

question was why? What would it prove? Were they nearby? Had they kept an eye on me all these years and remained silent, or had they sold me and never looked back? Did they ever think of me, wondering how I was doing, or forgotten all about me and moved on with their lives? For all I knew, I could have passed them on the street a hundred times and never recognized either one. Perhaps they had done the same without recognizing me. It was painful to think that it might have happened, but even more painful than the realization that my parents had actually abandoned me was the fact that the woman I had called Mom for 47 years hadn't thought enough of me to tell me that I'd been adopted. Did she think I would have loved her any less because she wasn't my birthmother? As my anger grew, I was beginning to, and I hated the feeling. Moreover, there was nothing I could do about it. It felt as if my life was spiraling out of control.

Amazingly, Gloria seemed to reach into my mind and collect my very thoughts, putting them into words. The icy crystals of each syllable stung at my soul. "Honey, would you like to find your biological parents?"

"No!" I snapped. "Why would I want to find the people who discarded me the first year of my life? Sold me like a dog breeder on a puppy farm. Why would I ever want to meet people like that?"

"I'm sure it wasn't like that!"

"How would you know?" I already didn't care how it happened; the fact was it had.

That evening I joined Barbara in the bar for a drink and wound up getting smashed, something I hadn't done in more than ten years. I'm not exactly sure when I first became addicted to booze — in high school it was just a cool thing to do. Then, in college, I drank to be sociable at first; later it actually seemed to help me study. Ironically, the only semester I didn't make the Dean's honor roll was the semester I quit drinking. Naturally, I rectified that situation immediately. In the corporate world, I drank because of the vocational isolation and constant job pressure to beat last year's figures. However, that night in the Jersey Bar, it was just because I felt sorry for myself.

SEVEN

"You're drinking too much," Gloria told me as I sat down to breakfast the Saturday morning a week and a half after we buried the woman who'd adopted me. I'd called my attorney before leaving Sedona and he was able to get Bobby's bail reduced to $25,000 for a first offence felony DUI with injury. We'd returned to San Diego via Needles with Bobby and a box of his personal effects and taken him directly to an inpatient drug rehab center downtown, which was just fifteen minutes from our house.

Barbara had returned to Maine with the personal items she wanted and indicated she wouldn't contest the will even though M... ah, make that Jenny had been her birthmother and not mine. It was difficult, but I just couldn't seem to call her *Mom* any more. Surprisingly, Barbara even phoned a couple of times to see how I was doing and somehow her words didn't seem as slurred as usual. Whether that was because I was listening to them from inside my own bottle I really didn't know nor did I care.

With each burning swallow the painful reality seared itself into the empty hollowness in my chest: Jenny had lied to me and now she was dead. The vodka didn't change a thing and I didn't know which was worse — the deception or the adoption. I glared at Gloria and replied that I was fed up with my meaningless life. I hated my job and hated the fact that I had been weak enough to fall off the wagon after more than ten years of sobriety. Why she remained faithful during my first bout of alcoholism I'm not sure, but I knew she wouldn't put up with another. The truth of the matter was I didn't really like myself when I drank and the booze wasn't helping me forget why I started again. I was tempted to join my son downtown.

"Ralph Larson called yesterday," Gloria said, surprising me with my district manager's name during breakfast. I was having a bowl of corn flakes and a little hair of the dog in a glass of orange juice. "He wanted to know what was going on with you."

"Whatever do you mean?" I asked, reaching for the OJ with a shaky hand.

"You know damn good and well what I mean. The alcohol isn't making you fit in, Morgan, it's making you stand out. You're not hiding anything from anyone and your drinking on the job is going to get you fired if you're not careful. Then where will we be?"

"I'm not drinking at work," I said. Technically, that was true. A couple of beers with my noontime meals outside the store didn't count, not enough to impair my performance, or so I thought.

"Well, evidently someone noticed the smell of alcohol on your breath and e-mailed Ralph. He called because he was concerned."

"Bullshit! He wants me out of there because my numbers have been down for three consecutive quarters. But so has every other store's, and there's nothing anyone can do in this economy. He knows it, yet he has the temerity to accuse me of drinking on the job?"

"He got a report. He's following it up same as you would if someone complained about one of your department managers or salespeople. I told him about Bobby, burying your mother, finding out that you were adopted, and how all of it was affecting you."

I set the OJ down hard, sloshing it over the rim onto my hand. "You had no right, Gloria. It's none of his damn business," I said, licking the orange liquid from my skin.

"He's your boss."

"He should have talked with me, then."

"If you would have come home after work last night you could have taken the call yourself. What did you expect me to do? Lie?"

"I expect you to mind your own business."

"Your drinking is my business."

"The hell it is!"

"Fine," Gloria said, rising and placing her fists on the table. "Why don't you just shoot yourself. It'll be a lot quicker. And, if it'll help, I'll load the gun for you."

In 27 years of marriage she'd never spoken so callously, even in jest. I knew she'd hit bottom even though I still had a way to go.

"Just because you happened to find out that Jenny Hamilton wasn't your biological mother, it doesn't change who you are, Morgan. Who was it that said, 'A rose by any other name is still a rose?' Not that it really matters. The only thing that's changed about you is your attitude. It really sucks." She told me that, if that was who I thought I was, she never would have given me so much as a second look. The fact that Barbara had developed into an alcoholic didn't give me the right, because we now knew she and I weren't related and couldn't possibly share a common biological predisposition for it. "Either you can go out and find your biological parents and put your mind at ease, or you can go out and not come back. I didn't marry a drunk, Morgan, and I'm not going to live with one any more — better or worse be damned!"

She picked up her half-eaten breakfast and stormed into the kitchen, where the garbage disposal whirred to life.

Thank goodness Debby and her family lived in Palm Springs, three hours away, and they couldn't just drop in and find me this way. Nevertheless, if I kept drinking, it was only a matter of time before they would. Much as I hated to admit it, Gloria was right. If my biological parents were still alive I had to find them — if for no other reason than to learn about the genes I had passed on to my kids. Was my biological mom or dad an alcoholic? If so, it might help explain Bobby's drug addiction and my alcoholism, but not Barbara's. Neither Jenny nor Leon ever took a drink in all the years I'd known them.

Had either of my biological parents died of heart disease or cancer? After Gloria drew the line in the sand, my genealogical heritage suddenly took on a whole new light. If my birthmother had died, say, from breast cancer, Debby would need to tell her doctor because, from everything I'd read, early detection was the key to survival. If either parent had died of colon cancer or cardiac arrest, I needed to notify my doctor also. But where would I begin to look?

EIGHT

"Gloria, I am a complete shit," I said, joining her in front of the sink and twisting the top off a one-liter bottle of Stolichnaya vodka that just minutes before I'd opened and poured from into the glass of orange juice. Without another thought I dumped it down the sink, recalling that I'd done it once before with less provocation. I could damn sure do it again.

I asked her if she would please brew a pot of coffee while I took a cold shower. It might not speed up the metabolic process of purging the alcohol from my system, but drink-sodden logic told me I could function more effectively as a wide-awake drunk, which, after all, was how I'd made it through college. I gritted my teeth against the cold water jets, their icy needles biting into my back and trickling painfully down my legs as Gloria opened the shower door and handed me a steaming mug of black coffee.

"Morgan," she said, "I want life the way it was before Jenny died."

So did I, but it never would be until I took positive action to find my past. How could it?

After toweling off and putting on sweats and tennis shoes, I sipped the coffee and called my attorney, Duke Taulbert. He was one of my best friends from high school who had become a lawyer following his retirement from the Navy. After passing the Bar and opening a small practice in Alpine, California, Duke had talked me into becoming one of his first clients a little more than six years ago. That wouldn't have been difficult no matter where he'd opened it because everyone needs a lawyer occasionally and I trusted Duke implicitly. Besides my sister... ah, Barbara, he was also one of the few people who still called me Harry. I made an appointment to see him later in the day and went for a run.

✖ ✖

I gazed at the professional shingle tastefully stenciled on the pebbled glass door: DUKE TAULBERT, ATTORNEY AT LAW. The black lettering was edged with gold. Who would have ever guessed? Certainly not me; but after the obligatory cup of coffee and rehashing old times, I thanked him for getting a reasonable bail set for Bobby and wanted to know what was in store for my son after he finished rehab.

"Well," he said, leaning back in his chair and clasping his hands behind his head. "You've already taken the first step by hiring an experienced California DUI defense lawyer."

"I hired you because you're my friend and not a public defender."

"With your income you wouldn't qualify for a public defender."

"Bobby would."

"Granted. Even so, public defenders are good lawyers. Unfortunately, they sometimes get a bad rap because they're so overworked and can't choose the cases they take the way private attorneys who specialize in those areas of the law can."

"I didn't know you specialized in defending DUI cases."

"Not intentionally, but I have gotten a lot of experience out here. Think about it, Harry; if you were going to have open-heart surgery, you wouldn't want a proctologist operating on you, would you?"

"No. But Bobby graduates, if you will, from rehab next week and wants to get all this behind him. From what I gather, you told him his trial is scheduled next month."

"That's correct; in Victorville, which is about a hundred seventy-five miles closer to us than Needles."

"Does that really matter?"

"Well, it's not so good for me."

"How so?"

Duke laughed. "Billable hours, my friend, billable hours. Not to mention the mileage reimbursement."

I frowned. "I was talking about the outcome. What's he looking at?"

"First offense for a DUI with injuries is anywhere from sixteen months to four years in state prison, one to five thousand in fines, and restitution to the woman he hit. Fortunately for him, Harry, she'll make a full recovery and didn't suffer any permanent injuries."

"Thank God for that."

"Amen, brother," he said, and handed me a bill for what he'd already done for my son, which was more than fair.

As I wrote the check I told him about the adoption papers and Florida birth certificate I'd found in the bottom of Jenny's trunk.

Duke listened attentively. "Each state has its own laws," he said, "and Florida's are different from the ones in California, particularly fifty years ago."

"I'm not that old," I said.

"Close enough. Anyway, up until recently you wouldn't have had a chance of finding your parents without a court order predicated on some type of medical emergency. However, a couple of years ago the Supreme Court changed the law, unsealing the files to adoptees who've reached adulthood. This is a good thing, I think. Unfortunately, many of the older civil servants still bristle at helping adoptees find their birth records and will drag the process out until they either give up or give out."

"Give the hardest job to the laziest man and he'll find the easiest way to do it," I said, throwing a quote I've often heard Duke use back at him.

"Which is, I suppose, why you've come to me?"

I laughed, feeling a bit more at ease after sharing Jenny's long kept secret with someone besides Gloria. "Precisely."

"On a Saturday afternoon?"

"You need to find that easier way?"

He chuckled. "Of course I'll work with you on this, Harry, but you can't afford to employ me full time."

I questioned him with a glance.

"It literally could take years. Suppose I handle the letter writing, giving you the legal clout of my letterhead, and—"

"Yeah, right," I interrupted, and glanced around his tiny office with a short chuckle, "clout!"

Duke looked at me and grinned. "I'll grant you a sole proprietor law firm is not going to garner much attention, especially one from Alpine, California. But with the right tone it just might fake out the GS-5 who is stuck in a dead end position and waiting out his or her last three years, two hundred and seventy-one days—"

"But who's counting?" I interrupted again.

"—to retirement into responding," he said, looking somewhat annoyed. "Did you bring your birth certificate?"

I nodded. "Can't see what good it'll do; it's a fake."

He held out his hand. "Just let me see it. You never would have gotten into USC if it were. I suspect what you have is an amended birth certificate issued after the court sealed your adoption record."

I handed him the certificate I'd been using all these years.

"The names of your biological parents and other identifying information that might have helped you find them have been eliminated for obvious reasons. However, almost every county in the country retains the original birthdate on the amended certificates."

"Yeah, so?"

"So, if you know your birthdate and one other piece of information, which I'm about to show you, you might be able to match it up with county birth records."

"I'm listening," I said, leaning forward.

"Each newborn is issued an official number filed by date of birth. Most of the time, this number is unchanged on amended birth certificates. Since birth records are public information and maintained at both the county and vital statistics offices, matching your amended certificate by date and official number could help you find the name you were born with."

"Not on this one."

"What do you know about it?"

I handed him the Florida certificate.

He glanced between the two. "Well, kiss my ass," he said.

"Now what?"

Duke laughed. "This does complicate things a bit."

I nodded. "That's what I've been trying to tell you."

"Hard to tell which one is the original," he said, turning my California birth certificate over in his hands. "Whoever had this done must have been very well connected and had lots of money."

"Not my parents," I said, handing him the remaining paperwork. Someone had gone to a lot of trouble to ensure that I would never find my biological parents. It looked like a corporate shell game and, mixing metaphors, I would have to peel away the layers much like eating an artichoke to get at the holding company's heart. "Leon worked for the post office. They didn't begin to pay him enough for something like this. If it isn't real, why did Jenny hold onto it all these years?"

"I don't know. Are there any others?"

"Are you kidding?"

He looked at me and shook his head. "I'm dead serious."

"That's all I found."

"Have you checked everywhere, including safe deposit boxes?"

"She didn't have one."

"Are you certain?"

"Yeah."

Duke pored over the documents a minute or two, which seemed a lot longer, before looking up. "As I said, it does complicate things. Two certificates will take longer to track down than one, but—"

"Longer than years? I'll be dead before you find out who I am."

"*We*, Kemo Sabe," he said, leaning back. "I already told you, you can't afford to hire me full time."

I slumped back in the chair beside his desk. "Some friend you are."

"Hey. As far as I or anyone else is concerned, you are Harry Morgan Hamilton. Always have been, always will be. I couldn't care less who your parents were. They could have been Jacqueline and Aristotle Onassis for all I know, but it wouldn't change who you are, Harry. You're still my pal and I'm going to help you because I have a feeling how important this is to you. However, you're the one who'll be doing all the legwork."

Duke was right. It really was my quest and, beneath all the pain, I appreciated his honesty. "So, what do we... ah, I do first?"

"Have some genetic testing done. Find out for sure whether or not Jenny was your biological mother, or Leon your biological father. Then start with this." He held up my California birth certificate.

"Why? It's obviously not real."

"We don't know that for sure. It very well may be the amended certificate. The Florida paperwork could be the fake, designed to throw you off. Although why they'd go to all that trouble is beyond me. Starting with this will require less travel and you might learn something in the process. Bureaucracies are the same everywhere and you're going to have to make a few trips to LA, maybe even Sacramento. While the information you want might be sealed to you, it isn't sealed to everyone. The doctor who delivered you, for example, can review hospital medical records any time he wants and isn't legally bound to keep the information that concerns you confidential. That is, if he's still alive, and if you can find him."

"What are the chances?"

Duke shrugged. "It's a place to start."

"I thought you said less travel."

"You could be traipsing back and forth to Florida."

"I might have to anyway."

"True, but by then you'll be more familiar with the system and how it works, which could save you from making extra trips. Besides, the success of your search could very well begin and end with your California records — if they exist. Have you thought about the consequences?"

I looked at him and wrinkled my brow. "Consequences?"

NINE

Gloria didn't have any trouble empathizing with the mother who'd abandoned me, and that really bothered me. How could the woman I married even consider the feelings of anyone so heartless? Nevertheless, it was one of the things that attracted me to her, although at times like that it drove me crazy.

"What if that woman was raped and found herself in the family way, as they used to say," she said. "Back then abortion was illegal and women couldn't get them unless they were ready to risk their lives with backstreet butchers who used knitting needles and coat hangers, or could afford to go to another country where they were legal."

"Spare me the histrionics," I said, not wanting to think that maybe that was how I began life — so much for the idea of being conceived in love. There were far more reasons why women sought abortions than I cared to think about and I pushed the painful thoughts from my mind as I sat down in front of my computer.

Gloria glared at me with hands on hips. "I'm just trying to point out how she might feel if you unexpectedly show up on her doorstep; it has nothing to do with you as a person. If it was a violent rape she may still be trying to forget. Your presence will be no more welcome than that of the rapist. Are you prepared for such a situation?"

I rocked my head forward, closing my eyes, and thought of Duke's cautionary advice.

"What if you do find your parents?" she asked as the old clock I'd wanted so badly began chiming on the hour. "If they're still alive, they're going to be old; they might even have other children and grandchildren who don't know about you. How do you think they'll feel when you come barging into their lives? What will they think about their parents and grandparents then? You could cause a lot of people to become embarrassed, or hurt, or extremely angry. This isn't just about you, Morgan, and I think you ought to think seriously about it before you do something you might regret."

"I thought you were the one who suggested I do this." My pulse raced and my breathing felt labored, conscious of the all too familiar Westminster melody pealing in the background as Gloria rehashed the same concerns as Duke. "Besides, they should have thought about that before giving me up."

"It's not a decision most people would make lightly."

"Then they can suffer the consequences," I said, throwing my head back in defiance.

"You're not listening to me," Gloria said. "They might have another family. Innocent children—"

"If they have children, they have to be darn near as old as me, maybe even older. I'm sure they can handle discovering a long lost brother," I said, turning on the computer, "I know I could."

"You don't seem to be handling it all that well from where I'm standing."

"Gloria, I have to find out who I am and where I came from. I'll deal with confronting whoever I have to after that."

"You do see the problem then?"

I shrugged and stared at the blue screen waiting for the computer to finish booting up. What did my wife know? She knew who she was and where she came from. How could she possibly understand what I was going through? It was worse than any midlife crisis I could have imagined and I'd observed a few. My previous boss, Tom Crossman, showed up at the store one day in a bright yellow Porsche 911 with a cute little redhead hanging on his arm to collect his final paycheck, then drove away from his job, wife, and family. Bad as it may have been for them, it was the break I'd been waiting for because corporate headquarters moved me into his position on an interim basis. After six months of proving myself, I was officially promoted to store manager.

The last I heard, Tom was up in Klamath Falls, Oregon, selling real estate to Californians who'd taken the capital gains from their homes and moved north, driving land prices in the Beaver State into the ozone, and making him rich. Regardless,

Tom's ex-wife told Gloria she'd heard from her kids that old Tom wasn't so happy with the little redhead any more, which I suppose came as no real surprise.

I couldn't imagine walking out on Gloria, Debby, and Bobby that way, but I guess many men do, and a few women, also. Retailing is a tough business that's more lucrative than most, especially in upper management. However, I hadn't made all the personal sacrifices required to get there, figuring that I'd made far too many just reaching a mid-level position. In many ways, I suppose, the insidious way annual sales and inventories have routinely pulled me away from Gloria and the kids wasn't any different than having an affair. Not to mention the drinking. Nevertheless, it was an accepted form of infidelity in business — even condoned. Unfortunately, come to find out, somewhere along the line I'd lost Bobby to drugs.

A good father would have taken his son to church, Scouts, and Little League. He would have attended all the games, even if it meant leaving work early and finishing an inventory late. "The customer is always right" is a motto we live and die by at Nordstrom, but they're damn sure not the most important people in *my* life. It was a lesson I learned far too late. Instead of taking Bobby to Little League games, I'd spent *quality* time with my son at corporate functions such as annual picnics and Christmas parties, slipping him a sip of beer or wine when the bosses weren't looking. What harm could it do? Drinking was the way I coped with the daily pressures of retailing and it seemed an easy way to bond with my son.

Bobby was 14 the first time I took him out on a business dinner with buyers. Gloria and Debby had gone down to Rancho la Puerta for the weekend and I didn't want to leave the kid home by himself all night. Bobby really seemed to enjoy the evening and acted a lot more grown up than I could have imagined. Even the buyers were surprised that he wasn't legally old enough to drink and, of course, I looked the other way when they snuck him a taste of theirs. By the time he was 17 Bobby had developed a taste for Scotch and would order it with water. Six months later he was drinking it on the rocks, which really impressed the buyers who would pick his brain on current fashion trends in school. I was proud of my son's ability to handle his liquor without getting sloppy and didn't give his drinking a second thought until we arrived home one night and I had to run interference with his mother.

Sometime before my desktop popped into focus with all the little icons neatly arranged along the left side, Gloria left the room. After my earlier conversation with Duke, I tried to quell the growing excitement of actually having some idea where to begin and soon forgot my failure as a parent as I began my search.

The Internet is a wonderful thing and it never ceases to amaze me how much information is available to just anyone. Of all the subject directories and search engines available I used Yahoo! Even though it sometimes took longer to find the information I needed, it was faster than trying to learn a new system, which inevitably frustrated me to no end. After twenty minutes of picking through a maze of web pages with keywords and phrases, I found the California Vital Statistics, Birth Records Section, under the Department of Health Services, and downloaded their request form. I quickly filled it out and stuffed it into an envelope with a check for eight dollars.

All I had to do next was mail it off and wait for my birth certificate. If it came back without a hitch, maybe I was who I thought and the adoption papers in Jenny's chest were someone else's — maybe an adopted brother who hadn't survived. Yeah, right! Who the hell was I kidding?

I turned back to the computer and began searching for genetic testing labs. Not surprising, they all wanted genetic samples from me and both my parents. Now, where in the world was I going to get those? Leon had been cremated, Jenny was six feet under, and all their personal effects were gone. At least all that I thought might possibly contain a DNA sample, such as combs and toothbrushes. Gloria had located a company that handled estate sales to auction off those items none of us wanted, and the rest had gone to Goodwill or the dump. I turned off the computer in frustration.

✖ ✖

Monday morning the first thing I did before heading off to the store was phone Ralph Larson at corporate headquarters. Although Seattle was in the same time zone as San Diego, upper management in the retail world synched itself with the opening and closing bells of the New York Stock Exchange, so I knew he'd be there early and felt it best that I acknowledged my error and assure him it would never happen again.

"It's a good thing it wasn't a customer who complained, Hamilton, or you'd be looking for another job. As it is, I'm somewhat reticent about keeping you on without sending you to some kind of rehab program. Your record indicates you've had a similar problem in the past, does it not?"

"That was more than ten years ago. I had a small relapse by having a couple beers with lunch two or three times this week. It's not a problem any more," I told him. "A regrettable mistake; it won't ever happen again."

"It better not. You're skating on thin ice as it is with your sales figures. If they don't show an improvement this quarter, I'm going to have to consider making some changes down there. Do I make myself clear?"

Oh, yeah. Loud and clear, I thought.

TEN

Summer came and went and, right in the middle, Bobby was incarcerated for three years in California Men's Colony, a male-only state prison a few miles northwest of San Luis Obispo, for his felony DUI conviction. Unfortunately, as we found out, it turned out not to be Bobby's first DUI and the judge's options were limited by the state's statutes. It could have been worse, a lot worse.

One weekend a month Gloria and I would drive up Interstate 5 to Los Angeles and fight our way around the 405 to Pacific Coast Highway en route to San Luis Obispo, where Bobby was serving his time. We'd usually talk on the way up about anything and everything. Going home was a different story and I'd be fighting to stay awake about the time we reached Ventura. Knowing our son was in prison is one thing, seeing him there quite another. Gloria and I both knew it was my fault and each trip was another painful reminder. This was our third trip and I was unusually silent as my mind was elsewhere.

Ralph Larson's changes could only mean one of two things: either I was going to be moved to a smaller store or let go. Neither of which was a pleasant thought since I'd turned down a career opportunity into upper management by refusing to leave San Diego because of my family. Thus, at 48, I was too young to retire with any kind of meaningful benefits or collect Social Security, and too old to find another job with a salary close to what I was then making. By the time we reached CMC I was wishing we'd just sent Bobby a letter telling him that Jenny hadn't been his real grandmother and I was back at the store working on the upcoming Labor Day promotions to boost my sales figures.

Clustered cellblocks assaulted my eyes each time the minimum security compound came into view, and as we topped a small hill just north of the quiet little college town, its harsh surroundings were a grim reminder that my son was isolated from civilized society. Two 30-foot fences topped with razor wire and evenly spaced guard towers, each housing searchlights and armed guards, made up the perimeter. Although I'd never seen attack dogs between the two fences I couldn't help imagining that K-9 sentries prowled the enclosure at night like some profane beasts out of a Stephen King novel.

The gatehouse was the only access to the prison as far as I could tell, and it seemed odd that more people were lined up trying to get in than out. The first time we went to see our son, visiting hours were almost over before we finished the paperwork and were allowed inside. Removing belts, shoes, jewelry, and emptying our pockets, Gloria and I stepped through a supersensitive metal detector and were greeted by a guard we'd come to know as Sergeant Kraft. He had less than a year to go before retirement and constantly talked about the ten acres in Idaho he'd bought, where he planned to build his dream house. I usually listened because Bobby had said on more than one occasion that Kraft was one of the few *bulls* who treated inmates with dignity.

I retrieved my clothing, accessories, and pocket change, which, per prison regulations, could not be more than $10 in quarters. Then Gloria and I followed another guard, who was much younger than Kraft, through the track between those formidable double fences before entering the compound. The sound of that gate slamming shut and locking behind me was always unnerving, but it was particularly so on that tropically bright Chamber of Commerce Day that makes Southern California such a desirable place to live. While the chain-link fences didn't block out the sunshine, the thought of being locked up behind them had a considerable dimming effect on its brightness.

My heart really wasn't in it as I stood wondering how to break the news about my son's grandmother. Because no matter how much I didn't want to be there, Gloria was right. It just wasn't something I could put in a letter. Bobby would undoubtedly have questions and she felt it best that we told him in person and wondered why I hadn't told him months before.

We were in the middle of another discussion about it when Bobby came into the visiting room.

"He's got to find out some time," Gloria said.

"I know, but right now he's got enough to deal with. It'll keep."

Bobby's eyes danced between us, following the exchange with keen interest. "What?" he asked, taking a seat across the table from us.

"Until he's your age?" Gloria asked, with a little too much sarcasm.

It would be a relief not to have to tell him, but his curiosity was already piqued and it wouldn't be fair not to.

He stared at me, knots the size of Bing cherries formed at the back of his jaws. "What?"

"We'll talk about it before we leave," I said. "Promise."

Bobby suddenly smiled. I hadn't seen him smile much recently, but the dark and sinister smile wasn't a happy one. With nothing but time on his hands, he was used to waiting. "You'd be surprised how easy it is to have someone snuffed in here," he said, radically changing the conversation. "A pack of cigarettes will do it."

"Bobby Leon Hamilton!" Gloria said. "What on earth are you talking about?"

"Someone took out Ron last week. Actually, I'm surprised they opened the gate to visitors so soon. Especially when they don't know who's responsible."

"What do you mean, someone took out Ron?"

Ron was Bobby's cellmate, who'd been serving a life sentence without the possibility of parole. He was only about five foot eight but extremely muscular from working out every day for the past fifteen years. Physical fitness enhanced a con's chance of surviving in the yard and Ron had taken our son under his wing, encouraging him to bulk up after he first arrived. We'd shared a portion of our past couple of visiting hours with Ron, listening to him brag how big and strong Bobby was becoming in such a short time. In fact, most of the prisoners seemed younger and stronger than their actual age which, except for the alcohol, tobacco, and drugs that got smuggled in, was a result of the regimented lifestyle behind bars.

"Took him out, you know, killed him."

49

"Why?" I asked.

Bobby shrugged. "Obviously he pissed somebody off. Someone shanked him out in the yard. That's all I know."

"Oh, that's just great," Gloria said. "Now I have to worry about someone sticking you with one of those things because you upset him and he gave someone else a pack of cigarettes to do it."

"It doesn't work that way."

"Well, you just said—"

"It's got to be righteous."

"Don't interrupt your mother," I said, feeling a cold shiver run down my spine. What could ever be righteous about sticking a knife in anybody? Bobby was an intelligent young man who would never kill anyone. But the hardness in his voice gave me pause. He'd said that it was possible to get heroin inside the prison and it was heroin that had put him there. Listening to him talk about snuffing someone, I wondered whether he'd relapsed and might be hanging around with the wrong people. I raised an eyebrow. "You're not doing anything stupid?"

"It's cool, Dad. Everything's cool."

I loved Bobby, but never really felt that close. He'd been more like a very young colleague than a son, and the distance between us since his accident had dramatically increased. If Gloria weren't insistent on our visits, I doubt that I would have ever brought myself to make the trip alone. We either sat inside the visiting room beside a bank of vending machines watching other inmates and their family members make fast-food and drink selections, or sat on the patio outside beneath one of the guard towers and consumed ours. Occasionally, we'd talk with other cons, and most seemed like regular guys. I often wondered why they were in prison but none of them ever volunteered an explanation. After talking with a wholesome-looking young man, or playing checkers with a sleepy-eyed grandfather type, Bobby would shock us with the gory details of their crimes. It was difficult to judge the dangerous from the harmless because some of the most hardened-looking inmates were doing time for far less serious offenses than Bobby.

I took a second look at my son, who was in jail because I'd set him on the road to addiction and hadn't recognized the signs after having been there myself. Jenny died because I hadn't been more insistent she move in with us. There was nothing I could do about either. I felt like a failure as a father and a son, yet couldn't share my feelings with Gloria. It all seemed to be chipping away at my security as a husband as well. Never before had I felt so alone and I shuddered inwardly with the realization that Bobby seemed to harden a little more with every visit.

Bobby stood when the other prisoners began lining up against a wall across the lounge as visiting hours came to an end. I glanced between my son and Gloria, stood, and placed a hand on his shoulder. "I don't have any easy way to tell you this," I said, trying to keep my voice from cracking, "because I'm still dealing with it myself. But—"

"Morgan," Gloria interrupted, "must you do it now? There's no time to answer any of his questions."

I glared at her. "Like I've got any answers."

"To what?" Bobby asked.

I couldn't stall any longer. "That I was adopted," I said, sliding my hand off his shoulder, "Jenny wasn't my real mother, which also means she wasn't your real grandmother."

He glared at me. "Thanks a lot for waiting until the last minute to drop that bomb."

Our brief conversation left me so shaken that I headed for the gate without remembering to collect my visitor's pass, only to discover that getting out of a correctional facility is impossible without the proper paperwork. Gloria would have made it because she's a woman, but in a men's prison I wasn't going anywhere.

ELEVEN

The prospect of not being allowed to leave the prison coupled with the emotional ending to our visit had me too distraught to drive back to San Diego that night, so I stopped at the Embassy Suites just south of San Luis Obispo. After checking in Gloria said she needed a glass of wine, which wasn't normal. So, I imagined she was also rather distraught. I remembered a package store we'd passed on the way and returned for a bottle rather than going out and sitting in some bar. I never drank wine because I just didn't like it, but decided that since my wife had suggested it I'd join her. A less expensive domestic brand would have served us equally well, but I picked out a Hungarian import and was pleasantly surprised.

Gloria settled into one corner of the oatmeal-color upholstered sofa before taking a sip and voicing her approval. I nodded in agreement as the alcohol more than the dry bouquet excited my taste buds. "Maybe I should have bought two bottles."

"I don't think so," she said, swirling the wine around inside the hotel glass tumbler.

I set mine on the coffee table and stretched out on the sofa with my head in her lap. "He isn't the same boy we raised."

She stroked my hair. "No, he isn't."

I rolled over on my back and looked up past her bountiful bosom at the bottom of her chin. Gloria had classic beauty from every angle and I think for the first time I noticed a few tiny timeline creases across her neck. "Somehow I get the feeling there's a difference between being macho to survive and being macho to prosper."

Gloria sipped her wine, stared straight ahead, and continued stroking my hair. "Bobby's not a predator."

I wasn't so sure. "As far as I'm concerned, his attitude about Leon and Jenny adopting me was more dismissive than it needed to be."

"He seemed more relieved to me," she said. A tear splashed out of the corner of her eye and rolled down her cheek, leaving a glistening trail. She lifted the wineglass to her lips again. "Why did you wait so long to tell him?"

I shrugged, unsure myself.

"Oh, Morgan, where did we go so wrong?"

"You didn't go wrong anywhere," I said, reaching up and wiping the teardrop hanging from her jawline with my index finger. "I did."

"Don't be absurd; he's *our* son. We're both responsible."

I sat up and grabbed the wineglass from the table and tossed it back. "He was driving on the wrong side of the road because he was stoned out of his mind. Where do you think he got his habit? From me, Gloria, he got it from me! You never even let him taste your wine at picnics or parties, but I did. I'm also the one who took him out on the town with buyers and let him drink hard liquor. I'm the one who introduced him to alcohol... the one who gave him his first buzz!"

"And he went on from there, Morgan. You wouldn't recognize heroin if you tripped over it."

"Maybe not, but he wouldn't have tried it if he first hadn't experienced getting high on booze. And to think I was actually proud of the way he could handle his liquor."

She closed her eyes and shook her head. "You don't know that. Everybody's different. Besides, you had nothing to do with him running head-on into that woman's car."

"I disagree," I said. "I have an addictive personality. I should have stopped to think that Bobby might also."

"You weren't thinking clearly; alcohol does that."

I jumped up from the sofa and glared down at her. "Quit defending me, damn it! I failed to act responsibly. I thought a few drinks might help us bond faster. In the beginning it really seemed to help."

"There is no love like that of one alcoholic for another," Gloria said, glaring back up at me, "is that what you're trying to say? Well, I was sober and knew what you were doing, yet said nothing. If anyone's to blame, it's me. But don't think for one minute that I'm going to beat myself up over it. Bobby's predisposition for drugs and alcohol would have come about no matter what we did, if not with you then with someone else. In college he would have discovered beer in a frat house, or experimented with whiskey in the armed forces. Who knows?"

She stood and came over to me, taking my hands in hers. "I don't like what Bobby's done any more than you. However, I don't love him any less and neither should you. That poor woman will recover, but it will take time, and who knows if she'll ever be the same. We're not responsible for what he did, Morgan. Oh, we might have contributed in some small way by how we raised him, or in the genes we passed on, but Bobby is an adult and responsible for his own actions. You can feel justifiably proud that he took that responsibility and accepted his punishment like a man; that's how we raised him. Which is why I can forgive him, but I'm not so sure about myself... not totally."

She dropped my hands and stepped back. "Look, right now we're both upset, but I think Bobby understands."

"Does he?"

She stepped closer, resting her head on my shoulder and hugging my waist. "The best thing we can do is give him our love and support."

Maybe Gloria could ignore my contribution to our son's alcoholism, drug addiction, and ultimate criminal behavior, but I couldn't. If he was a product of his environment, then I'd created it and Gloria ignored it. She was the classic codependent who always made excuses — first for me, and then for Bobby. Neither my wife nor I had driven the car that injured Kathleen Okrepkie, yet we both felt just as guilty. Bobby's imprisonment was Family Business — a dirty little secret we kept from friends and neighbors as we went about our daily lives, embarrassed by our failure as parents.

TWELVE

Between Bobby's legal problems, the demands placed on me by upper management at Nordy's, and my writing, there seemed precious little time to devote to looking for my biological parents. Fortunately, the previous quarter had shown a slight improvement and there'd been a three percent bump over last year's Independence Day sale figures. Ralph Larson had grudgingly kept me in place and we were gearing up for the annual Labor Day sale. I'd just finished another grueling day and it was 10:30 p.m. when I arrived home exhausted, but not sleepy. The nagging question *Who am I* remained just below the surface no matter how late or how hard I worked. It was far easier to put in the hours of being in charge of something and forgetting the negative bureaucratic responses to the inquiries concerning my biological parents, which seemed incredibly similar to the rejection slips to query letters from New York editors and agents.

While I waited for a response from California's Department of Health Services, I received a dozen more rejection letters to my time-travel novel *Syzygetic Journey*.

"Well written and gripping, but not what we're looking for," one said.

"A particularly noble effort at a different kind of book," said another.

"Great story, but not quite right for us."

The reasons went on and on. If it was such a gripping, well-written, great story, then why weren't they buying it?

Jenny used to say that anyone could write an exciting story and make it interesting. "The trick is to write a quiet story and make it interesting. If you can do that, son, you won't have any trouble when you get an exciting story." She also said that the whole world loved a lottery winner, but looked with ambivalence on anyone who earned the same amount of money by putting in the hours and working hard. "The only way to learn how to write is to write. If it was easy, Harry, everybody would be doing it. The reason they pay good money is there aren't many people who can."

I sorted through the mail and ripped open an official-looking envelope as quickly as any of the self-addressed, stamped envelopes I'd included with query letters about my manuscript. California didn't have anyone born on April 4, 1950 named Harry Morgan Hamilton; not in the entire state, let alone at Kaiser Foundation Hospital in Los Angeles. They wanted more information. However, I believed that would be a waste of time because the birth certificate I'd been using all these years was obviously a fake.

I pushed the stack of unopened mail aside and reached for the phone across the hand-carved mahogany roll-top desk I'd bought from the store after a holiday sale years ago. Even though it was late I needed to talk with Duke about what to do next. I'd only been at it a few months, but already I was getting frustrated and needed to rev up my positive self-talk. I'd always been able to define the goals in my life and visualize pathways to achieving them. The goal of finding my biological parents was perfectly clear; it was the pathways cluttered with innumerable, well-hidden obstacles that weren't. Just like getting published, I thought, and something else I was determined to do. However, with Jenny now gone, it had lost some of its urgency.

"Genetic testing is out of the question," I said, in response to Duke's interrogative, "unless you know a way to have Jenny exhumed."

"It shouldn't be a problem if Barbara agrees. We'll just petition the court with her consent."

"That's all there is to it?"

"Of course you'll have to pay for it."

"Besides that?"

"Don't sweat the small stuff, Harry. I'll handle the legal paperwork after you get Barbara's okay and it'll be a done deal. In the meantime, I have to go to Los Angeles tomorrow. I'll stop by the hospital and ask a few questions."

"Thanks a lot," I said, and hung up with the thought of

calling Barbara, but realized it was three hours later on the East Coast and she'd probably passed out hours ago.

While the laws in most states had changed in favor of adoptees, and I had a ton of willpower as well as Gloria and Duke on my team, entrenched old-school bureaucrats had bigger, stronger teams with decades of home field advantage.

For an instant I thought it was some kind of cruel trick as I stared at the clear looping script on the front of a red, white, and blue priority-mail envelope peeking out from the stack of unopened mail. It wasn't until I glanced at the return address that I was able to exhale. My sister rarely wrote, in fact it wasn't unusual for her to skip two or three years between Christmas cards. Naturally, I'd forgotten how closely her handwriting resembled Jenny's. Since my birthday wasn't for another seven months, and it wasn't close to Christmas except in the retail world, whatever was inside had to be important.

I slumped back in the comfortable swivel armchair and reached for the small stainless steel pocketknife I always carried. The blade sliced through the fibrous envelope like a razor and in no time flat I was looking at the contents: a note from Barbara, two non-sequentially numbered letters Jenny had sent to Leon while he was in Korea, and his replies. Normally, he went by Randall and everyone called him that except for two childhood friends he allowed the familiarity of Randy, and Jenny who, as far as I know, was the only one who used his first name because not even my grandparents called him Leon.

Barbara's note said that she'd read all Mom and Dad's letters and that I would find these four particularly interesting because they contained references to my recently discovered situation. Apparently even Barbara had trouble with the word *adoption*. She told me that the other letters covered many subjects and emotions and I was thankful that she didn't go into any more detail. I'd already made my feelings known about her parents' right to privacy. Still, if the letters contained anything about my adoption I wanted to know. The fact that they had raised me didn't change the fact that they had also lied to me. Jenny always said that anyone who would lie to you would steal from you. I just never realized she meant my life.

I muttered my appreciation to Barbara under my breath, while selecting the one with the earliest postmark to read.

April 4, 1951

My Darling Leon,

Today is Harry's birthday and we are having a party. Mother baked a wonderful angel food cake and I decorated the house with lots of pretty blue and white crepe paper streamers and matching balloons. I invited the old gang over and Opal brought her new boyfriend, Niles. I think you would like him, although he does seem to play a lot of golf and tennis, which I know you don't particularly care for, however, he did seem rather nice. Rosa didn't come as you might imagine, but I don't really blame her. I don't know if I would be strong enough if the situation were reversed. Anyway, we all had a wonderful time and everyone was amazed that little Harry is almost walking.

It's the cutest thing. Have I told you? The little fellow crawls over to Father's club chair and pulls himself up on the apron and slowly turns around. He gets the biggest grin on his face just before letting go, then sort of stumbles forward with his arms outstretched and runs across the room to keep from falling. It's adorable to watch, but I'm always afraid he'll get hurt because he can't slow down without losing his balance. The wood floors are so hard it makes me cringe, but each time he falls he crawls back to Father's chair and pulls himself up again. He wants to walk so badly and I haven't the heart to stop him, even to keep him from hurting himself. It's something he's got to learn for himself and I'm afraid the little guy is destined for a lot of stitches in his lifetime.

Leon darling, I miss you so much it hurts. I don't know why President Truman got us in this dumb old war anyway, and it scares me so to think that you might never be coming home. Ever since you left I've been throwing up and Mother says I've been terribly cranky, but I'm really just tired all the time. Besides, she'd be cranky, too, if Father had gone off to war. She just refuses to admit it. Why do you have to be away when I need you the most? I have such wonderful news to share with you, yet I can't seem to get the words down on paper fast enough. I hope you're as excited when you read them as I am writing them right now.

Well, darling, I went to the doctor last week because, as I said, I've been feeling tired all the time. I thought maybe I was just depressed, like Mother said, because you were in that dreadful place, but today he told me I am pregnant. Can you believe it, Leon? We're going to have a baby. And all this time we didn't think we could. Isn't it wonderful? If it's a little boy I want to name him after you. Do you mind terribly, darling? Oh, I hope not. Leon Randall Hamilton, II. Doesn't it just sound wonderful? I don't think Junior would be a good idea considering Harry is older and I think he might become suspicious if we do. Besides, "The Second" has a nicer ring to it than "Junior," don't you think?

If it's a little girl you can pick the name, but I do so hope that you'll be home before our baby is born. Do you think I should write General Ridgway and ask him if he thinks it's possible? I know he probably doesn't know you personally with all the thousands of boys we have over there, but surely he knows when the war will end.

Until then, may the Lord watch over you and bring you safely home, my love.

Your loving wife,
Jenny

I folded the letter in half along its sharp creases and stuffed it back into the powder blue envelope. How Leon had been able to hang onto the stack of mail Jenny sent, I have no idea. There's only so much room in a knapsack for items needed to survive. Yet somehow Leon had made room for a year's worth of letters, probably at the expense of dry socks, which could be why he'd lost his toes during the winter of '52 and was sent home long before President Eisenhower ended the war as promised. Fortunately, he hadn't been killed. Thousands had.

Feeling as if I had just shoplifted a Butterfingers candy bar, I looked around nervously and picked up the second letter, which was postmarked five days later. Two lessons I'd learned early in life were not to look in someone else's purse or wallet, or read someone else's mail without permission. Since

neither Jenny nor Leon was around to give permission, I believed that what I was doing was wrong. If they had wanted me
to know about my parents they would have told me.

I'd just finished reading how Jenny sat and watched me
bash my face against the floor learning to walk. Over the years
she watched me lose more fights than I won and never broke
them up until I'd gotten the upper hand, regardless of how
badly I was losing or how bloody I'd become. And as she'd
predicted, I was stitched up many times. It never seemed to
bother her, yet she'd never told me the truth about my identity. Why? What could she possibly have thought she was pro-
tecting me from? And why did I have to feel like I was stealing
information I was entitled to?

I opened the second letter.

THIRTEEN

Dearest Leon,

Every day I ask God to watch over you and all the boys fighting over there and bring you safely home to me. But every day I'm afraid to check the mailbox because I might find a letter from the government telling me that you're missing in action or, worse yet, that you've been killed. I can't bear the thought of never seeing you again, my darling.

Today wasn't any different; however, today the mailman brought good news and I'm so excited I just can't stand it. Are you sitting down? I am, and I wish you were here beside me to see the paperwork from the courthouse. It just arrived and little Harry is all ours. Isn't it wonderful? Mother surprised me by saying she was relieved that no one could ever take our little boy away. I didn't know she felt that way about the adoption, but she's even more excited about our baby than I am, if such a thing is possible. I'm going to be sorry to leave, but a deal is a deal and now that the paperwork is finally here we have to honor it.

Father can't take off work, but Mother said she would drive out to California with me and help me find some place decent to live until you return. I know it would be easier for everybody if we could just stay here, especially financially, but my parents understand why we have to go and are trying to help the best they can. Mother hates the idea of being so far away from her first real grandchild and plans on coming back when the baby's born. I hope you'll be home then too, *my darling.*

This afternoon our son, Harry — doesn't that sound wonderful, Leon? — our son! This afternoon he got five stitches in his little hand after sticking it through the front of our oscillating fan while I was reading the adoption papers. Blood went everywhere and scared me half to death. Fortunately, the doctor said he didn't do any permanent damage, and I'm sure his cuts will heal long before my jangled nerves, but I'm finding that I can't turn my back on that boy for a minute. Much as I want another, I'm not sure I can handle it. Maybe a little girl would be nice instead. Would you be terribly disappointed?

Well, it's getting late, my love, and our son is sleeping peacefully. I must get my beauty sleep when I can. Sending you all my love.

Your devoted wife,
Jenny

As I replaced the letter in the envelope I glanced at the nearly invisible scars running across the back of three fingers on my right hand. Like so many other scars on my body, to which I'd never given a second thought, it was momentarily interesting to try and recall how I'd gotten them, however I had absolutely no memory of the event. Setting the letter down and turning my hand over, I stared at the white line with tiny dots along each side; a scar from the day I met Gloria — the luckiest day of my life.

It seemed apparent from the Miami, Florida return address Jenny was using, along with the Final Decree of Adoption issued by the State of Florida, that that was where I was born. So, why did my adoptive parents have to move to California? If they had to take me out of Florida as a condition of the adoption, they had 47 other states at the time to choose from. Unless, of course, my real parents were from California and the deal depended on Jenny and Leon Hamilton moving closer to them so they could watch me grow up. Why else wouldn't USC have questioned my California birth certificate? If that was the case, why had Florida issued what Duke called an amended birth certificate? Maybe Leon's letters would shed some light.

A May 1st postmark above his heavy scrawl was stained brown, probably from coffee, which had sloshed out of his canteen while writing home. His handwriting had always taken some getting used to and more than once I thought it ironic that he hadn't become a doctor. I hoped the letter inside wasn't going to be all mushy, which would put my — ah, I almost called him Dad — put Leon in a whole new light, because I wasn't sure if I could handle that. Confronting him had always been intimidating, and opening his mail without permission was even more unnerving than opening Jenny's. It didn't matter that he'd been dead more than nine years; he was still a father figure whether I wanted him to be or not. *Does a boy ever truly escape the shadow of his father?* I wondered.

The summer Duke and I ran off to Woodstock without his permission was the first time I'd challenged Leon's authority successfully, but it was only because there was nothing he could do to change it. That first feeling of independence was truly wonderful. However, it took several more years before he and I were able to converse routinely on an equal basis. Even though Duke and I returned from the rock festival safely, Leon had a hard time allowing me to make life-changing decisions without his input. Fortunately, I'd matured enough not to see them as a challenge and our relationship mellowed. Logic told me I had to read the letters regardless of how I felt. The onionskin paper crinkled in my hands.

April 29, 1951

Dearest Jenny,

I don't know why the mail seems to be so slow these days, but it does. I just received your letter telling me I'm going to be a father. I can't believe it. However, I don't think having a baby is reason enough to qualify for a humanitarian transfer, so pa-leeease don't write the general. There're a lot of guys here who are much worse off than we are.

Right now, I'm in Tokyo, Japan. Seems like I no sooner got to Korea than they sent my company back for R & R. Far be it for me to complain, even though there's not much for a married GI to do besides go to the Service Fleet Club, take hotsy baths, and drink saki. So, I go to the club and take a lot of hotsy baths because, as you know, I'm not much of a drinker. Maybe it would be easier being over here if I was, but I just don't like the taste. Irregardless, as soon as I read your letter I got so excited that I took a bunch of the guys into town and bought them all the saki they could drink, which is why the money order is five dollars less than usual this time. I hope you don't mind.

Of course I like my name. Why wouldn't I? I think naming the baby after me is a swell idea if that's what you want to do. But my mother always told me it's a good idea if both parents pick out the baby's name because the chances are better that the child will like it if both the parents do. So, if it's a girl — I like Barbara, Cathy, Jill, and Rachael — in that order. If you don't like any of them, please let me know. In the meantime, I'll be thinking of some more in case you can't.

It sounds like Harry has an adventurous spirit, which I'm sure he gets from his father. Stop and think a minute about all the crazy things that man does. No wonder he can't stay married. How many wives is it now, four? Certainly not the kind of example I want to set for Harry and my children. I'm counting the days until we're together as a family again. In the meantime, you'll have to watch that boy carefully so he doesn't grow up as reckless or irresponsible as you know who.

Lots of love,
Leon

The back of the envelope had a P.S. that was nothing more than a group of meaningless letters: *T.S.T.S.T.S.A.* I was sure they meant something to my adoptive parents, but didn't give them much thought as I mulled over the last paragraph. Such interesting descriptions of my biological father were so different from the methodical man who'd raised me. And the perplexing question for me was, which of his previous wives *was* my mother? Or was it the present Mrs. you know who? I certainly hoped so because, even though I didn't know them, I didn't want to think of my parents as being divorced. Besides the obvious reasons, it would also complicate trying to locate them.

The last letter of the four was dated more than a year later and postmarked in Honolulu, Hawaii where Leon had spent several months in Tripler Army Medical Center recovering from frostbite and undergoing physical therapy learning to walk with three missing toes.

July 14, 1952

My Darling Jenny,
Only ten more days to go until I'm in your arms again; I can hardly wait to hold you and Harry again. I can't believe he's talking in sentences already, isn't that unusual for a two-year-old? Undoubtedly something else he got from his father because the man always struck me as extremely smart even when drunk, which was two out of the three times we met. I certainly hope that isn't a trait that's hereditary. Anyway, do you think the little guy will remember me? I've lost quite a bit of weight this past year — so much, in fact, that you might not even recognize me, although it would break my heart if you don't.
I'm so excited about meeting Barbara for the first time I can hardly stand it. I'll bet she's beautiful just like you. I hope she won't cry when I hold her and I can't wait for this darn troop ship to get underway. It's maddening knowing I'm four thousand miles closer to you than I was in Korea, yet have to sit and wait for the Navy to have their "liberty," as they call it, before the next troop ship leaves for the States. If it weren't for that, I'd be there in less than a week.
Eisenhower is promising to clean up the "mess in Washington" if he's elected and that he will come to Korea, which I imagine means to win the war. Although that won't affect me because I'm being discharged, I think we should vote for him instead of that Stevenson fella so we won't have to keep sending our boys over there.
This war has taught me that except for God, there isn't anything as precious as family and I couldn't bear to think that our votes might prolong it. You wouldn't believe what it has done to family men who come from homes that aren't as strong as ours and I can only im-

agine how it will ultimately affect those who wait for them, to say nothing of those who have been killed.

I've given a lot of thought to your letters concerned with telling Harry he's adopted. I hope you haven't already told him. Since we can't ever let him know who his real parents are, which I'm sure someday he'll want to know, I think giving him only part of the story isn't fair. Lord knows if my parents ever told me that I'd been adopted I would have done everything I could to find out where I came from. But you know as well as I that if he does, we'll lose him. And anything we tell him will only weaken whatever family bonds we hope to establish. I'm sorry; I know it's not what you wanted to hear, but the less Harry knows the better.

All my love,
Leon

FOURTEEN

Leon's letter had been a shock since he always did whatever Jenny wanted and, from my perspective, seemed relatively uninvolved with raising Barbara and me except in matters of discipline. He was the keeper of the belt and, after coming home from work and talking over the day's events with Jenny, would take it off and hand it to her. She administered the spankings that encouraged us to learn from our mistakes. It was surprising to learn where Leon had taken a stand and how much control he had because, in the nine years since his death, Jenny hadn't said a word about my adoption. Since neither was alive, I had no one at whom to vent my anger. At least no one who was responsible and Gloria flat wouldn't put up with it.

I hardly slept at all that night, aware of the family clock's incessant chiming every fifteen minutes and thinking about the letters Barbara had sent me. Instead of answering questions they'd spawned a thousand more and I was already awake when the alarm went off the next morning. After brewing a pot of coffee I called Barbara, who answered on the first ring and sounded surprisingly alert for 7:30 a.m. her time.

"Harry?" she said, "you're up early."

"It's my writing time, but I'm having a little writer's block at the moment. I, ah... I read the letters you sent me. They were a real surprise. Thanks."

She laughed. "For the letters or the writer's block?"

"The letters, of course," I said. "Writer's block comes and goes."

"I hope they help."

"I'm not sure if they will or not, but—"

"Weren't they just wicked good? Couldn't you just hear

their voices, Harry? You should read the rest of them."

"I don't think so. I felt kind of funny reading those four."

"I'd like them back, you know."

I took a deep breath and nodded even though she couldn't see it, or hear my head rattle. "Sure. I have to ask you another favor, Barbara. I need to exhume Jenny to get a genetic sample for testing."

"Are you out of your mind?"

"Just to make sure she isn't my biological mother. Duke says it's one of the things I need to do and all a court order requires is family consent. Of course, I'll pay for everything."

"Well, you can just forget that, Harry. Mom is resting peacefully and I'm not going to let you dig her up for any kind of testing."

"Barbara, there's no other way. We threw out everything else we could have used... her comb, her toothbrush, her—"

"No way, Harry!"

"Don't make me fight you on this."

"You're unbelievable, you know that? Won't read a letter she wrote to Dad without getting all wigged out, yet have no qualms about digging her up and cutting off a piece of her body just so you can confirm something you already know from reading those letters. You do what you have to do, but there's no way I'm giving my consent to let you dig up *my* mother."

After she hung up, I had an even more difficult time concentrating on the story I was working on, which united the recipients of a donor's organs in retribution against the man who murdered her. Since the only time I had to write was early in the morning, I'd force myself out of a nice warm bed at the impious hour of 4:30 just to type a few pages before heading off to work. It didn't matter that I hadn't gotten to sleep until well after midnight; it was something I just had to do. Some mornings the stories would flow onto the screen without any effort, and others I would sit in front of it staring at the blinking cursor on a blank screen until it was time to go to work.

About an hour and a half later I jumped when the phone rang.

Duke had some good news but hadn't wanted to phone when he returned from L.A. late the night before. However, he thought everyone should be awake by six and had no problem calling his clients that early. "The early bird catches the worm," he said.

"That's such a cliché."

"Which is why I'd never use it in a legal brief."

I chuckled. "Glad to hear it. But you won't have clients to brief if you keep calling them this early."

"You want I should call back later?"

"Not unless you want to die."

"Yeah!" He laughed. "I'm sitting here getting ulcers worrying about that."

I chuckled. "Okay, so tell me."

"Well, I stopped by Kaiser Hospital, found the admin clerk, and told her that I was investigating a murder and needed to see the victim's original birth record. I told her that the one filed at the Vital Statistics Office appeared to have been altered and it was critical to the investigation that I verified the date and number on his amended certificate."

I almost choked on my coffee, which by then was cold. "And they believed you?"

Duke snickered. "You can get almost anything you need at lunchtime. All the supervisors are gone. Cute little thing appeared to be a recent hire and easily persuaded. I really hated taking advantage of her but I didn't have any choice."

"Sure you did."

"Like what, Sherlock?"

Any news Duke had, no matter how small and no matter how he'd gotten it, would rekindle the spark of hope I so desperately needed. Even before discovering that I'd been adopted I had occasionally wondered if I was just "another brick in the wall," or did my life really have purpose? Would I ultimately be defined by my writing, as were the great literary figures of the past? If so, to this point, it meant nothing. The adoption papers only intensified those negative feelings. "Never mind; what did it say?"

"What say?"

"You know damn good and well."

"Maybe I *should* call back later... like when you're not so uptight."

"Duke!"

He chuckled. "It said your parents' names were Nelson

and Dixie Simmons. Sounds like an old vaudeville act, if you ask me." He laughed again, this time with more gusto. "How hard could it be to find a couple with names like those?"

"I don't know."

"Well, be sure and let me."

"Let *you* know?"

"This is where the gravy train stops, pal. If you want more information, you're going to have to pay for it. How many ways do I have to tell you that you can't afford to have me doing your grunge work? Get on the Internet and find them yourself. Almost everyone leaves a data trail a mile wide unless they work for the CIA or are in the Witness Protection program."

"So what's my name?"

"Harry Morgan Hamilton, same as it's always been."

"That's what it said on the hospital copy?" I asked, unable to contain the sarcasm.

"No, but now that you have your parents' names you don't need it."

"Duke!"

He laughed. No matter how serious the situation, Duke always enjoyed pulling the other guy's chain.

"C'mon, Duke," I said, not wanting to beg.

"David Patrick Simmons. You were born April 4, 1950 to Nelson and Dixie Simmons."

The knots in my back eased and I slowly exhaled. "Are you positive?"

"The date of birth and official hospital number match; that's as good as it gets, Harry old pal. Now, if I were you, I wouldn't be wasting time arguing with me about it. Those folks are old and getting older by the minute, if you get my drift?"

"Yeah, thanks. I owe you."

"Big time, David," he said with another chuckle. "Or would you prefer I call you Patrick?"

"Just fax me the copy."

I hung up, excited with the prospect of getting my real name and automatically hit Control S before exiting WordPerfect, leaving Carla Martinez shot and car-jacked the same as the day before, and logged onto Yahoo! Hopefully, the subject directory would lead me to Nelson and Dixie Simmons's current address — if in fact they were still alive. But what if they weren't; what would I do then? Find out if they had any other children and locate them? The idea seemed ridiculous. Chances were good that Nelson and Dixie never told them about me, and why should they? According to my adoptive parents' letters, it sounded as if no one was ever supposed to find out.

My fax number rang and the machine began to hum as I waited impatiently for the copy to print out. When it finished I snatched it from the tray and the warm paper sent a shiver down my spine as I stared at my actual birth certificate. David Patrick Simmons. April 4, 1950. Mother, Dixie Louise Simmons. Father, Nelson Chandler Simmons. Just like Duke said.

The big red ball of my Logitech Trackball slid rather than rolled between my sweaty fingers as I repositioned the curser over the Advanced Search box. I typed in Census and clicked. Instantly the screen changed, indicating five categories and 243 sites. It was more information than I could reasonably process. Without any controls on who could post what on the Internet, separating the useful from the useless, and valid from invalid, was extremely difficult without wasting a lot of time.

Scanning the list of categories wasn't like researching fiction, where finding the exact answer had to be tempered with spending all day looking for it. Although a few readers would catch technical errors no matter how small, most would not. After all, besides Duke who'd pointed it out to me, and a few helicopter pilots, how many readers caught the twist-grip throttle on the CH-53 in Tom Clancy's *Red Storm Rising*? Making stuff up that sounded good and moving on often proved more expedient, which, in retrospect, could be the reason my work wasn't selling. I vowed then and there to remedy that lazy writing habit when resuming my story — after locating my parents.

I waded through a plethora of advertising, noting how the Census Bureau was unable to provide genealogical information, locate missing persons, or provide recent information on individuals. I then hyperlinked to a site with a database of 600 million names derived from telephone and e-mail directories. It was more than twice as many people in the United States and N. Simmons came up 110 times in Southern California alone with 22 in the Los Angeles area and five in San Diego. Unfortunately, none were listed with either a Dixie or a

D., which although frustrating wasn't totally unexpected. Somewhere in the past 47 years, Nelson and Dixie might have divorced, or she may have died. Not everyone lived to be 76, which, according to the fax, Dixie would be since she'd been born June 1, 1922, making her 27 when she'd given birth to me.

Keying the mouse and letting my computer dial the numbers would have been quick and simple, but what would I say. "Hello, Mr. Simmons, you don't know me but..." or, "Is this Nelson Simmons who used to be married to Dixie?" What if it was? Would he immediately become suspicious, thinking I was perhaps another of his ex-wife's attorneys seeking additional alimony, or an insensitive telecommunication salesman unaware of his grief because she'd recently passed away, causing him to hang up? Besides, it was much too early to begin calling people on the West Coast.

I printed out the list of Simmonses and thought about how to proceed, trying to quell the stream of unanswered questions bubbling up inside my head. Was I the reason they got divorced? Or, worse yet, did my birth result in the death of my mother? Back then it certainly happened with more frequency. What if one was the Nelson who'd been married to Dixie? Could I really have found him so easily? Certainly not without Duke's help. Yet it was the spark I needed and I was determined more than ever to meet my biological father and confront him regardless of how he felt. "The hell with early," I said, taking a series of deep breaths and picking up the phone. I punched in the first number.

FIFTEEN

N. Simmons number one lived in Malibu and was attending Pepperdine University, his name was Norman and he was much too young to be the man I was looking for. He assured me after much prodding that neither his father nor his grandfather were named Nelson, and neither had been married to anyone named Dixie. The second resided in Ventura, sounded old enough, and although actually named Nelson said he was only 59. I couldn't very well call him a liar but without meeting him I had my doubts. Why wouldn't the man who sold me for $6,200 lie?

The Simmons in San Diego didn't answer and didn't have an answering machine like the one that picked up when I dialed another number in Indio. "Hello," a sexy young female voice said. "This is Nicole. Sorry I missed your call. Please leave your name and number at the tone and I'll get back to you. Promise!"

And so it went. After a dozen or so such calls I sighed and returned to my census search, surfing into The Record Room with another hundred plus choices from which to select. Hyper-linking to U.S. Vital Records and forward through California to L.A. County, I somehow wound up checking the Social Security Death Index for Dixie's name. Thankfully, she wasn't there. At least not in the past 48 years and that was all I cared about.

Nelson was a different story. Sixteen had died in Southern California since my birth and I wondered whether one of them might not have been my father. A nagging sense of loss tugged at me as I stared at the names, which was odd because I didn't know any of them from Adam. My emotions were roller-coasting after my conversation with Barbara and the other dozen calls. My mainspring felt ready to snap and if I didn't find the right Simmons soon it just might.

The thought of having to expand my search upstate and outside California loomed ominously in the back of my mind as I thought about tracking down the wrong and disconnected numbers, not to mention the unlisted Simmonses who weren't in phone books and e-mail directories. I felt as if I was getting nowhere fast and I was just getting started. It was a tedious project, much like writing query letters to editors where each rejection slip was one step closer to publication and each name crossed off the list was one step closer to finding my biological parents. Nevertheless, how many of them were out there?

Recalling how easily Duke had accessed the same information that had been refused to me, I flipped open the Yellow Pages and began looking for a private investigator who would have the experience and, more importantly, the chutzpah necessary to find Nelson and Dixie Simmons. While I'd never backed down from a fight, I'd never lied or cheated to win one either. I couldn't just go up to some clerk and say that I was investigating a murder in order to gain access to public records to which everyone in the world but me seemed entitled. Ultimately, I'd wind up asking the wrong questions and they'd see right through the ruse. It was time to call in a professional, reduce the pressure on myself, and get some results.

I was both surprised and impressed when Tommy Peterson, the investigator I'd spoken with, phoned back three days later with the information. Nelson and Dixie Simmons lived in Manhattan Beach and the $125 Peterson charged for their address was worth every penny. I told him that if I'd known it was that easy I would have hired him long ago and saved myself a lot of anguish.

"All in knowing where to look," Peterson said, and casually suggested that rather than risk spooking the Simmons by calling, I drive up first thing in the morning after the rush-hour traffic subsided and knock on their door with birth certificate in hand.

It was uncharacteristic of me to skip work without notifying Justin Forsyth; however, a blast of cerebral flatulence blew every coherent thought except meeting my folks out of my mind as I backed my Corvette out of the garage into the alley-way. I should have called the night before, but wound up surfing the Net trying to find the same information Peterson had given me. It was one thing to pay for information but another not to verify it. By the time I had, it was too late to call my assistant and I was too excited to remember.

I turned right onto Sunset Boulevard, leaving the quiet streets, craftsman bungalows, and stately homes of Mission Hills, and drove down through historic Old Town, the birthplace of San Diego. Within five minutes I was heading up Interstate 5 with 280 horses galloping under the hood and rumbling through tuned headers and twin Glasspacks. No one did the speed limit any more it seemed as cars whizzed past. There wasn't a cloud in the sky and I turned up the volume on the cassette deck, my hair whipping in the 70-mile-an-hour breeze. I was thankful that I hadn't left before nine as I cruised up the busy freeway listening to Rare Earth's "Get Ready." Behind the driving 4/4 beat of John Parrish's electric bass guitar, Pete Rivers hammered out rim-shots on the snare drum, and I smacked my palms against the steering wheel in cadence with each and every one, simultaneously rehearsing what I would say to my biological parents. "Hello. My name is David Simmons. Remember me?"

The constant jangle of Gil Bridges' tinny tambourine sounded wonderfully nostalgic on the Bose speakers as I exited the San Diego Freeway onto Rosecrans and headed west across Aviation and Sepulveda Boulevards to Highland before turning south again to 30th. But the nostalgia did little to dull the ever-sharpening edge of anxiety the closer I got. The Simmons lived in a small corner house four blocks up from the beach and I imagined that the only thing that kept it from being designated an apartment or condominium was the narrow strip of overpriced dirt between it and the next small house. San Diego may be crowded but it was nothing compared to Manhattan Beach.

I debated whether to park under a shedding bottlebrush tree in what might be called a front yard, or return to Highland and feed a 30-minute meter. A sign in the front window of the house said the space was private and violators would be towed. However, the oil-stained, herringbone redbrick lawn that might at one time have been grass was the only empty space on the block and it appeared that the Simmons were gone. I pulled in anyway and shut off the engine, then raised the top to keep the falling autumn leaves out of my car.

The entry was on the side and separated from the cross street by a six-foot cedarwood fence and another foot of over-priced dirt. I stood on a small concrete stoop under the same sun which moments before had felt much more pleasant, waiting apprehensively after ringing the bell a second time. The soft sounds of someone stirring inside abruptly made my heart jump and, as the inner door opened, my hands were suddenly wringing wet.

A short plump woman in a blue calico dress with white bib apron tied in front stood behind the screen, drying her hands on a plaid dishtowel. She didn't look 75.

"Good morning," she said, with a pleasant smile, "isn't it a lovely day?" She wore little or no makeup, save a light blush or rouge under high cheekbones, and her tightly curled gray hair shimmered with a whisper of blue highlights from a recent rinse.

The cheerful greeting caught me completely off guard and I floundered to respond, forgetting all my sarcasm and wondering why, if it was so lovely, she didn't have the door open? Never mind that Manhattan Beach was a suburb of Los Angeles and she didn't need any reason other than that. While people from her generation were smart enough to keep doors closed and locked, as a whole they were more trusting than those from mine and subsequent generations and would open them to anyone who knocked. Dixie Simmons didn't know me from Ted Bundy. Not that he would have attacked a 75-year-old woman, but there were those around who would and they probably looked no different from me.

"Yes, it is," I said, half choking, unexpectedly overcome with emotion. I wanted to open the screen door to both hug and slap my biological mother. I refrained, however, from doing either and it was a good thing, too.

SIXTEEN

"Who is it, baby?" a frail voice asked from somewhere behind Mrs. Simmons.

She turned away. "I don't know, dear," she said, then turned back and asked, "What can I do for you, young man?"

"I'm not sure," I said, patting the left breast pocket in my tweed sports jacket with my right hand as if beginning "The Pledge of Allegiance" and feeling that I'd made a big mistake. "I'm looking for someone and I was hoping maybe you could help me. Would you mind if I asked—"

A kitchen timer jangled before I could finish my question and distracted her as she fumbled with the lock. "You'll have to wait 'til I tend to my baking," she said, pushing the screen door open and turning away again.

The sweet aroma of fresh baked cinnamon rolls seemed to lift me right off my feet as I stepped through the door and followed her across an early American dining room into the kitchen. Without waiting to be invited I took a seat on a padded barstool by the counter and watched as she pulled two trays from the oven. She quickly slathered four huge golden brown rolls on the first with white glaze icing then flipped the second onto a sheet of waxed paper where caramel and chopped pecans oozed down the sides of four more rolls. Suddenly, my mouth began watering and I forgot all about my sweaty hands.

"I like mine with coffee," she said, "and if you'll wait just another minute while I take Nelson one, I'll fix us a cup unless, of course, you prefer milk like my Nelson does."

I nodded as she took a spatula and lifted one of the caramel rolls off the paper and slid it onto a snow-white bone china plate. She licked her fingers and winked at me with a nervous little smile, then opened the icebox and pulled out a half gallon of whole milk. I actually preferred it to the two-percent Gloria always bought for health reasons. The only time I ever drank whole milk after getting married was when we went to Jenny's. Gloria would glance disapprovingly every time Jenny had her back turned, but my wife knew better than to argue with her mother-in-law about what was and was not good for me.

Mrs. Simmons disappeared around the corner into the living room and I heard her husband's frail voice ask again who was at the door.

"He didn't give me his name."

"Well, ask! How many times do I have to tell you, you can't be too careful these days?"

"Shhh, now, you watch too much TV. He looks like a very nice young man and he needs our help."

He snickered. "Doing what? I can't even help myself any more. How's he expect us to help him?"

"I'll handle it, Nelson; you just enjoy your caramel roll while it's nice and hot."

It seemed to me that all women prior to Jenny's generation believed the way to a man's heart was through his stomach and, while they may have perfected the art, they somehow failed to pass it on to the next generation. Barbara would never spend time baking cookies or cinnamon rolls for her former husband, Brice, and neither would Gloria except on birthdays and holidays, and then she'd pick up an apple pie or chocolate cake from the Price Club and serve it in one of her dishes, making it appear homemade, or make something from a mix. Debby would go over the top and bake something from scratch, unlike other women from Generation Me who were interested only in three things: what's in it for me, how fast can I get it, and it better not interfere with my time off. It was the same at work as employees stood idle in those times when business was slow, not bothering to restock, dust, or acquire product knowledge that ultimately might help them to increase sales. And then they left because they had to work a weekend or two and didn't get a raise every other month.

In all fairness, it was a double-edged sword — it seemed that corporations only cared about the bottom line, not their employees. Retailing was particularly brutal and I couldn't

wait for the day when I could retire and leave the rat race behind. But that was at least another 12 years away if I remained with "The Store."

"Would you like caramel or iced, Mr. ah..." she said, coming back into the kitchen.

"Simmons," I said, "David Simmons."

She hesitated ever so slightly, as if trying to recall where
she knew me from, then put it out of her mind and continued
across the kitchen. "Did you want coffee? It'll only take me a
minute to boil some water."

"No, thank you."

She turned on the stove and moved the kettle to a back
burner.

"I'm not very hungry," I lied again. Who could eat at a time
like that? My stomach was doing flip-flops as I watched her
scoop another caramel roll off the paper. "Only half, please,
and a small glass of milk, thank you."

"A big man such as yourself?" she asked, setting the whole
roll in front of me. "Eat what you can and take the rest home."

Why argue? I thought and shrugged. Although encouraged
to eat while it was hot, I waited for her water to boil. As I
watched her peel the green foil from a naturally decaffeinated
Folgers Coffee Singles bag, the milk became even more appealing. Drinking decaf coffee was like drinking non-alcoholic
beer. Why bother?

She stood at the end of the counter, cut the frosted roll on
her plate with the edge of a fork, and took a bite. With her
mouth half-full she told me that she preferred standing in
case Nelson called. Also, the stool was too high and she'd tak-
en a spill from it the year before. "Thank goodness I wasn't injured. I couldn't afford to be laid up because who would take
care of Nelson?"

It was a natural opening and I took it. "What about your
children?"

She looked sadly away. "Our son died when he was only a
week old and giving birth to him almost killed me. Nelson
didn't want to risk trying again. Said if he lost me he'd kill
himself and the child would grow up an orphan. Well, I didn't
want that, either. So we never had any more."

"I'm sorry," I said, but wasn't sure if I believed her or not.

"His name was David, same as yours. Had he lived he'd be

just about your age."

"I know," I said, reaching into my breast pocket and pulling out a copy of her son's birth certificate along with my amended one and laying them side by side on the countertop for her to read.

The fork fell from her hand and clattered on the imitation wood grain Formica beside her plate, and her eyes began to water as she stared at the underexposed, drab-black copy of the original. "Where did you get that?"

"It's mine," I said, a bit more defensively than I meant.

She covered her face with her apron.

I reached over and placed a hand on her arm trying to comfort her, but she pulled away and mumbled something through the cotton. But all I could make out was that her baby was dead.

Nelson's voice filtered in from the other room, still sounding feeble, but a little louder. "Dixie, baby, what's wrong?"

She sniffled into the apron, muffling the sound, and then lowered it from in front of her mouth long enough to say, "I'll be there in a minute, dear."

"No, he's not," I said, jabbing my finger at the certificate. Since talking with Duke, I'd done my homework. "Look at the number. Every baby born is given an official number, which is filed in the county registry by date of birth. If the child is put up for adoption the state reissues what they call an amended birth certificate, eliminating all identifying information that might help an adoptee find his or her parents such as their names and ages, place of birth, et cetera. Oddly enough, because it sort of defeats the whole purpose, L.A. County retains the same date of birth and official number on their amended birth certificates. By matching them up I was able to find my given name, David Patrick Simmons, and it wasn't difficult to find you after that."

She buried her face in her apron again and began to sob. "It c-can't be... I watched my baby die. He stopped breathing and turned blue. There was nothing I could do to save him. By the time the ambulance arrived, he was dead. It was my fault... If only I had known what to do... I was just too young."

If she was acting it was a darned good job.

Still sobbing into her apron, she trundled past, knocking over the barstool beside me, and disappeared around the cor-

ner. Gloria would have hurried after, trying somehow to ameliorate the pain I'd just inflicted — as if it was my fault. All I
was trying to do was find the people who'd abandoned me
without any expectations of ever seeing me again. My arrival
on their doorstep 47 years later had to be a shock, but any
pain they felt, I believed, was self-inflicted. The six grand
they'd received, long since spent, obviously did nothing to as-
suage it, unless Dixie Simmons was actually telling the truth?

Could it be that I had been resuscitated after the ambulance took my body away and then secretly black-marketed by
some sort of underworld hospital syndicate that issued a pho-
ny death certificate? If so, what about the body? They would
have had to bury it and it didn't sound like the kind of death
that would require a closed casket. Surely Dixie would have
recognized her own child, regardless that he was only a week
old — unless of course he'd been cremated, which seemed unlikely since the Neptune Society hadn't revived the custom until sometime in the late 60s or early 70s as cities grew and
cemeteries became more crowded. It was too bizarre for even
me to believe and I wrote fiction. Somehow I had to find out
and I wasn't leaving until I did.

I followed Dixie into a tiny 1940s white-on-white, movie-
set-looking living room with white shag carpeting. Nelson was
lost under a white crocheted afghan on a creamy white upholstered sectional pressed against the far wall, which was covered with 8x10 black and white photographs of old movie stars
in black metal picture frames. I recognized some of the newer
ones: Elizabeth Taylor, Humphry Bogart, Marilynn Monroe,
Cary Grant, Grace Kelly, and John Wayne.

In front of the couch was a five-foot round of thick glass
set atop a gilt wrought-iron pedestal that held the remains of
Nelson's half-eaten cinnamon roll. Alabaster walls, with satin
white trim on the baseboards and window-shutters, and a
bright white acoustical ceiling that appeared covered with ex-
ploded popcorn, completed the Hollywood effect. A polished
aluminum walker stood sentinel as Dixie squeezed beside him
and collapsed into his feeble arms.

Dixie's sob-wracked body looked as if it would crush the
poor man as she cried on his chest, but Nelson's bony, liver-
spotted hand never faltered as he stroked her permed hair,
waiting for her to regain enough composure to tell him what

I'd said. He glared at me over her shoulder and I stared back, contemplating the likelihood of coming from such unlikely stock and worrying about the emotional trauma giving him a stroke after Dixie cried herself out and conveyed the purpose of my visit.

When she did, color flooded into the old man's cheeks as he sat up beside her, swung his legs out from under the handmade blanket, and stretched a shaky arm toward the walker. "I want you out of here, mister. I don't care who you say you are, but you darn sure aren't our son. David was buried in Hillside Memorial Park a long time ago. You can drive up to Inglewood and check it out yourself and I suggest you do. We visit him on his birthday, Christmas, and Easter every year and have done so for the past 48 years; nothing's going to change that. You walking through our door waving some fake piece of paper isn't doing anything but causing my wife grief and I won't stand for it. Now, get your sorry ass out of my house before I have to hurt you."

I looked down on him and wanted to laugh as he stood with one quivering hand on the walker and the other in his pajama pocket where the old coot just might possibly be holding a small pistol. Leon's letter said that my father had done a lot of crazy things and I would be hard pressed to cross the room and get a gun away from him before he pulled it out and shot me.

All of a sudden my worst fears came to life as Nelson's face contorted and his body stiffened. His hand came out of his pocket clutching at his chest as he fell away from the walker and toppled backward onto the couch.

SEVENTEEN

"Nelson!" Dixie screamed and tried to catch him, which, of course, was impossible. Light as his decrepit old body might have been, it was enough to send her sprawling sideways onto the floor. I knelt to help her, but she pushed my hand away and crawled toward her husband. "Don't just stand there, young man," she said as she pulled herself up on the couch beside him, "call 911."

It took the ambulance somewhere between ten and fifteen minutes to arrive. All the while Dixie rubbed her husband's arms, attempting to ease the pain within them.

"If Nelson was your father," Mrs. Simmons said to me as one of the attendants helped her into the back of the ambulance, "which he isn't, you may have just killed him. I hope you're satisfied. Whatever someone may or may not have done to you in the past isn't our business and I don't ever want to see you again."

The driver closed the door and sprinted around to the cab. Red lights flashed, bouncing off the surrounding houses. Some neighbors peeked out from behind closed window shades, while others stood in their minuscule front yards, likely speculating in hushed voices about the possibility of an upcoming estate sale, as the ambulance drove away with siren blaring.

Turning the lock and pulling the front door closed, I couldn't seem to move as I stood on the front porch recalling Duke and Gloria's warnings. I waited until the ambulance was out of sight before heading to Hillside Memorial Park. Not that seeing a grave marker would prove anything because, if in fact I had been sold on the black market, the child buried there could be anyone but David Simmons. Moreover, while I was glad to be alive, an ominous feeling swept through me as I stood over the embossed bronze marker:

David Patrick Simmons
Beloved Son
April. 4, 1950 – April 11, 1950

Where had he come from, this child who had taken my place? As I looked out over the sloping hillside, past the oleander hedges muffling the din of the afternoon commuter traffic beginning to wend its way home, I wondered how Dixie Simmons knew for certain that it was really her son who was buried beneath my feet. For all the damage I'd just done, had I learned anything useful?

EIGHTEEN

Graciously, Duke refrained from telling me "I told you so" the next time we met, although he was intrigued with Dixie and Nelson's reaction.

"Obviously, they believed you were dead," he said.

I sat in his office on a comfortable couch, the soft floral-patterned fabric something his wife, Susan, had picked out, and it wasn't difficult to distinguish her touches, which stood in stark contrast to the mounted service memorabilia on the wall behind his desk. Brass plaques and shadow boxes filled with medals encircled a framed poster in the middle of his *I-love-me* wall, as he called it, with a camouflaged Navy SEAL rising out of green swamp water holding an algae-covered assault rifle across his chest. Although impossible to recognize even by those who knew him, Duke had posed for the famed Navy recruiting poster and the picture made my skin tingle every time I saw it.

"Why wouldn't they? Maybe they aren't my folks after all."

"I'm not convinced," Duke said, swinging his feet up to the corner of his desk and crossing his legs at the ankles. As always, he looked comfortable with himself. "I saw the official documentation at the hospital. The records might be old but they didn't look as if anyone had tampered with them."

"Maybe not, but I'll bet you didn't check for a death certificate, did you?"

He laced his fingers behind his head and leaned back in the chair. "It really didn't occur to me."

"No reason it should. It wouldn't have occurred to me either, but isn't it something we need to check out?"

"Unquestionably," he said, kicking his feet off the desk; they thudded on the beige and green industrial grade carpet somewhere behind his desk. "Tell you what, Harry, I have to return to L.A. next week and I'll be happy to check it out. But only because you've got me curious."

"Not that I mind waiting all night for one of your crack-of-dawn phone calls," I said, feeling maybe I could kill two birds with one stone, "but I'm going with you."

He frowned.

I shrugged.

"You know," he said, rising out of the chair, "just because those folks had the right name, doesn't mean they're the right people."

"Are you trying to make me feel worse?"

"I'm just saying—"

"Come on, Duke. How many Nelson and Dixie Simmons can there be?"

"I don't know, but you might want to continue looking for another couple with the same first names. Simmons is a fairly common surname and it's a big country."

"I don't think there's any point. The Simmons woman recognized my birth certificate and it upset her so much the old man had a heart attack. Even if there is another Nelson and Dixie Simmons—"

"Yeah, yeah, yeah," Duke said, dismissing my denouncement with a wave of the hand. "Right names, wrong people. I think maybe the California birth certificate is a fake and you should concentrate your efforts in Florida. But not until after we get a look at that kid's death certificate."

"And maybe Nelson's?"

"Probably too soon for that, if in fact he died. But you can always check the obits in the L.A. Times. Library should have copies for the past few days."

I pursed my lips and nodded.

He came around the desk and momentarily placed a hand on my shoulder. "If this is too tough for you, Harry, maybe you should call that Peterson fellow again and see what he can dig up. He did a good job for a fair price, which, by the way, was much more reasonable than I would have charged — even for a friend."

Sometimes it amazed me that Duke actually seemed to know when he was coming on a bit too strong, because most of the time he didn't. A year after his wedding, Susan told Gloria and me about an incident that happened on their honeymoon while riding a glass-bottom boat in Disney World's Frontier Land.

"We were standing somewhere close to the side when a riverboat with a giant paddlewheel passed in the opposite direction," she said, making an undulating motion with the tip of her crutch, "and sent its bow wave washing across the deck of the boat we were riding on.

"'Hold this,' Duke says, handing me the new Polaroid camera we'd gotten as a wedding gift. Well, silly me. I thought he was going to pick me up so I wouldn't get my braces wet, and what a sweet man I'd just married. But nooo... what's he do? He hops up on the guardrail and leaves me standing there to get soaked.

"'Hell,' he says, 'I had on my new two-hundred dollar boots, an' you were too weak to get up there yourself.'"

We all laughed, including Susan, who had taken about three weeks, according to Duke, to "get over her mad" before realizing there had been nothing malicious in his actions. He'd just reacted like he might have if he'd been with one of his SEAL Team buddies instead of his new wife.

"It's not too tough," I said. "I just want answers now. I get frustrated spending days looking for information any high school kid can find on the Internet in a matter of minutes."

"Don't sell yourself short, pal; it's not that simple. Government bureaucracies are complicated mazes filled with little bureaucrats who defend their dead end jobs with red tape tied up in more red tape — even on the Internet. Professionals like Peterson have been in the system long enough to know just where to cut it. But that information is available to you, too; try not to be so impatient. What you're looking for has been there 48 years. It's not going anywhere."

Regardless, I phoned Peterson when I returned home and got his answering machine. I left a message for him to get in touch with me.

NINETEEN

It felt like I was back at square one and vowed to work smarter, not harder, which meant I needed to get more organized. When Peterson called he'd probably want to see the letters Jenny and Leon had written to one another along with my adoption papers and amended birth certificate, and I didn't want to waste time looking for them.

I went to the garage knowing I'd squirreled away a three-ring binder with marsupial pockets somewhere among the morass of unmarked cardboard boxes filled with Jenny's stuff that we'd brought home and stacked along the inside wall. In hindsight it would have been faster driving to the Office Depot downtown and purchasing one.

Each time I opened another box without finding the elusive binder, I wondered why we hadn't taken the time to label them, or kept those contents in the first place. A lot of it was either sentimental or useful, but there were boxes of Jenny's books I'd never read, and a carton of her favorite jigsaw puzzles that undoubtedly would have pieces missing. In one of Jenny's kitchen drawers Gloria had found Ziploc sandwich bags with stray puzzle pieces sealed inside. Evidently my wife thought that one day she might reunite them with the appropriate puzzles.

We also had an attic full of boxes that hadn't been opened in years. Probably all good stuff that still worked, but when would we ever use a rotary dial telephone or CB radio again? I darn sure didn't want our kids to have to deal with the quagmire of crap Gloria and I saved after we passed away, let alone Jenny's. I got so sidetracked digging through those unmarked boxes that I lost sight of my original mission.

I began moving the boxes I'd opened to the outside garage

wall and labeling them with a black Sharpie marker. It was tedious going, but in the long run it would help my wife and I make a decision on what to do with the contents, or so I thought. The last box I opened stopped me cold. It was filled with Bobby's personal effects from the Needles jail. Evidently I'd set it in the garage after dropping him at the rehab center and forgotten all about it. Bad enough were the memories triggered by pulling out my son's bloody and puke-stained clothing, which I immediately threw in the garbage can to save Gloria from experiencing the same emotions.

Bobby had come into the lobby carrying that particular box after we'd bailed him out of jail. Evidently the investigating officer had salvaged the vehicle registration and insurance paperwork from the glovebox and valuable personal items from the trunk of my son's totaled car before a wrecker towed it to the junk yard. Bobby had seemed particularly attached to the box and wanted to take it with him to rehab; however, they hadn't permitted him to do so. I had no idea how my son had explained the wooden cigar box filled with art deco, antique, and estate jewelry to the cops and gotten it back, but the sight of it suddenly made me sick to my stomach.

✖ ✖

Most of the PIs I'd talked with before hiring Peterson to find Nelson and Dixie Simmons had indicated that their fees would range in the hundreds of dollars a day or any portion thereof plus expenses. Peterson's flat $40 an hour plus expenses seemed more than fair considering the $90 my auto mechanic charged. Although after a while, even $40 an hour added up to a pretty good chunk of change. Nevertheless, Peterson's first bill had been a pleasant surprise, as was he when we finally met.

"Time-slicing," he said. "If I have to make a trip to L.A. for any reason, I try to combine it with other cases and split the bill between my clients. Most dicks would charge each one separately, I know, but I got me a pretty good pension an' don't really have to work. Besides, most people who need my services can't afford 'em, anyway. So, because I love what I do so much, I give 'em all a break."

"You're a hell of a guy," I said, trying to keep from staring.

Character observation is critical for writers who must quickly sketch them with a word or two. Peterson looked just about as I imagined from listening to his smoke-damaged voice on the phone. A cliché of broad shoulders and barrel chest with square, butt-crack chin and full head of salt and pepper hair combed straight back. His gray eyes twinkled as we stood just outside the store's west entrance. I had difficulty concentrating on the character study with everything else on my mind.

"Yeah, so what can I do for you?" he asked, exhaling. A plume of smoke sailed out the side of his mouth adding to the cloud around him. "Simmons moved or something?"

"No... " I said, weighing whether to ask his opinion about the cigar box in Bobby's personal belongings. I hadn't yet shared my discovery with Detective Meadows or Gloria. "...the address was good, but they weren't the ones I was looking for."

"Ain't any others, Mr. Hamilton, least ways married to each other. Not in the whole damn state."

Duke might be interested in that wee bit of information but I already knew it didn't matter. "That's good to know," I lied. Peterson wasn't a friend like Duke who, I was sure, wouldn't turn me in for tampering with evidence and also give me advice on what to do. "But they weren't my parents. Their baby died a week after it was born. I saw the grave site."

In our original conversation, I'd only shared the fact that I was adopted and had tracked down the names of my biological parents but was unable to find them. This time I went into more detail, telling him the whole story, beginning with finding my adoption papers in Jenny's old cedar chest. "So, I thought if you could find the Simmonses as quickly as you did, maybe—"

"It's like this here, Mr. Hamilton," he interrupted. "For the most part, I depend on personal contacts from when I was on the job. Not everybody I know is retired yet, but they're getting real close. An' I also still got me some confidential informants on the street, not that they're any help in a case like yours, but it took me a lifetime of work to build them relationships and I ain't about to give 'em up. Anyhow, that's neither here nor there, but that's the difference between me and you. For instance: letters you send — if you ain't got no clout — they're shuffled from department to department before winding up in some two-bit bureaucrat's pending file and they'll sit in there until the loser is damn good and ready to do something about it. An' your phone calls probably don't do no good, neither. I'll bet you've spent hours wading through voicemails and leaving messages which didn't get answered. Or if you actually did reach somebody, it was a secretary screening the calls of the person you wanted to talk to and they was out to lunch and never returned your call. Am I right?"

I nodded but he didn't give me time to answer.

"Well, I don't put up with that crap. That's how I was able to get the information you needed before, 'cause I had the right connections. But Florida? I ain't got no connections in Florida, so you're going to have to find somebody who's got the right connections down there."

"How do I do that?"

"How'd you find me?"

"In the phone book."

"An' you was real lucky, too. Not every dick in the business is as honorable as me. While I might use a legal ruse or two to get the information somebody needs when I ain't got the right connections, I ain't going to jail for nobody. I don't pull no illegal subterfuges like you seen 'em do on TV. Saying stuff like I'm some sort of government official or something could get my license pulled, an' I ain't about to do it. But a lot of guys who used to be on the job will just sort of wink at the law and do anything they need to do to get the information, which could come back an' bite you in the ass. Others are just out to take your money. They put in a token effort — stuff like you can do yourself on the Internet an' such. They never even leave their desks and have the gall to charge as if they're going out in the field."

"So how can I be sure if—"

"You can't. But let me give you some free advice."

"I think you already have."

"An' it's worth every penny, too, ain't it?" Peterson chuckled. "So, let me give you some more, Mr. Hamilton. I've helped a lots of folks in your situation looking for lost relatives. An' maybe I wasn't always successful, but I always gave 'em a day's work for a day's pay. Anyhow, first thing you got to know is that for the past fifty years or more, Florida has been the leading state for black market adoptions. So, as I see it, you've got a whale of a big job ahead of you. If you're lucky you might be one of 'em Cole babies. I seen some information about 'em on the Internet recently, so evidently somebody's got a handle on it."

"Cole babies?"

"Yeah. From the Cole Clinic down in Miami. Laws weren't as strict back then and private adoptions went largely ignored. Now, as I understand it, some unscrupulous doctors and lawyers teamed up and made a fortune selling babies from unwed mothers who were fast-talked into giving 'em up. Anyhow, if you ain't one of 'em and came from, say, a reputable agency, you just might need one of 'em unscrupulous dicks down there.

"I wish you luck, Mr. Hamilton," he said, grabbing my hand and crunching it goodbye. It was my turn to laugh as I watched him saunter into the parking lot, if only to keep from acknowledging the sinking feeling in the pit of my stomach. How in the hell was I going to find a Sam Spade caliber private investigator in Florida? Even if I could, I probably couldn't afford him.

On my way home I swung by the Liquor Locker on Morena Boulevard and sent Peterson a bottle for his unsolicited free advice. He sounded like a man who drank Scotch and I really hoped so because the 21-year-old GlenDronach cost almost as much as I'd paid him for the Simmons' address. If he didn't, his friends would undoubtedly be impressed when he served the aged single malt whiskey.

A week later Duke picked me up in front of the store en route to L.A. He had a little Honda CR-V four-wheel-drive that got about 26 miles per gallon. It was comfortable, but not a car I would have thought a former Navy SEAL would own. I also realized that he didn't listen to music as Rush Limbaugh blathered from the radio for most of the trip up the Interstate. By the time we reached the County Recorder's Office it was almost noontime and I wondered if Duke had planned it that way, or if that was just the way it worked out.

Most of the desks behind the counter were empty and the only bureaucrat around to help was a crotchety old man who should have retired decades ago. I was amazed that Duke actually sweet-talked the geezer into finding David Patrick Simmons' death certificate and making a copy for us, which essentially proved that my California birth certificate was a fake.

"Well, I guess that's that," he said.

"Yep," I said with a shrug. "Looks like I was born in Florida."

"That'd be my guess. But before you go running off tilting at windmills, have you checked with Barbara about exhuming Jenny's body for a DNA sample?"

"'Out of the question,' she said. And Leon's cremains were scattered in the high desert of Arizona. So I'm S.O.L. there, too."

"What about those letters you told me about? Were they still in their envelopes? If so, there'll be DNA on the flaps and stamps."

I smacked my forehead with the heel of my hand.

✖ ✖

The drive back home seemed a lot longer than the drive up. I was excited about the possibility of extracting Jenny and Leon's DNA from the stamps and envelope flaps, but so torn with anxiety for the past week about finding Jenny's jewelry in Bobby's belongings that I didn't know what to do next. Had my son accidentally killed Jenny when she caught him stealing her jewelry, or had he done it on purpose? The medical examiner had ruled Jenny's death as *undetermined*, not *natural* or *accidental*. Detective Meadows hadn't ruled it a homicide, but he hadn't closed the case either. I still hadn't notified him about finding the missing jewelry, and in order to do that I would have to tell Gloria where I found it.

"I need your help, Duke," I said. "I have a friend who—"

He slid into the inside lane to pass a pickup truck loaded down with hay that was only going the speed limit. "Don't try to sugar coat it, Harry," he interrupted.

"What do you mean?"

"What's really bothering you?"

"Okay, let me rephrase it this way: I have a problem, which I could ask you about as a friend, but I think it would be better if I asked you about it as a hypothetical."

He chuckled as a car behind us laid on the horn. "That

bad?"

"Yeah."

"Or maybe ask me about it as your attorney."

"Is there attorney/client privilege when it's not just about me?"

He looked across the car, checking the rearview mirror. "Is this a criminal matter?"

"I'm pretty sure it is."

Duke pulled back into the outside lane and flipped off the driver who'd honked and had accelerated past. It didn't matter that we were doing 70 in a 55. Other cars were flying by like we were standing still. "But you're not a hundred percent sure?"

"No, I'm sure. I just don't know what to do about it."

"Have you talked to Gloria about it?"

"I don't want her involved."

"But it's okay to involve me?"

I smiled half-heartedly. "Attorney/client privilege."

"Depends," he said. "The privilege protects most communication, but there is a crime/fraud exception, which renders it moot if your intention is to further the crime or fraud, or to cover it up. I can certainly advise you on a legal course of action, but I cannot and will not help you continue committing a crime if that's what you're contemplating, or become an accessory after the fact if you're covering one up. I won't lie for you, Harry."

TWENTY

The house was dark when I arrived home from work and parked on the street. I really needed to go for a run. The physical break between the mental strains of writing in the morning and then dealing with customers and staff the rest of the day was the way I coped without alcohol.

Unlocking the front door, I was surprised not to hear the familiar, annoying high-pitched signal that sounded for thirty seconds before the alarm went off, unless of course I entered a four-digit code on the keypad to secure the system. Although Gloria didn't usually forget to set it, on rare occasions I have found it turned off. "I'm home," I said, closing the door and glancing at the keypad. I didn't get a response from my wife, but a flashing red light indicated one of the security sensors had been activated. I waited a moment, thinking that it might be the front door that I'd just closed, but the light continued to flash. The thought that maybe someone had broken into our house slowly crept into my mind.

Every day the newspaper reported one or more burglaries in San Diego, and every day I wondered what were the chances of our home getting hit? I'd taken every precaution suggested by security experts with the exception of putting iron bars across our windows. I wasn't about to become a prisoner in my own house. Nevertheless, I stopped in the tile entryway and listened very carefully.

What was it you were supposed to do — leave and call the police? By the time they arrived, whoever was in there would be long gone and so would all our stuff, and I wasn't about to let that happen. So I stepped cautiously onto the carpet, made my way through the living room to the swinging door leading into the kitchen, and found it closed, which was odd because

Gloria and I never closed that door. I put my hand against it, took a deep breath, and held it as I listened again for any faint sound that might indicate someone was on the other side. Every creak an old house makes in the dark plays on the imagination and mine was running wild as I stood with my hand on the door — every sense heightened and every muscle strained taut.

Impetuously, I shoved open the door and burst through. Silhouetted against the glass French doors leading to our backyard were the figures of two men, who immediately turned toward me.

"Surprise!"

My knees buckled as the two silhouettes were joined by a dozen more and someone snapped on the kitchen lights. I heard myself say the F word, one I rarely used any more, as I fell back against the doorjamb and slid down to the floor on my butt.

"Happy anniversary, sweetheart," Gloria said, kneeling down beside me and wrapping her arms around my neck.

"W-what?" I asked, abruptly realizing, but not believing, that I'd been so wrapped up in my own little world over the past few months that I'd totally forgotten our silver anniversary. I still felt weak in the knees as she helped me to my feet and thrust a stemmed goblet filled with sparkling cider into my hand. "I'm sorry," I whispered in her ear as I raised my glass to accept the toast Duke was somewhere in the middle of making.

"...To Harry and Gloria and the next 25 years!"

Everyone cheered and raised booze-filled glasses to their lips, while I sipped my non-alcoholic cider and swore silently to myself. How the hell could I have forgotten? Nevertheless, it didn't take long before I was in the swing of things, attempting to enjoy family and friends as we drank, conversed, and munched on the party platters Gloria had hidden away from me in the fridge, which Duke's wife couldn't believe I hadn't opened in three days.

"Morgan never goes in the refrigerator, do you, sweetie-face?" Gloria said, using one of two terms of endearment in a tone reserved to express her anger or displeasure with me in public; this time I imagined it was for using the earlier expletive.

"It's the safest place to hide anything from me, isn't it, precious?" I asked, using the other.

She scoffed. "Not always."

"I guess from now on I'll have to start looking," I said, aborting my reach for another peeled oxymoron — jumbo shrimp — because my appetite had just been completely squelched.

Susan shifted uneasily on her crutches. "I think I'm going to go sit down for a while, if you don't mind." She motioned to Duke. "Honey, would you get this for me?"

Duke followed her into the living room carrying a plate of hors d'oeuvres and returned shortly for another beer, saying that we needed to talk before he got too wasted. It's never taken much to get him drunk and by the time I extricated myself from Debby, Bud, and a few other guests to get back to him, it was too late. Susan was saying goodnight to Gloria and prodding Duke out the door with the tip of one of her crutches.

"I'll phone you in the morning," I called out after them.

"Yeah, yeah, yeah," Duke said, waving one arm above his head while steadying himself with the other around Susan, who'd had polio as a child, wore heavy braces on both legs, and walked with crutches, yet was holding him up. "Great party!"

I slipped my arm around Gloria's waist and squeezed her close to me. "It sure was, honey. Thanks."

She smiled sweetly and closed the door behind the Taulberts. "If you'd gotten home sooner, you might have had time to talk with him. Now, why don't we go to bed so the rest of these nice people can go home," she said, loud enough for everyone in earshot to hear.

The party broke up shortly after 10 p.m., which seemed late for a weeknight, and I thanked Gloria again for the wonderful surprise.

"I'm glad you enjoyed it. But you really shouldn't have, you know — considering that you completely forgot our anniversary," she said, pulling a cotton nightshirt over her pulchritudinous body.

Even though I always said fridge for refrigerator, there was nothing lazy about my vocabulary as I considered the five-syllable word. Beautiful was beautiful, but older and more bountiful women deserved the extra two syllables. "It doesn't mean I love you any less."

"You could have fooled me. You may not be drinking, Morgan, but you're so wrapped up in your writing and the search for your biological parents that our relationship is virtually nonexistent. We never go anywhere or do anything together any more besides visit Bobby. Then it's like pulling teeth to get you to go."

"That's not true. We go grocery shopping together every Thursday evening. And—"

"Oh, that's supposed to make me—"

"And I do my writing in the morning while you're still asleep."

"You just don't get it, Morgan, do you? Who are you writing for anyway, you or Jenny? You certainly aren't doing it for me. We used to make love in the morning occasionally. I miss that. And I can do the grocery shopping by myself, thank you very much; it's not exactly quality time. I understand you've been through a lot recently, but so have I. I want you to take me on a date and be interested in me, not what I can fix you for dinner every night."

"I'm sorry," I said, feeling just about completely worthless. "I don't know how I could have forgotten our anniversary because you're the best thing that ever happened to me. I guess I just take you for granted and I shouldn't."

"No, you shouldn't."

"And I won't," I said. "I promise. But don't you ever do that to me again; my heart won't take it."

"Your heart's as strong as a lion's," she said, wrapping her arms around me and pressing her body against mine. She cupped my bottom with her hands and squeezed. "Come to bed and I'll show you."

✖ ✖

As I lay holding Gloria in the warm afterglow of loving her, my mood slowly began to change. I loved her too much to divulge that I'd found Jenny's jewelry in Bobby's personal belongings, even though Duke said I should. But without evidence to the contrary, I realized that Jenny might have given Bobby the cigar box long before she slipped and fell in her living room. Not that I hadn't tried to consider all the possibilities of how it came into his possession before telling Gloria.

I gazed into her warm brown eyes and wondered, who was I to be loved by this wonderful woman that I knew everything about, or at least thought I did, yet couldn't even tell her a simple little thing like who my parents were. Was I one of the black-market Cole babies Peterson had mentioned? I wasn't sure, considering the fake birth certificate from California. Regardless, the identity of my biological parents was going to be impossible to find without a court order. It seemed trivial and insignificant compared to my suspicions about Bobby.

"Don't tell me it wasn't any good for you," Gloria said, from somewhere in the distance.

"It's not that," I said, still gazing into her soft brown eyes.

"What, then?"

I swallowed hard and told her how I'd been sending Jenny a dozen pink roses every year on my birthday in appreciation for giving me life. "I still can't believe she accepted them without ever telling me it wasn't her."

"I'm sure it bothered her."

I rolled away. "And how would you know?"

"Because I'm a mother; maintaining such a fabrication with my children would tear me apart. Living a lie... I mean, honest to God, I could never feel completely honest, no matter how many years went by. Those flowers were probably as painful to Jenny as what you're experiencing now, yet she never violated your father's request. You've got to let go of the anger, Morgan. What's done is done. None of us wants to die the way she did without time to say goodbye to family and friends. Sometimes life just gets in the way. Suddenly, the people we love are gone without a chance to set the record straight. Take Bobby. There are things we both want to say to him and haven't. Things he needs to hear. But if I died tomorrow I wouldn't want him to spend the rest of his life hating me for something I left unsaid."

"It's a little different, Gloria."

"It's no different. You need to love Jenny for all the things she did for you. Not hate her for the one thing she didn't. Obviously, she loved you as much or more than any mother could possibly love a child, but she made a mistake. What parent hasn't? And you don't have to look any farther than a mirror for the answer to that. So it's time to let it go, Morgan, and move on."

"She wasn't my mother."

"Fine," Gloria said, reaching into the headboard and pulling out a white envelope. "Go to Florida. Find your biological parents... if they're still alive; but for heaven's sake, get over this feeling sorry for yourself. You aren't the first kid who's ever been lied to and you won't be the last."

I opened the envelope and stared at an airline ticket to Tallahassee. "What's this?"

"An anniversary present."

"I can't go to Florida. Not now. I—"

"Fiddlesticks. October is the perfect month. You won't start the Christmas holiday promotions until after Halloween and Justin is more than capable of running the store until you return."

"He's just a kid. He doesn't have the experience."

She laughed. "He handled the Memorial Day Sale, didn't he? If he wasn't capable, you never would have promoted him to assistant manager. I know you better, Morgan. Besides, you haven't been eating or sleeping right since Jenny's death and I'm worried about you. You've never let others solve your problems, and we can't afford to send Duke or Tommy Peterson."

I nodded in agreement. "How did you know?" Two days was extremely short notice to give Justin, but he was motivated to excel and was chomping at the bit to get his own store.

"I already told you. I know you."

"No, I mean about Florida."

"Oh," Gloria said, rolling on top of me. "I talked with Duke again. He said ever since you confirmed your California birth certificate was fake that it was time for you to go to Florida. But you've been dragging your feet. He told me that bureaucracies are the same everywhere and of course you're going to be frustrated, but the experience you got in L.A. will serve you well and he's only a phone call away. Now, you want to go again?"

I tossed the tickets on the bedstand, wrapped my arms around my wonderful wife with a prayer of thanksgiving, and took a deep breath before sharing the terrible secret I'd been carrying around for weeks.

"And that's the real reason I can't go to Florida now. We have to go see Bobby and ask him about Jenny's jewelry."

Gloria wiped the tears from her cheeks on the sheet. "Jenny's dead and he's not going anywhere. We can do it when you get back."

"Aren't you afraid of what he might say?"

"You've had a lot more time to think about this than I have, Morgan," she said, turning on her side with her back to me. "How about extending the same courtesy to me?"

TWENTY-ONE

In Tallahassee the driving rain needle-gunned the exposed skin on my face and hands as I climbed the concrete stairs in front of the Florida State Capitol Building. I counted the steps to myself as always, knowing the number would be long gone upon reaching the information desk where I asked my first question: "Where's the Office of Vital Statistics?"

It was quite a change from the balmy weather I'd left in San Diego the day before and I brushed the dampness from the sleeves of my lightweight jacket as a disabled woman turned her battery-operated cart to face me. She smiled sweetly. "What are you looking for, sir?"

"The Office of Vital Statistics!"

She had pretty features and a sexy voice, which would have been very easy to listen to on the phone but didn't fit her character the way Peterson's did. "I heard you, but what specifically are you looking for? Perhaps I can save you time by directing you somewhere local."

I wrinkled my brow.

"Because that office happens to be in Jacksonville," she said.

"I didn't know," I said, raising the packet in my hand. "These are my adoption papers; I'm trying to find my parents."

Her face grew more somber. "Department of Health and Children's Services is located at 1317 Winewood Boulevard, and Record Archives are in the State Library in the R.A. Gray Building here in Tallahassee. Birth and death records and marriage and divorce records are all located with the Bureau of Vital Statistics in Jacksonville. But you're going to need a court order for them to release the names."

I raised the packet again and pursed my lips. I wasn't

about to discuss specifics with an information clerk, and consequently spent the rest of the day asking directions, counting stairs, and batting my head against the bureaucratic wall before deciding to drive to Jacksonville the following day. My return ticket was open because Gloria hadn't known how long I'd need and, since I'd come this far, what was another couple hundred miles more or less? In 48 hours I could be on a flight home after visiting my original destination, which, to my chagrin, wasn't in the capitol city after all. I gulped down two aspirin before calling Gloria and then Duke to share my plans. At least Gloria was still speaking to me even though she hadn't made up her mind what to do about Bobby.

The wipers of the rental car slapped against the drops hitting the windshield as I drove across I-10, a flat asphalt thoroughfare cut through dense pine trees and shrouded under a low ceiling of dark gray clouds. At one point, it appeared as if I were flying beneath them when a heavy fog hovered six feet above the road, threatening to drop to the ground and reduce visibility to zero at any moment. With no one in front of me, I kept my speed up, aware of the impending danger that hitting a sudden fogbank might entail. I arrived in Jacksonville in a little more than three hours, which left most of the day to bang my head against the Sunshine State's bureaucratic wall again. How Peterson enjoyed this type of work was beyond me. Wasting time talking with record clerks who stiffened with resistance at the very mention of the word adoption was like pouring money down a slot machine without ever getting a little back to reinvest. It was a direct affront to my civil rights as a citizen of this country, not to mention against the basic human right to know from whence I came. I was mad as hell after having flown all the way from San Diego, California to Tallahassee, Florida and then driven half way across the state only to be told that anything relating to an adoption could not be released without a court order.

"I thought this was the Bureau of Vital Statistics," I said, glaring at a frumpish, middle-aged woman behind the counter. "It's a violation of my Constitutional rights to deny me access to a public document."

"I'm sorry, sir, the law is the law."

"I want to talk with your supervisor," I said.

She clenched her teeth and nodded, then disappeared into

a maze of cubicles. I hadn't yet learned not to challenge a government employee who had the least little bit of authority. The resistance encountered was inversely proportional to their pay grade, but I wasn't about to be turned away by some entry-level clerk. Fortunately, I didn't have to wait more than a couple of minutes, though it seemed longer, before the supervisor appeared out of the maze with his clerk in tow. It was obvious he wasn't happy about having his day interrupted.

I took a deep breath, trying to ignore the throbbing in my temples, while he perfunctorily introduced himself and ushered me to the end of the counter before sending the clerk back to help the next person in line.

"I agree our laws aren't as liberal as in some states, such as your own, for instance," he said in a condescending tone, "but they exist to protect the rights of people who have given up their children."

"Well, your laws are antiquated," I said, trying to keep my voice calm. "My lawyer says that not since slavery was legal, if in fact it ever was, has there been any law binding a child to a contract made between adults after the child reaches majority."

"I don't make the laws. You'll have to take that up with your congressman. Now, if you'll excuse me, I—"

"No," I interrupted and raised my voice. "I want to talk to *your* supervisor."

He rolled his eyes. "The department manager doesn't have time to talk with every customer and the law isn't going to change. Mr. Witherspoon is a very busy man and he's only going to tell you the same thing I told you."

"I don't care how busy he is. I don't like your attitude and I want him to know just how rudely I've been treated."

"Sir, do you know how many people we get—"

"I really don't care," I interrupted again.

After waiting close to thirty minutes, I handed the department manager a copy of Randall and Jenny Hamilton's petition to adopt baby boy Harry Morgan. All I wanted was a copy of the page in the official record book from the day I was born.

"I'm sure my people explained why that isn't possible," Witherspoon said.

"The book is a public record, isn't it?"

He acknowledged that it was, and available to any American who could claim bloodline parents.

"So, if the person who was born before me wanted to get a copy of the page, he could?"

Witherspoon placed his hands on his hips and frowned.

"And my name would be available to him?"

He nodded ever so slightly.

"So what's to prevent me from claiming I'm that person and seeing the record?"

Witherspoon wrinkled his nose before looking down it. I was beginning to see where the rest of the employees got their attitude. "We do check IDs," he said.

"That shouldn't stop me from seeing the record book."

"That's correct, it is a public record. Tell you what. Since you've come all this way, I'll just have Judy make a copy of the page you want as soon as she finishes with the next customer."

I thanked him and sighed as I took a seat against the wall across from the counter and watched Witherspoon instruct the clerk. Finally I would learn the name I was born with and it would all be worth the flight, drive, wait, and hassle. After she handed me the document I would head over to Susan Taulbert's parents' and spend a restful night before beginning the next leg of my search — finding my biological parents.

Or so I thought.

TWENTY-TWO

Susan's parents, Mr. and Mrs. Nicholson, lived in Lakewood Estates, a post World War II suburb developed across the St. Johns River from downtown Jacksonville. Duke had given me directions to his in-laws' house after suggesting that staying with them would be better than sitting alone in an empty motel room. He promised to phone ahead and pave the way for me. What he didn't tell me was that Susan's father was a retired clinical psychologist.

I crossed the Fuller Warren Bridge and got off I-95 at the first exit, wound through the quaint municipality of San Marco to Hendricks Avenue, and continued south to Cornell Road, where I turned left into the mid-century Lakewood development, still pissed off at Witherspoon and the whole governmental bureaucracy. After finding Emory Circle I turned left again and began looking for the Nicholsons' house number.

All the last names on the page Judy the clerk had given me had been blacked out, along with the page number. The only legible indication that it was the correct page was my birth number and date, which corresponded with the information in the adoption papers. I was certain that if I hadn't given everyone in the department such a hard time, they might only have taken time to black out my parents' last name and I could have later hired someone to get a copy using another name on the page. As it was, I couldn't get anyone to ask for that specific page without using my birthdate and number and having them run into the same bureaucratic wall.

"Petition the Court of Jurisdiction in Miami with good cause," Witherspoon had said. "But I can tell you that a mere desire to learn who your parents are isn't good enough."

I smacked the steering wheel. Why the hell wasn't it good enough?

The Nicholsons' house sat on a corner lot carpeted with Bermuda grass and shaded beneath a soggy grove of majestic old elm trees. The rambling red-brick ranch house, apparently built in the mid-1940s and enlarged with subsequent additions, was covered with a white gravel roof. I parked in the iron-stained concrete driveway and walked to the door under an umbrella of flaming yellow and golden leaves without getting wet.

Warren Nicholson greeted me at the door wearing a green-plaid flannel shirt and jeans; Edna Earl stood behind him wiping her hands on a waist apron. "Come in, come in. It's so nice to see you again, Morgan," Warren said. We'd met the first time at Duke and Susan's wedding where I'd been the best man.

"Duke told us why you're here," Edna Earl said, "you poor boy. We didn't know exactly when you would arrive, but supper is ready any time you are."

Warren glanced at me with hopeful expectation. "Maybe Morgan would like a drink first, dear."

"I could sure use one," I said as he closed the door behind me, "but I think I'll pass."

Warren looked disappointed as he led me through formal living and dining rooms painted a pastel shade of lime green with matching carpet and drapes that must have been popular in the late 50s or early 60s, into an expansive Florida room with red shag carpet and knotty pine walls. The sharp contrast between the pristine antique furniture in the front of the house and the well-worn early American out back made it easy to see where the Nicholsons spent most of their time. It was a comfortable room, heavily scented with a perfumed air freshener, and Warren headed straight to the bar, while Edna Earl attempted to strike a match and light the cigarette stuck between her recently painted bright red lips.

"I'm going to mix myself a little toddy for the body," he said. "Are you sure I can't fix you one?"

"No, thank you."

"I have coffee and tea in the kitchen," Edna Earl said, puffing on her unlit cigarette and moving the lighted match, that was about to burn her fingers, in front of the unfiltered cigarette until she finally found the end. "Or maybe you'd just like a nice cold glass of water."

They obviously weren't going to let me alone until I accepted something. "Do you have any Coke?" I asked.

"Diet or regular?" Warren asked, clinking ice around in his glass.

"Regular is fine."

Edna Earl left the room, leaving a trail of blue smoke behind, and returned shortly with a tall rose-colored plastic glass half filled with foam. After thanking her, I took a seat in one of those comfortable wooden glider-rockers and kicked back with my feet on the matching glider-footstool before taking a sip of foam. Warren settled into a big red club chair with matching hassock, which was obviously his chair, and punched a button on the remote, turning off the muted console TV. As the picture faded, Edna Earl sat in the center of a grand four-person sofa tucked beneath a built-in knotty-pine bookcase that filled most of the north wall, puffing away beneath a billowing cloud of smoke.

"Duke tells us you're having trouble finding your parents," Warren said.

"Poor dear," Edna Earl said, flicking her cigarette above an ashtray overflowing with lipstick-covered butts. "Is there anything we can do to help?"

I daubed the Coca-Cola foam from my nose, while Edna Earl took a tissue and wiped up ashes that had missed the ashtray on their maple wood coffee table. "I don't see how," I said, "but it's wonderful of you to put me up like this."

"Nonsense, Duke is family. We were so happy when he married our little girl. Any friend of his is a friend of ours," Warren said. "Besides, we don't get much company any more, so it's a real treat for us."

Edna Earl stubbed out her half-smoked cigarette and pulled another from the pack. "It's only when you smoke them all the way down that they're bad for you," she said, sticking the next one in her mouth and fumbling with the matchbook. "Warren used to counsel people occasionally who'd been adopted and couldn't find their folks. It's a terrible thing, you know, but he's very good at it."

"Well... " he said, setting his drink on an end table beside his chair, "I don't know that I did much other than listen.

However, over the years I have become familiar with several organized and semi-organized volunteer support groups—"

"People who use support groups as crutches are incapable of taking responsibility for their actions," I interrupted. All I needed was to hear about another mealy-mouthed twelve-step program. I'd kicked alcoholism without one on two separate occasions and I damn sure didn't need one for this. "They're weak and lack the willpower and stamina to finish anything themselves. So, when they fail, you can bet your bottom dollar they'll blame the group instead of themselves. I don't need any crutches, thank you very much."

"I think you have the wrong idea, Morgan. I'm talking about professionals who specialize in legal advice and uncovering information sources, not someone to hold hands and wring hankies with. There are dozens of groups, each offering support and assistance to people in your situation, and they've saved my patients many weeks and months of research by giving them orderly, step-by-step procedures to follow. Groups like ALMA, just to mention one. The Adoptees' Liberty Movement Association offers a computerized, multi-level cross-reference system, search assistants, workshops, and guidebooks to its members. If you'd like, I'll be happy to look in my files for their address... might have some others, too."

"Well, from that perspective," I said, sipping at the Coke again after the foam had dissipated, "it sounds like something I could have used a long time ago."

"I can't imagine what it must be like not knowing who your parents are," Warren said, shifting in his chair. "It's got to be tough. I found counseling dying patients and their loved ones far easier."

I wished I'd taken that drink.

"You see, people who know they are dying go through a series of stages, though not necessarily in this particular order," he said, enumerating them on his fingertips, "denial, anger, bargaining, depression, and acceptance, which are usually intermingled with hope, anguish, and terror. When a person's told they are terminally ill, most will deny it or become extremely angry. 'Why me?' they ask. Then somewhere along the line they turn to God, promising to repent and change their lives if He'll only let them live. When that fails, they usually become depressed. But the amazing thing is, and I've seen this many, many times, with proper counseling and strong family support, they usually accept their fate and wind up dying very peacefully."

It was way too much information and I felt the anger bubbling up inside like the carbonation in my drink.

"Those who are left behind go through a more predictable sequence of denial and acceptance beginning before the loved one dies, which usually helps ameliorate the posthumous distress unless, of course, their death was totally unexpected, in which case the bereavement stages are longer and more severe."

"I think maybe I'd better leave now," I said, getting to my feet and setting the Coke on the coffee table beside Edna Earl's ash-filled crumpled tissue. I understood completely after being hit with the double whammy of Jenny's totally unexpected death and finding out that she hadn't been my mother.

"Nonsense," she said, struggling to get off the sofa while balancing a long ash at the end of her cigarette over the carpet. "Supper is ready and your room is all made up. Please don't run off before you've had something to eat and a good night's sleep."

"My wife is a terrific cook," Warren said, raising his drink to his lips. "However bad your day has been, her chicken-fried steak and mashed potatoes are guaranteed to make you forget all about it. And her green beans and black-eyed peas are the best you'll find south of the Mason-Dixon Line, to say nothing of her cornbread and shoe-fly pie. If nothing else, Morgan, you've at least got to stay for the pie."

My stomach growled, reminding me that I hadn't stopped for lunch, and it overcame all the unwanted armchair psychology being slung at me. Whatever Duke had told his father-in-law, he undoubtedly meant well. But I hadn't asked for his or anyone else's help dealing with the aftermath of Jenny's death and found the unsolicited advice upsetting.

"Why don't you help me in the kitchen while Morgan washes up," Edna Earl said, stubbing out another half-smoked cigarette before the ash broke off and then spritzing the room with a can of air freshener that merely added to the pollution. "Follow me, Morgan. I'll show you to the bathroom."

Surprisingly, the house, which had three bedrooms and

was about 2,000 square feet, only had one bathroom at the end of the back hallway and it made me feel a little uneasy about spending the night. I'd heard older people usually had to make several trips to the john during the night and in the past couple of years had begun to visit it once or twice myself. Nevertheless, after washing my hands and swallowing two aspirin tablets I found in the medicine cabinet above the sink, I joined the Nicholsons in the kitchen at their yellow Formica-topped table with chrome trim, where Witherspoon and all his bureaucratic minions melted away with the first bite of Edna Earl's chicken-fried steak. Obviously, the older generation's axioms about food had merit.

I listened politely while Warren continued his psychoanalysis of orphans looking for their biological parents. He seemed to think of most as zealots, expressing almost a bipolar manic and depressive cycle of highs and lows with each success or failure in finding information about themselves. It wasn't difficult to understand why his 30-year medical career hadn't netted more than an overdeveloped tract house in a middle-class neighborhood.

The unleaded coffee after supper, which I learned somewhere between the main course and dessert was what they called dinner in the South, did nothing to offset the shoe-fly pie-induced hyperglycemia. I excused myself to the guest room and attempted to read the next chapter in a paperback I'd purchased at an airport newsstand before leaving San Diego. Anything heavier would have crushed my sternum when it slipped from my hands as I nodded off. Obviously, the stress from the past few days had been more than I realized.

The next morning after a hot shower, bacon, eggs, toast, and three cups of high-octane coffee, I thanked the Nicholsons and walked out to the mid-sized car I'd rented, only to find the left rear tire flat. Steam rose from the driveway beneath the canopy of damp trees and birds chirped noisily in the branches as blue sky peeked through the colorful leaves. Rather than listen to any more of Warren Nicholson's psychobabble while I waited for Budget Car Rental or my Triple A insurance company to send someone to fix it, I changed the flat myself. It felt good to torque the wheel's lug nuts tight as I pretended to wring Witherspoon and his minion's necks with each and every twist.

In the clearness of the new day, I once again pondered my three choices. Head to the airport north of town and fly home, return to Tallahassee for I wasn't sure what, or drive to Miami and try to petition the Court of Jurisdiction that handled my case 47 years ago. If it was anything like the courts in California, it could take weeks or months before I got an answer. I shot across University Boulevard to I-95 North and followed the signs to Jacksonville International.

TWENTY-THREE

I don't know why San Diego, a coastal city like Jacksonville, is far less humid, but it is, and my head began to unclog shortly after arriving home. It's probably why people on the East Coast are stuffier than on the West, or at least seem to be.

I'd only been gone four days yet it seemed like the whole week was shot. Although flying is a much faster and safer way to travel than driving, I never have liked it. Neither do I like riding buses or trains or any other mode of public transportation, for that matter, where I'm not in control. Being the pilot or driver or engineer would be different, I'm sure.

Be that as it may, Gloria met me at the gate and gave me a great big hug. The knots in my shoulder loosened as she squeezed me close and a tingle shot through me. After all these years she still affected me that way and I often wondered if other men were as lucky in their marriages. She wanted to hear all about my trip and offered to drive out to Duke and Susan's in Alpine to get him started on the petition after I told her, but I said I'd call him from the office the next day. All I wanted then was to go home and pick up where we'd left off the night she handed me the ticket.

✘ ✘

Just before Thanksgiving I received a letter from Gen-Tech, the laboratory to which I'd sent my swab and the envelopes from Leon and Jenny's letters. Barbara would undoubtedly be upset that they hadn't returned the envelopes as I'd requested, but no more than me to discover that neither of her parents were one of mine. However, from the discussions within the letters they once contained, I hadn't expected it and neither

113

had Duke. Nevertheless, it was something that needed to be done.

I stopped winding the old clock after getting the DNA results and it sat silent on the mantel above my kids and grandson's stockings a month later when Bud, Debby, and little Morgan drove over from Palm Springs for Christmas. Gloria asked them to stay an extra few days so we could all visit Bobby, but they declined, so Gloria and I went by ourselves. We still hadn't agreed on how to broach the subject of finding Jenny's jewelry among his personal belongings, which made the visit unusually awkward, to say the least. I probably would have been accusatory and Gloria would have been making excuses for him. He still had two and a half years left to serve on his sentence and Gloria said we had plenty of time to present a united front and get it right. But we had to agree on that first.

I finished writing a couple of chapters for the story I was working on in early January and sent a dozen copies to readers for their perspective. Meanwhile, I waited for the court in Miami to respond to Duke's petition on my behalf.

Gloria circled a notice for a writer's conference at San Diego State in the arts section of the paper and left it on my desk. I glanced at it, skeptical about paying $400 for the prospect of meeting anyone interested in what I was writing. Writer's Market was $30 and had hundreds of listings specifically categorized by genre, which I'd used to select editors and agents with whom to pitch my time-travel novel.

Writing allowed me to escape from reality much more thoroughly than reading because, as a writer, I'm usually looking for the mechanics behind a story and the author's techniques in telling it rather than losing myself in his or her work. Although writing does require a certain amount of research to provide authentic sensory background, which establishes and maintains credibility with the reader, it is purely make-believe. Writing gives life meaning through cause and effect relationships, unlike reality where, more often than not, it seems formless and without resolution; very much like Gloria and my differences on how to deal with Bobby's guilt or innocence in Jenny's death. But they weren't going away by not dealing with them.

Slice-of-life articles like the one adjacent to the conference ad resolved nothing. Yet that sad story had sparked my imagination, and I set the newspaper down and began typing feverishly, trying to get a thousand words complete before heading off to my day job. Somewhere in the middle of page three the phone rang. I glanced down at the clock: 6:15 a.m. It could only be Duke.

I snatched up the receiver on the first ring, hoping it hadn't disturbed Gloria, who normally didn't awaken before eight o'clock. "I thought I asked you not to phone me this early."

"Yeah, but this is important," my friend said, and his familiar and cheerful voice, for some unexplained reason, irritated me. "Or would you rather I have waited until later to give you the court's response? You want the good news or the bad news first?"

He didn't give me time to answer. "Seems they didn't view your alcoholism as a compelling medical reason and refused to release your parents' names. But the good news is that Florida law grants authority for the adoption agency or, in your case, the attorney who handled the adoption to contact your birth parents if you petition them and they're still alive. There's also something called a mutual consent registry down there where you may leave your name and address and your folks can get back to you if they like. However, the law prohibits you from contacting any subsequent offspring of theirs if they don't."

Hope swiftly replaced irritation. "Yes!" I said, hitting Control S on the keyboard to save my work and then pumping my fist in the air. I didn't use a normal mouse unless I absolutely couldn't avoid it.

"Well, don't get your hopes too high, old buddy. If your folks are still alive they may or may not agree to respond, and without the court order you aren't going to get access to any identifying information in your record. And that would be bad news because, if they don't respond, I'm not sure where to turn next. So, soon as we hang up, I suggest you track down the lawyer who handled your adoption and give me his current address. I've got a letter ready to go."

"Wouldn't it be easier if you—"

"How many times do I have to tell you? Friend or no, you can't afford to have me do the grunt work. Once you tell me where to send the letter, I know what to say. Pay me for professional legal help, Harry. If you want to throw your money away, hire that Peterson fellow again. But the quicker I get something in the mail, the quicker you're going to get an answer."

Duke's news made me too excited to think about Bobby or concentrate on my story. Deep down I knew what Jenny would have done; I just didn't want to go there or fight with Gloria about it again. I exited the WordPerfect program and clicked on Internet Explorer. The court might not have unsealed my record, but they had given me another avenue to travel in the quest to find my parents. How hard could it be to find a law firm now that they all advertised on TV and in the Yellow Pages?

I pulled open the bottom right-hand desk drawer filled with hanging files and flipped through the alphabetical folders to find one I'd labeled Important Papers. The letterhead on the adoption document inside was simple: Carmine Manzoni, Esquire, Attorney at Law. His Biscayne Boulevard address and telephone number were centered beneath. My shoulders sagged. Chances that the independent attorney was still practicing were slim to none, and who knew where his records would be? Hopefully Manzoni had taken his case files and joined another firm, or passed his practice on to a son or daughter. I prayed for anything but another dead end as I surfed the Internet looking for attorneys in Miami.

More than 4,700 matching listings came up and I quickly scrolled down to the Ms. When the index jumped from Mann to Marzyck I slumped back in the chair and took a deep breath before clicking a New Search box and typing in Manzoni's address. Forty-seven years ago the attorney worked out of an office building on Biscayne Boulevard; today it was a pub. I smiled at the irony in the food chain of lowlife bottom feeders and exited the program without bothering to search by phone number, because there wasn't a listing in the country any more that began GLendale.

I hopped on the Net and began searching for anyone named Manzoni in Miami, again without any luck. The little clock in the lower right-hand side of my computer screen read quarter to eight and I swore silently at having let so much time slip away unnoticed. It was now impossible for me to get to work on time. Normally it wouldn't have been a big deal, but that morning I'd scheduled a meeting with Justin and all my department managers to review our sales goals for the coming year before the store opened.

Gloria walked past the doorway and looked in. "You haven't left for work yet?"

"Does it look like I left?"

"Good morning to you, too," she said, turning and heading in the opposite direction.

"Gloria, I'm sorry," I said, but it was too late as our bedroom door down the hall slammed closed.

How could such an auspicious beginning to the day have turned to crap so fast?

I phoned Justin and asked him to reschedule the meeting but decided, at his suggestion, to let him run it and brief me on the outcome. And then out of sheer frustration, I phoned Peterson again.

✖ ✖

A couple of weeks later, the soft melodic tinkling of "September Song" being played on the grand piano opposite the shoe department floated through the escalator opening to the second floor and into the men's sportswear department. As the pianist tickled the ivories on the floor below, I gradually stopped berating the housewares department manager for not having displayed the items in the next day's two-page ad on the front racks. *Oh, it's a long, long while from May to December—* The words to my adoptive father's favorite song echoed in my head and, regardless how I felt about his having lied to me, it brought back painful memories of happier times. Leon and Jenny had saved for months before bringing home their first High-Fidelity record player, unlike my best friend's parents who had saved for a television set. I recalled that they were as excited as two kids on new bicycles.

Leon slit the seal and opened the demo record box that came with the Philips turntable, carefully placed the long-playing black vinyl disc on the thin chrome spindle, and lowered the needle arm. He turned and stood in front of the record player with his arms wide open as Bing Crosby, or Frank Sinatra, or some other big-name vocalist from that musical era who I can't quite remember crooned the bittersweet chorus.

I visualized my adoptive parents waltzing around our small living room staring into one another's eyes, totally impervious to the fact that Barbara and I were seated on the sofa watching them dance and wishing they'd bought a TV set instead.

—and these few precious days, I'll spend with you. In retrospect, there wasn't any wonder Jenny had wanted to fulfill their dreams by moving to Sedona after Leon died. Over the years I tried to convince her several times to move in with Gloria and me, especially after our kids had grown and gone and we had the extra room, but she never would consider it.

A soft, pealing double chime in the overhead public address system speakers repeated throughout the store, signaling me to call the office, and I left the housewares manager, feeling totally frustrated as I went to the nearest register and picked up a phone.

"Hamilton," I said.

"You've got a call from someone named Peterson, boss," Justin said. "He said it's important."

"Is he still on the line?"

"Yes, sir."

"Tell him I'll be right there," I said, hanging up and heading for my office. Passing by the department manager, I stopped, placed a hand on his shoulder, and nodded at the shelves. "I know you're shorthanded, Walter, but I don't pay you for excuses. Before you go home tonight, okay?"

I didn't wait for a reply. Peterson obviously had something important to tell me and I didn't want to keep him waiting.

TWENTY-FOUR

"Sorry to take so long in getting back to you, Hamilton," Peterson said, his voice filled with smoke. "But that attorney you wanted me to find died back in 1986."

I propped an elbow on the cherry wood desk in my office and leaned forward, resting my forehead in my hand.

"He lived quite a colorful life, though. *Six wives,* if you can believe it. Apparently Manzoni never met a woman he couldn't marry." Peterson laughed at his own joke. "Probably why he got sixty-two hundred for handling your adoption."

"Huh?"

Peterson chuckled. "Alimony, Hamilton, alimony."

"Look," I said, "all that's very interesting, but it really isn't why I hired you and it doesn't help me one bit."

"Relax, Hamilton, I ain't charging you for the background info; that's my thing. People are fascinating and sometimes I get carried away when they spike my interest. Anyway, Manzoni sold his practice in 1975 to four lawyers fresh out of the University of Miami law school. He then moved to Asheville, North Carolina with wife number five and opened another practice. About a year and a half later he closed it, got divorced, and went into real estate. Did pretty good, too, because he left wife number six about a one-point-two million dollar estate when he died."

"So how does all this help me?" I asked, glancing up at the solid brass ships clock tick-tocking on the wall. It read 8:49 p.m. The store would be closing in eleven minutes. Most of the other store managers had probably long since gone home but, to me, it wasn't what I expected that got done, it was what I inspected... and I still hadn't completed my pre-sale inspection of all the departments.

"Simple. The records you're looking for are either somewhere in a storage shed in Asheville, or down in Miami with Cohen, Garcia, Jurwitz, and Rosenthal, the partnership that bought him out. You know his widow is still alive and never remarried. Ain't that something?"

"Yes. But so what? What good would it do to talk to her? She wasn't married to him when his practice folded."

"Naw, but maybe she knows what happened to the records. He's supposed to keep them just about forever and I'm sure Mrs. Manzoni number five didn't agree to lug them back to Miami after the divorce which, by the way in case you're wonderin', is where she went."

"I sure hope you're right."

Peterson laughed. "Have I ever let you down?"

After hanging up I sat there wondering whether Duke had it all wrong. After 48 years my biological parents, if still alive, had to be in their late 60s or early 70s — maybe older, which didn't leave a whole lot of time to get to know them. Peterson was good, but I'd hired him to help me, not do the job for me. In that respect Duke and Gloria definitely had a point. Surfing the Internet wasn't so daunting that I couldn't ride an information wave or two. The worst that could happen was I'd wipe out and find nothing. However, at that point, I felt capable of finding the right Mrs. Manzoni and the partnership that had bought out her former husband without Peterson.

The phone on my desk jangled and I grabbed it. "Yeah?"

"Yeah?" the voice on the other end of the line said. "Who the hell is this?"

"Who wants to know?" I said, immediately becoming defensive.

"Ralph Larson, district manager. Now, who the hell is this?"

Oh, crap, just what I needed. I wanted to pitch my voice up two or three octaves and say, "I'm sorry, my mommy and daddy aren't here right now," and hang up. I felt foolish at not having recognized my immediate supervisor's voice, or having been more professional when answering the call. "Sorry, Mr. Larson, it's me, Morgan. How may I help you?"

"Answering your own phone these days, Hamilton?"

"Yes, sir."

"That's good. Keeping costs down?"

"Yes, sir."

"Actually," he said, "you've saved me some time because you're just the person I wanted to talk to."

During my tenure as store manager half a dozen different people had filled the district manager's position and I could count the number of times they'd called on one hand. Although Ralph and I had talked before it had been at least six months ago. No wonder I hadn't recognized his voice. "About?" I asked.

"Performance... yours in particular."

I swallowed the lump forming in my throat. "I know the holiday numbers weren't exactly what you were expecting, Ralph, but the figures were still better than last year."

"Percentage wise, your store is running two-tenths of a percent better than the others. However, I don't believe that's through any personal effort by you because you haven't been around enough to make that happen, according to the buyers I've been talking with. How long before you retire, Hamilton?"

Well, that caught me by surprise. "Not any time soon," I said, thinking that even in my wildest dreams retirement was a decade or more away.

"That young assistant of yours, Justin Forsyth... I've been hearing a lot of good things about him. How soon do you think he'll be ready for his own store?"

The tone in Larson's voice made me uneasy. "I was sort of grooming him to move up in a year or two but—"

"It could be a whole lot sooner if you continue to fail at showing up for work and having your head elsewhere whenever you do. If not, you may want to consider finishing out your career in retail somewhere else. Do I make myself clear?"

✼ ✼

Saturday morning I was up writing at 4:30, same as every other day. My new novel was coming along without too much internal angst from Jenny, who still looked over my shoulder and edited almost everything I wrote. However, this time I was getting some help from the characters. Deshler Remmington, a New York City lawyer suffering from polycystic kidney disease, represented Marybeth Whiting in a divorce from her multimillionaire husband and was hard at work wooing the lavender-eyed divorcee hoping to share in her fortune. In an unexpected twist that I hadn't seen coming, Marybeth offered him one of her kidneys as a wedding gift. But Deshler's triumph was short-lived as his new bride doled out the money and the transplant slowly failed. I was writing, but Deshler was plotting and planned to murder his bride in order to gain control of her estate and get her other kidney. Meanwhile, Carla Martinez, blinded in a San Diego highway shooting, was learning to navigate her darkened world while running from the man who'd shot her. And three more characters were beginning to whisper in my ear. It was amazing how the story seemed to evolve after reading a small slice-of-life news clip about an organ donation.

Somewhere around six I stopped to read the newspaper and pour another cup of coffee. A writer's conference sponsored by SDSU caught my eye in the classifieds and looked vaguely familiar. I drew a circle around it and planned to phone the university later. Then as I thought about it I realized that it was the same conference Gloria had brought to my attention several weeks ago. Back at the computer, white letters popping up on the blue background were forming words and sentences, paragraphs and pages, as fast as my fingers could type. My characters seemed to have created lives of their own and were taking full responsibility for the directions they wanted to go, which was more than I could say for myself at the moment.

I loved Saturdays because I could spend more time in my make-believe world without having to rush off to a real job. In fiction there needed to be conflict *and* resolution; no one would read it if there wasn't.

It was 9:45 when Gloria came in with a fresh cup of coffee and quietly set it on the corner of my desk. She never interrupted me while I was typing, not wanting to disrupt any train of thought I might be struggling to get down on paper, so to speak. However, just after she left Peterson called and derailed everything. I hadn't talked to him in more than a month and wondered why he was calling. Although I'd been unable to locate Manzoni's former wife, I hadn't hired Peterson to help me again because, like Duke said, after 47 years the files weren't going anywhere.

"Well, Mr. Peterson, this is a surprise."

"Just called to see how you were doing."

"Really?"

"I also wanted to thank you for the Scotch. I don't believe I ever did."

"You didn't."

"Sorry. It was excellent." He cleared his throat. "But I was wondering if you were able to track down those files an' find your biological parents."

"Still working on it, I'm afraid," I said. "I have a hard time even finding myself on the Internet. But I haven't given up yet."

He chuckled. "Well, you have to do something first to garner a little public recognition, like getting your name in the papers."

"I think I'll pass."

"It don't have to be for something nefarious, Mr. Hamilton. Don't get me wrong. You could be recognized by a garden club or some such for having one of the ten best yards in the neighborhood. Something like that. The thing is to give the various search engines a place to find your name other than the phone book. So let me help you out a little."

"Let me get this straight," I said, feeling a bit leery. "You want to help me do what exactly?"

"Tie up a couple loose ends, if you don't mind. The last time we talked I thought you sounded a little befuddled. I sure figured you would have called me back long before now. But if you're still plugging away at this thing without some sort of resolution, let me save you a whole lot of frustration." He went on to tell me that Manzoni's wife had a garage full of files, but they were all from the law office he'd opened in Asheville. Far as she knew, all the files in Miami had been sold with his first practice. "No good news there either, because two years after Cohen, Garcia, Jurwitz, and Rosenthal bought his practice, the building and all its contents burned to the ground, which is probably why a pub currently occupies that address."

"Thanks, but I didn't hire you to find all this out."

"I know. But as I told you before, people are fascinating and some of them even spike my interest. I can't help it if you're one who did. I looked this stuff up on my own time because you got my curiosity up, nothing more. However, I'm afraid that's the end of the line as far as I can see. I just wanted to let you know. Anyway, I wish you luck finding your folks, Mr. Hamilton. If there's anything else I can do for you, don't hesitate to call."

"Thanks. There is one thing... "

"Yeah?"

"I'm curious why the date and numbers on my fake California certificate matched those of a dead baby and was wondering how that could have happened."

"You in a hurry?"

"It's a piece of the puzzle."

"Maybe so, but it looks like a dead end when it comes to finding your parents, if you ask me. However, I'll be happy to do a little digging next time I'm in L.A. Time-slice it, if that's okay with you?"

I thanked Peterson and turned off my computer, but not before backing up the day's work on a floppy disc. In all the years since I transitioned from my trusty Smith-Corolla typewriter to that first Epson 8086 computer, I'd only lost two or three chapters, and each time it was because I hadn't backed up the work. In a way I missed the sound of that old manual typewriter, but computers had long since spoiled me with more applications and system software on them than I would ever need. Buying one just for word processing was sort of like purchasing a howitzer to swat a fly. However, when the laptop's battery kicked in and prevented me from losing my work every time one of those damn rolling blackouts came through without warning, I was thankful for the overkill.

As soon as I can afford to retire, Gloria and I are getting the hell out of the Golden State, because it's taking too much of our gold to live here. Property taxes aren't too bad, but only because they're tied to the purchase price of our house, not its current value. There's a state income tax on top of the federal, and license plates for our cars are more than $1,000 each year. Then every time there's an earthquake, legislators hike the sales tax another quarter percent to pay for the damage. The weather isn't good enough, in my opinion, to justify paying premium taxes for the rest of my life.

In fact, our house was still shrouded in a dense fog when I went out for a jog. After my conversation with Peterson, I needed to do something to relieve the pressure building inside.

TWENTY-FIVE

Gloria had made me a sandwich, peeled an orange, and left them on the kitchen counter next to the mail. After all the years we'd been married, she knew I'd go hungry before opening the fridge to find something to eat. Her note said that she'd run down to Alpha-Beta to pick up a couple of items she needed for dinner and wouldn't be gone long. I took a bite of the pastrami and Swiss on 12-grain and glanced at the mail: a bill, two self-addressed stamped envelopes returned from agents, and a letter from Bobby. I opened them in that order, saving what I hoped would be the best for last. SDG&E had the audacity to bill without offering a discount for the many disruptions to our electric service. I shook my head, thinking Nordy's would never survive with such shoddy customer service.

Two form letters from the agents rejected my time-travel novel with the same mundane platitudes: not right for us, but keep trying, and... Perhaps another agent would be interested. Rejection letters were dismal reminders that I still wasn't published, but they no longer stung my soul as they had in the beginning. Just part of the process, I thought, setting them aside before picking up the phone. Rather than spinning my wheels writing queries to faceless names in a book, I'd attend the upcoming San Diego State University Writer's Conference and meet an agent or editor or two personally.

Talking with a friendly young lady from SDSU re-sparked my enthusiasm and I signed up, giving her my credit card number over the phone, something else I rarely did. Maybe my time-travel manuscript wouldn't wind up as a doorstop after all. It cost an extra $50 because I hadn't made the early registration deadline when Gloria had first given me the ad. Nevertheless, I elected to spend another $30 to get a ten-minute personal interview with a New York editor who handled science fiction, and thought it was money well spent, seeing as how I didn't have to leave town.

Bobby's letter sounded upbeat as he wrote about his prison vocational training. Not that he wanted to repair shoes after his release, but sewing new leather in the workshop smelled much better than scrubbing greasy pots and pans in the galley. Mindless manual labor allowed him time to think about writing poetry. He included one of his poems, wanting to know what I thought:

> *If peace were a flower,*
> *Open and shared,*
> *Wouldn't someone come along and pick it?*

It sounded like something from Woodstock and I flashed on memories of the Vietnam War protests and Jimi Hendrix winding up the historical musical festival, to which Duke and I had gone, playing a freeform solo guitar rendition of "The Star Spangled Banner."

Poetry was something I knew little about other than it was damn hard to sell, harder even than the stuff I was writing. At least Bobby wasn't writing prose. But where had his sudden interest in poetry come from? Had it always been there and I'd just not seen it? I made a point to ask Gloria after my jog.

✖ ✖

Mission Hills wasn't all that large when it came to avoiding vertical inclines on a beneficial jog of any distance, and my knees really hated the hills. I headed east on Sunset Boulevard until it forked into Fort Stockton Drive. Running on concrete sidewalks was supposedly also harder on the joints than running on asphalt in the streets. But due to heavier traffic on the main thoroughfares, I ran on the sidewalk until turning left onto Goldfinch. I looped around St. Vincent Catholic Church and headed west on West Montecito Way, intending to run around Presidio Park before heading home. I'm not sure my knees felt a difference running on concrete or asphalt the way they did ascending or descending any kind of incline. My mind was mostly on Bobby and his little poem as I picked 'em up and put 'em down for the next 45 minutes.

Gloria was in the kitchen putting away the groceries as I came in through the dining room from our front entry. "You have a good run?" she asked, closing the refrigerator door and crossing back to the island.

I went to the sink and held a large drinking glass under the tap. Until we installed the reverse osmosis purification and softener system a few years back, we all drank bottled water. "I got a letter from Bobby today," I said, turning the cold water faucet on.

"How's he doing?" she asked, standing in front of an assortment of paper grocery bags on the counter.

I gulped down half the glass and wiped my chin on the back of my hand. "He sounds good," I said, breathing hard. "Probably thinks he's gotten away with murder." I guess his little poem wasn't the only thing on my mind.

"You can't be serious."

"Then where did he get Jenny's jewelry? I don't know, Gloria, I just don't know, but it's been eating at me ever since I opened the box of his personal effects from Needles. We can't just keep burying our heads in the sand."

"I'm sure he has a good explanation."

"Then why haven't we asked?"

A tear spilled out of her eye and trickled down her cheek. "Because I really don't want to know... what if she died because he pushed her and she hit her head on the table?"

"If he did, he needs to own up to it."

Another tear spilled out of her eye. "He'll never get out of prison if that's what happened. Is that what you want?"

"You know it's not. We didn't raise him to spend the rest of his life behind bars, but we did raise him to tell the truth and take responsibility for his actions, successes as well as failures. How are we any better if we ignore what happened, lie for him, and try to sweep it under the rug?"

She wiped her cheek on her sleeve and sniffled.

"We should let Detective Meadows know we found Jenny's jewelry."

"Gloriosky, Morgan. Where are we going to tell him we found it?"

"He's probably been canvassing all the jewelry stores and

pawn shops in and around Sedona since we told him it was missing."

"That's his problem."

"And ours is Bobby."

"He's a full-grown man; he's no longer our responsibility. If we've done such a good job raising him, then he'll do the right thing. We just have to wait and see."

I took another gulp of water. "We're still his parents."

"That's right, and we need to protect him."

"How, by sending him a carton of cigarettes every week so he can pay someone to keep someone else from sticking a shiv in him? I thought you just said he's no longer our responsibility."

"That isn't what I meant and you know it," she said, and ran upstairs sobbing.

✶ ✶

The following Friday I strolled into the Doubletree Hotel ballroom on Hazard Center Drive feeling like I'd just entered the first floor of my store — minus the clothing racks and cosmetic and jewelry counters. In their place were at least fifty round cloth-covered tables, each surrounded by ten padded, chrome framed, stackable chairs. A crowd had gathered around the finger-food table in the center and I joined them with sweaty palms. Nordstrom was just across the freeway and, although I'd left work early, it seemed that the writer's conference opening mixer was well under way. Most of the tables already had people seated around them in a wide variety of fashions: everything from evening gowns and tuxedos to cutoffs and tee shirts. I met another writer who wrote stuff similar to mine and had traveled all the way from Livingston, Texas to attend the conference. After two hours of idle introductions to free-spirited writers and serious hopefuls without meeting either agent or editor, I called it a night.

The next day at the registration table in the hallway I received a basic name tag and program of events where I discovered the code: name tags with ribbons attached indicated the attendee was an editor, an agent, a published author, or university personnel — a different color for each group. I recalled seeing clusters of ribbon-tagged conference goers the night before and it reminded me of a story Duke told about a formal social gathering he was forced to attend when he was in the Navy at the Singapore Sheraton in 1979, prior to the Iranian rescue mission.

"The required uniform for attendance was Gulf-rig."

I'd looked at him askance and had no idea what he was talking about.

"White shirt, black pants, and gold cummerbund; most of my team didn't have cummerbunds and hadn't brought them because they took up locker space. Even some of the junior zeros hadn't brought theirs for the same reason and they had a lot more storage space in their staterooms than we had in berthing. One of the jet-jock squadrons got a bit carried away and had red cummerbunds made up special for the occasion and the wing commander's people had 'em designed in a rainbow with a different color for each pleat. It looked like a regular damn circus in there.

"Well, I'm telling you, Harry old buddy, the chicks were scarce. Whoever went on the advance party to set this thing up either forgot, or couldn't get many of the local women interested. The few who did attend were primo but you couldn't get near them without fighting through a circle of red, gold, and rainbow cummerbunds. Something no self-respecting SEAL would ever do unless he was drunk out of his mind. But after a hundred and two consecutive days at sea—"

"I get the picture," I said, interrupting him.

"No, you don't. The officers had them surrounded and monopolized until I met a little brown-eyed beauty named Wind Song coming out of the ladies' room. She was curious about the different cummerbunds and I quickly explained that gold cummerbunds were like wedding rings. 'Guys wearing the gold cummerbunds are married,' I told her, 'and those without, like me, aren't.'"

"You haven't changed a bit, have you?"

He chuckled. "I guess not."

"So, what did you tell her about the others?"

"I had to think fast and the first thing that popped into my head was that anyone wearing a red cummerbund had a social disease. 'You want to stay away from them,' I said."

I laughed. "How about the wing commander's people?"

"Benny-boys, I whispered. She giggled and disappeared into the crowd. By the end of the night, cummerbunds were piled ankle-deep around the perimeter of the room and all the girls were gone. It was a short party but a good drunk."

I shook my head and checked my watch as I turned and headed off for the first seminar of the day. Many of the programs were basic stuff like developing characters, plot, or dialogue, but the ones I wanted to attend instructed *wannabe published* writers such as myself with what agents and editors were looking for and how to promote your book after it becomes published. Nothing that wasn't available in print through Writer's Digest, or other writing magazines, but the program participants offered current information straight from the horse's mouth. I kept watching the clock waiting for my one-on-one interview, while trying to glean as much new information about the publishing industry as possible.

I'd read that if you couldn't write your idea on the back of a matchbook, you probably couldn't interest anyone else in it, and I'd spent hours distilling the synopsis for my 100,000-word manuscript down to 33. "My story is about a twentieth-century Navy pilot who leads his crew on an epic journey across seventeenth-century America on a collision course with Cotton Mather and the Salem witch trials."

The editor sitting across the barroom table at my ten-minute, thirty-dollar appointment looked impressed. "What's it called?"

"*Syzygetic Journey,*" I said.

"Interesting title," he said, taking a sip of water and leaning back. "Tell me about it."

Time seemed to fly by and I'd barely begun discussing the plot and main characters when the interview was over. "The manuscript is complete," I said, standing and shaking his hand.

"Maybe you should call it *Return to Salem.*"

Although I'd become somewhat attached to my title over the years, it really didn't matter what he wanted to call it. What mattered was whether he wanted to read it or not. "May I send you a copy?" I asked.

"Sure," he said, reaching into his jacket pocket and handing me a card. "Sounds interesting. Make sure you put *requested material* on the envelope so my secretary doesn't inadvertently put it in the slush pile."

The appointment was over and the rest of the day passed uneventfully. I was elated that *Syzygetic Journey* wouldn't wind up buried for months among the thousands of unsolicited manuscripts that were sent to editors and agents every year.

That evening after the scheduled seminars were complete, attendees were invited to the ballroom for more finger food and socializing. I went to the bar and ordered a beer to calm my nerves before going home. As I sat there in the reduced lighting feeling guilty, I noticed a few of the other patrons were also wearing conference nametags, most of them with ribbons. Sitting by himself at the bar, two stools down, was a big-time New York agent who handled speculative fiction. My palms grew sweaty when I recognized him and I thought about Duke's story when, for no reason, it seemed, the ribbon on his nametag fell off and fluttered to the floor. He obviously hadn't noticed, and I couldn't believe that I actually got off my barstool and picked it up.

After handing it to him with beer in hand and schmoozing a few minutes, I hit him with the 33-word summation I'd prepared for my earlier appointment. Incredibly, he wanted to hear more and, two hours later, I surprised myself by going home completely sober with his and two more agents' cards requesting to see my manuscript.

Gloria was reading in bed when I arrived home and literally floated into our bedroom wishing I had recalled Duke's Singapore Sheridan story before signing up for the personal interview. "Who needs to spend thirty dollars to talk with an agent? I could have just sat in the bar and waited for them to come in at the end of the day."

"You haven't been drinking, have you, Morgan?"

I patted my shirt pocket. "I bought a beer and took a couple of sips," I told her, and I had done so because I was too keyed up at the end of the day. But I'd spent so much time pitching my book to the editors and agents who came in for a drink after the scheduled events were over, I never finished it. "I won't make that mistake again."

"It wasn't a mistake, sweetheart," Gloria said, laying the

book she was reading face down on the bedspread. "You learned something. Now, come to bed. You've got another busy day tomorrow."

"Who can sleep?" I asked, pacing at the foot of the bed. "I've got to write letters to those people and make them copies of my manuscript."

"I'm sure they don't want to take it back on the plane. If everyone at the conference gave them a three- or four-hundred-page manuscript to take back, their luggage would be impossible to manage."

I laughed, feeling a bit foolish. "I suppose so, but if I send it priority mail it will be waiting for them when they return to work."

"It's Saturday night, Morgan, nothing is going anywhere until Monday. Try to relax."

"I don't want them to forget who I am."

"They won't remember you tomorrow. The important thing is that they asked to see your work and it will stand on its own merit. I'm so happy for you. Now, why don't you come to bed and tell me everything that happened today and maybe we can find a way to burn off some of that excess energy."

TWENTY-SIX

Sunday morning I arrived early at the conference and drew a cup of coffee from the industrial-size urn in front of the ballroom. One of the New York agents, dressed in a Hawaiian shirt and jeans who'd given me his card at the bar the night before, was just biting into a Danish when I greeted him. We talked briefly about nothing in particular, and then other more interesting current events before the conversation rolled around to writing conferences and appointment fees. I hoped that I hadn't been too blatant in steering the conversation to that point.

"Maui is the granddaddy of them all and they charge eighty dollars there for a six-minute appointment, so the committee encourages us not to discourage writers after they've paid that much to talk with us." He chuckled. "You wouldn't believe the crap I let people send me."

My heart sank. Were they doing the same thing here? "Seems to me," I said, "that conferences are good places to discover new writers because they're serious enough to spend the money to attend in the first place. And since writers are basically a shy bunch, why is it that all you guys congregate and schmooze with one another instead of mingling among those of us who came to be discovered?"

He smiled over his Danish. "We aren't any different from you, Morgan," he said, glancing down at my name tag. "It's just another aspect of writing, and we too are more comfortable with whom we know."

As it turned out, meeting the editors and agents at a conference wasn't any different than sending them query letters. It only cost a hell of a lot more. At six cents a page my 400-page manuscript ran $24 a copy, not to mention eight more dollars and change to send it and another eight and change for the return postage. Multiply that by four and add it to the conference fee and I was out more than $650 for the weekend. If anything the experience renewed my resolve to see my books in print, but I wasn't quitting my day job — not just yet, anyway.

✖ ✖

My adoptive mother had died a little more than a year ago and Gloria and I were driving up Pacific Coast Highway en route to visit Bobby for our June visit. We'd finally decided it was time to confront our son about finding Jenny's jewelry in his belongings. I'd almost forgotten about the manuscripts I'd mailed off the month before, but my mind wasn't on questioning Bobby, where it should be. Instead, I was thinking about my latest novel and a new character who'd begun to emerge. Spike Williams, suffering from uncontrollable diabetes, had just been released from federal prison in Jessup, Georgia in exchange for an experimental pancreas transplant, and he was attempting to turn his life around after the surgery with help from a prison pen pal named Nelda. Maybe Bobby could help me add a touch of realism to the prison life in my story. Talk about a cop out. I'd also either temporarily forgotten, or set aside, the quest to find my biological parents because Peterson had reached the final dead end and I was having a lot of trouble dealing with it.

When my cell phone rang, I pulled it from my pocket and handed it to Gloria.

"Who?" I heard her ask, as if reception along the coast just south of Santa Barbara was fading. The road curved around the foothills by the sea and, out my window, a golden sunset illuminated the shimmering ocean surface in a fiery blaze of color. She listened attentively before speaking again. "He's busy driving at the moment; may I take a message?"

I glanced at Gloria.

"I'm his wife."

Red taillights ahead abruptly began to glow brighter as we rounded the next bend and I could see a traffic jam forming ahead.

"No, he can't; there isn't any place to pull over at the moment. May he call you back?"

Maybe if everything came to a stop I'd take the phone but, unless it did, Gloria did the talking while I was driving. California drivers always seemed in too big a hurry for me to let down my guard behind the wheel. It was difficult enough just to hold a conversation with my wife going through L.A. and she was seated right beside me.

"I'll tell him. Thank you very much," she said as traffic began picking up speed again.

"Tell me what?"

"Just a minute, I have to write it down before I forget."

I waited as she fished around in her purse for a pen and scribbled something that looked like a name on the back of an envelope.

"So, who was it?" I asked.

"He didn't say except to mention that he worked at the courthouse in Miami and was calling from a pay phone so you wouldn't be able to call him back. He said that while alcoholism wasn't a compelling medical reason to open your adoption records to you, there was something you should know and probably wouldn't be able to find out through the mutual consent registry."

I pulled over to the side of the road and stopped, letting traffic pass. "Like what?"

"He didn't say. All he told me was the name of the doctor who delivered you and said you'd have to approach it from that angle because, if anyone ever found out he helped you, he'd lose his job."

"Are you kidding me?" I asked, reaching for the envelope on Gloria's lap. "What else did he say?"

"That's all," she said, handing it to me. "It doesn't make any sense, Morgan. Why would some civil servant, who doesn't even know you, risk losing his job to tell you this?"

I stared at Dr. Julius Scarborough's name. I didn't care what the man's reasons were as I wondered what could be so important that he risked being fired and was willing to use his personal time and money to tell me.

TWENTY-SEVEN

"See de Convict," Bobby said, laughing as he gave us the inmates' definition of the large CDC stenciled on back of his denim shirt, which was standard California Department of Correction issue for prisoners. I had a difficult time focusing on my son's prison humor as thoughts about the clerk who'd phoned with Dr. Julius Scarborough's name flashed through my mind. Who was this conscientious bureaucrat and why had he called?

Duke once told me that "You never know where help is going to come from, or why. However, it's really not important — just be grateful and move on."

I disagreed. The why *was* important, at least to me. And, if I interpreted the message correctly, it had something to do with my parents' medical history, which could possibly affect my health and that of my children. That had to be why the clerk had called and it sparked a glimmer of hope. When Manzoni's records had gone up in flames, it hadn't been the end of the line after all. I wondered if the doctor who delivered me was still alive and, if so, the likelihood of him still being in practice. After 48 years it was doubtful and I briefly contemplated hiring Peterson to find him until realizing that I had become more adept at using the Internet for that sort of thing. I couldn't wait to get back home and begin, thinking how the clerk had just saved me a great deal of angst and quite possibly thousands of dollars and months, maybe even years, of work.

"I liked the poem you sent, Bobby," I said, trying to keep my mind off Dr. Scarborough and the primary topic of conversation Gloria and I had decided to have with our son. I'd wanted to turn the car around and head for home as soon as the clerk had called, but Gloria had come unglued when I suggested it because we were on a long overdue mission.

"Which one?" he asked. "I've sent several."

I swallowed. Gloria usually read Bobby's letters and summarized the contents for me. However, I didn't recall hearing about any other poems. "If peace were a flower..." I said.

"Oh, that one," he said with a dismissive wave of the hand, "a work in progress. I haven't got it into an acceptable form yet."

"What's wrong with it the way it is?" I asked.

"Too many syllables; I'm trying to hone it into a haiku, which in case you don't know is a Japanese poem with a total of seventeen syllables in three unrhymed lines with five, seven, and five syllables, respectively. Right now it's at six, four, and ten — three too many overall. It's a real challenge not to compromise the message when squeezing it into that particular form. Every word has to count and the constraint gives rise to creativity. But I have time — it's not like I'm going anywhere soon."

He laughed again and it twisted my gut into a knot realizing the possibility that he could be spending the rest of his life in prison. If Bobby had caused Jenny's death while burglarizing her townhouse, it would be enough to get him charged with first-degree murder.

I remember reading somewhere that almost anything that is bad for other people is grist for the writer. But I wasn't about to use Bobby's tragedy as sustenance for my story because it wouldn't help either one of us. Spike Williams would just have to develop by himself without relying on my son's prison experience for help. Bobby seemed more agitated than I expected and I wondered if he was on something but was afraid to ask. Anything I said on the subject would only alienate him further and upset Gloria, who was attempting to enjoy the company of our son despite the purpose of our visit.

✖ ✖

According to Peterson, anyone persistent enough could gain access to hospital records, as Duke had demonstrated when I accompanied him to L.A. But the trick in looking would be to know which hospital records to check. In Miami alone there were 57 hospitals listed on the Internet. But just because my adoption had taken place there, and the courthouse employee who'd called with Dr. Scarborough's name was from the south Florida megalopolis, it didn't necessarily follow that that was where I was born. Attempting to balance my leisure time between working on the new story and looking for Dr. Scarborough wasn't keeping me from dwelling on Bobby's reaction to our finding Jenny's jewelry in his personal effects. Nor was the fact that I hadn't heard back from the agents and editor who'd requested my time-travel manuscript at the conference. While surfing the Internet, I wondered if published authors had to wait as long.

Ironically, after visiting Bobby, Spike no longer spoke to me. However, researching technical and personal information about my fictional character was less stressful than having to deal with the reality of my son's situation. I'd told Bobby that his mother and I had decided to tell Detective Meadows where we'd found his *adoptive grandmother's* jewelry and let the chips fall where they may. Gloria had spent most of the visit crying and nodding in agreement, or shaking her head in disbelief. By the time visiting hours were over, she and I were totally wrung out and Bobby still had no idea how that jewelry box had wound up in his personal effects. However, he'd sounded genuinely remorseful about breaking his mother's heart.

On the way home Gloria and I had discussed hiring Duke to represent our son again.

"He didn't do such a wonderful job with his DUI conviction," she said.

"I thought he did pretty well, considering Bobby hadn't been totally truthful in not telling Duke about the previous DUI on his record. You can't expect any lawyer to defend someone without knowing all the facts."

"Don't give me that crap about a lawyer never asking a question he doesn't know the answer to as an excuse. Your friend blew it and Bobby's paying the price."

"He's paying the price for drinking and driving and lying about it. If Bobby shoots straight with Duke he'll—"

"He'll what?" she interrupted. "Get him off?"

"We both know that isn't going to happen," I said. "But I'd trust Duke with my life."

"Well, it's not your life we're talking about here, is it?"

Difficult as the conversation had been, it faded in my mind as the only Julius Scarborough I'd found from the Miami area was in the Social Security Death Index. Praying it wasn't another dead end, I searched the Physician's Reference Index by year a second time without success. I switched off the computer in frustration and went to bed.

✻ ✻

In August Gloria suggested we drive to Sedona and put some flowers on Jenny's grave. We hadn't heard anything back from Detective Meadows after notifying him about finding the cigar box in Bobby's personal belongings. It had been fifteen months since Jenny's death and I still hadn't forgiven her for deceiving me all those years. My wife thought it would help with the healing process and we were just walking out the door when Peterson called.

"Nothing to report, Mr. Hamilton, I'm sorry to say. Just checking in to let you know I haven't given up."

"I'm glad you called, anyway," I said, and told him about the courthouse employee who'd given me Dr. Scarborough's name and what little I'd been able to find out.

"Sounds like you're on the right track. You might try checking the Florida Medical Association's website and see what pops up. If that doctor had his own practice or was with a medical group, well, that's what you're looking for. Whether he's dead or not isn't going to matter. What you're trying to find is your birth record." Peterson chuckled. "An' that ain't something he'd take with him, if you know what I mean?"

"No, but if he's dead maybe his practice died with him."

"His records had to go somewhere. Most likely to the hospital where he delivered babies. Once you find that you'll need to get some doctor to go through 'em and find yours. As you already know, your birth record is sealed to you but open to others. Any doctor can review hospital medical records at will and is not legally bound to keep all the information confidential, depending on how—"

"What do you mean, not legally bound?" I interrupted. "I thought all medical records were confidential, and isn't there such a thing as physician/patient privilege?"

"Medical records are confidential — doctor/patient privilege and all that. But only information needed for medical care is shielded. Extraneous facts are not, even if they are part of the same statement. It's your medical record we're talking about here, Mr. Hamilton, and once you find the hospital where this Scarborough delivered you, I suggest you fly down there and make an appointment to visit one of the staff doctors personally. Tell him about the phone call you got from the clerk and convince him to take a look, because you suspect your parents may have a medical history you should know about. Why else would some two-bit clerk risk his job to give you that doctor's name? The worst he can do is say no, which I'm here to tell you is a hell of a lot easier over the phone."

I couldn't afford to run back and forth between California and Florida every time I needed another piece of information, but Peterson had a point. I could definitely make a stronger case in person. By convincing a doctor to find my birth record and make me a copy, I would be on the home stretch to finding my parents. I thanked Peterson for pointing me in the right direction. Putting my keys down, I told Gloria briefly about this new information.

"We'll just have to make this trip another time," I said. "I have some research to do before going to Miami."

Gloria placed her hands on her hips and squared off at me. "It wasn't just a trip to put some flowers on your mother's grave, Morgan. It was a chance for us to spend some time together."

"She wasn't my mother."

"Of course she was, and you're still trying to live up to her expectations."

"The hell I am."

"Oh, for heaven's sake, you are, too. It's apparent in everything you write. But you're so upset with her for one little transgression that you can't see it. At this point I don't care if you ever find who your biological parents are, or were. All I want is to have my husband back. I was so looking forward to this trip — getting you away from that damn computer and your job for a few days so we could maybe reconnect."

"You can come with me to Florida," I said.

She flipped her chestnut-brown hair back over her shoulder. "I don't think so. You wouldn't even know I was there," she said, in that sanctimonious voice of hers that had a way of grating on my nerves, particularly when I deserved it. "And I doubt that it would be any different than it is around here with you lost in cyberspace looking for a past that doesn't matter to anyone besides yourself. How many times do we have to tell you who you are anyway, Morgan? The only one who doesn't seem to know is you."

"That's easy for you to say. You know who—"

"Yes, I know who my parents are. And so do you. Leon and Jenny Hamilton raised you and loved you as much as their own child. Now, give it a rest and get in the car. We are going to Sedona."

TWENTY-EIGHT

Not that Sedona was ever home, but Gloria and I had visited Jenny enough after she took up residence there that it had a similar feeling. In reality the town hadn't changed since burying the woman who'd raised me, yet I felt like an interloper returning to the tony desert community. Even though Jenny's townhouse had plenty of room, we'd always stayed at Poco Diablo Resort because it was impossible for me to live under the same roof as she and Gloria. Invariably, I'd wind up getting caught in the middle of a petty disagreement and couldn't take sides without alienating one of the two women in my life. It didn't take a rocket scientist to figure out that our visits were much more enjoyable when Gloria and I had our own space, and it suddenly dawned on me that maybe it was why Jenny hadn't wanted to come live with us.

We did the obligatory trip to the cemetery and placed a dozen pink roses on Jenny's grave, which brought up painful memories of Jenny's faultfinding with Gloria. Unbelievably, she'd blamed all the difficulties Bobby encountered growing up on my wife for not breastfeeding him as a baby. Although we stayed at Poco Diablo Resort, it just wasn't the same any more and Gloria and I were physically and mentally exhausted by the time we reached home. Nevertheless, when she went to bed I headed for my office and booted up the computer.

I found Dr. Scarborough's name without too much difficulty on the Florida Medical Association's website and lost all track of time as I began hot-linking from site to site trying to find out as much about him as possible. Eventually I discovered that he'd given his practice to a young doctor named Rolando Diaz. Almost stranger than fiction, Dr. Scarborough had met Diaz in a hospital cafeteria where the adolescent Cuban refugee was washing dishes to put himself through college. Scarborough had offered the boy his medical practice as an incentive and amazingly Diaz not only put himself through college but medical school as well.

After completing an internship at the Mayo Clinic, Diaz returned to Miami, where the aging Dr. Scarborough brought him into his thriving obstetrics practice until Diaz completed the residency requirements at Jackson Memorial Hospital. Then, true to his word, Dr. Scarborough turned over his practice and retired. The article had made the front page of The Miami Herald above the fold. Two years later Dr. Scarborough's name appeared in the newspaper once again, only this time in the obituary columns.

I rechecked the Medical Association's website and verified Dr. Diaz was currently practicing in Miami Shores, then quickly logged on to Expedia.com and booked an early flight to the Sunshine State the following day.

TWENTY-NINE

I'd never been to South Florida, but other than the lack of mountains surrounding it, the high humidity, and the ocean being on the wrong side, Miami didn't feel any different than Los Angeles. It was just another sprawling metropolis of high-rise condos and office buildings with the same fast food chains and spray-painted graffiti on overpasses. The Miami Shores clinic where Diaz practiced wasn't difficult to find because the city was laid out in a simple cross-sectional grid structure much easier to navigate than L.A., but, as luck would have it, the doctor wasn't in. However, after I explained how I'd flown all the way from San Diego for five minutes of his time, his receptionist told me that he spent Tuesdays and Saturdays on staff in the hospital for deliveries. Then, for whatever reason, she told me in confidence that his breaks came at noon and six p.m., when he stopped for meals in the cafeteria where his medical career had begun. If I was lucky, I could catch him then because he usually lingered over lunch and dinner, encouraging the help to stay in school and continue their education.

Following her directions I shot down I-95 to 836 West, exited on Twelfth Avenue heading north, and passed by Cedar's Medical Center before pulling into Jackson Memorial Hospital's huge complex, where I began searching for an empty parking space in the crammed lot.

The hospital reminded me of a casino in a bizarre sense, because the impressive structure wasn't built with doctors' money any more than Harrah's in Las Vegas was built with Bill's money. I followed a sickly old man tottering across the parking lot and waited while he slowly lowered himself into a '64 Oldsmobile with peeling olive-green paint. I could have parked in the next lot over by the time he started the engine and backed out. A gray cloud of exhaust engulfed my rental car as he accelerated and drove away before I pulled into the empty, smoke-filled space.

I set the emergency brake and left the Toyota Camry's engine running because it was only 5:15, too early for Diaz's dinner break and too humid to sit without the AC. If Scarborough delivered babies in Jackson Memorial, chances were good that that was where I'd been born. It made sense only because Diaz had taken over his practice and that was where *he* delivered them. Nevertheless, I didn't get the sense of déjà vu I was hoping for and began to question the impulsiveness of coming to Miami instead of writing or calling. Not being one of Dr. Diaz's patients, or related to anyone who was, what made me think he would even speak to me without an appointment during the precious little time he had to himself?

While I waited for the dinner hour, I turned on the radio, took out a yellow legal pad, and began writing about Sharon Zdanowski, a high school student and Olympic swimmer from West Allis, Wisconsin, who'd suffered a cardio-myopathy during practice and would die without a heart transplant. The sound of an anchorman's voice delivering the evening news startled me from my work and I quickly set aside the pad and pencil, turned off the engine, and walked through the sweltering late afternoon heat toward the hospital entrance.

Normally I hate to ask directions, but time had gotten away from me the way it always does when I'm writing. I stopped at the information desk and asked how to get to the cafeteria, which turned out to be teeming with men and women in white lab coats and green surgical scrubs. The few patrons in street clothes talking quietly among themselves were obviously family members of patients and my eyes quickly scanned over them in search of Dr. Diaz. His receptionist told me to look for a short, stocky man who looked more like a professional wrestler than a doctor, and that he usually wore a pastel blue lab coat with matching stethoscope draped around his neck and navy-blue rubber Birkenstocks. I spotted three blue lab coats on my first walkthrough. None of the wearers looked anything like a wrestler, so I walked back toward the entrance and went through the buffet line and filled a large Styrofoam cup with coffee. As I paid the cash register attendant, Dr. Diaz came through the door.

He waved at the staff behind the food counter, stopped and talked with each, even when not selecting food items from their particular sections. From a distance he seemed gregarious enough and immediately my hopes went up. I tarried at the end of the line *doctoring* my coffee, so to speak, with cream and sugar. I normally used neither but needed to kill a little time while waiting for him to find a seat. Unfortunately, he joined a boisterous group of green-scrub-clad doctors and surgical assistants in the center of the room.

I found a seat nearby and my coffee was cold by the time the group broke up. Diaz was just getting to his feet when I approached him. "Dr. Diaz?"

At the mention of his name, a friendly smile broke across his acne-scarred and pockmarked face. Coal black eyes twinkled with life as he turned and faced me. "Yes. And to whom do I have the honor?" he asked, without the slightest trace of an accent.

I extended my hand. "Morgan Hamilton, writer extraordinaire. I'm currently working on a book about the tragedies of lives cut short and the miracles of life passed on through organ transplant surgery and I—"

"You don't want to talk to me, Mr. Hamilton," he said, laughing as he interrupted. "I'm an obstetrician, not a surgeon."

"I know. You're right, I don't want to talk with you about surgery."

"Then how may I help you?"

"I need a few minutes of your time to talk about Dr. Scarborough," I said, jamming my hands in my pockets. "I'm sorry for the ruse but I needed something to get your attention. Most of the time, I find that strangers will speak with me because I'm a writer. For some strange reason it interests them."

He sat back down and motioned me to join him. "I think most people would like to write a book someday. Maybe someday I will myself."

A nervous laugh escaped as I took the seat adjacent to him. "I think more people would like to have written one than actually write one."

He laughed. "You're probably right."

"That said," I said, "they're a lot easier to write than they are to sell. It seems you have a better chance of winning the lottery than being published, unless, of course, you're a celebrity or politician involved in any sort of scandal, or someone with alphabet soup behind their name. I'm currently working on my third novel. The others are doorstops at the moment."

"Well," he said, folding his hands in front of him and chuckling, "I won't give up my practice just yet. Now, what is it about Dr. Scarborough you wish to know?"

I felt somewhat more at ease, but only for a moment.

His eyes darted over my face as the smile faded.

"I believe he was the doctor who delivered me," I said, wondering why Diaz should even care. "Anyway, about fifteen months ago when, uh, Jenny Hamilton, who I thought was my mother, died, and I was going through her things, I discovered my adoption papers. It came as quite a shock to learn after 47 years that she hadn't really been my mother."

"I'll bet."

"You have no idea, Doctor. Since then, I've been trying to find my biological parents. I won't bore you with the details, but a couple of months ago I received an anonymous phone call from a courtroom clerk giving me Dr. Scarborough's name because," I said, adlibbing a bit, "he believed there was a medical history I should know about."

"But he wouldn't tell you what?"

"No. All he said was that he could lose his job if anyone found out he called and that I'd have to find my parents through the doctor who delivered me. Well, as you know, Dr. Scarborough died many years ago and without your help I have nowhere else to turn."

"So, let me see if I've got this straight. You want me to look in his files and tell you who your parents are. What makes you think they're still alive?"

"I don't know if they are, and I don't expect you to understand this, but I've got to find out who they are or were. Not just for medical reasons..." I blinked and swallowed, "it's... well, it's just devastating not knowing."

"I understand perfectly, Mr. Hamilton, but I'm not sure I can help you. Dr. Scarborough left me a ton of old medical records, many of them dormant, and after a number of years prescribed by law, which I'm not even sure what that number is because my staff handles it, have been destroyed. I seriously doubt that your record still exists after all this time."

I closed my eyes and shook my head, knowing I couldn't trust my voice to speak without a flood of emotion.

"Let me buy you another coffee and see if we can think this thing through," he said, taking my half-empty Styrofoam cup from the table and walking back toward the cashier.

He returned with two steaming coffees and, as we drank, told me how he and his family floated across the Gulf Stream on a raft made from four old inner tubes lashed together with clothesline. He didn't remember much of the epic journey because he was only four at the time and both his parents and sister had drowned in a turbulent rainstorm that broke the raft apart. "I know exactly how you feel about trying to find out about your parents. I wanted to know everything I could about mine. Why they left my homeland on such a flimsy raft. What were they like? I'm sure you know all the questions.

"But I was lucky," he said. "My father's brother and his wife were already in the United States and, because I had no one living back home, I was allowed to stay provided they adopted me, which, as I look back now, was really a political asylum adoption. My uncle told me stories about how my parents were imprisoned in the early fifties after attacking an army post with Fidel Castro. When they were released two years later they fled with him to Mexico, where they helped organize the revolutionary movement that eventually overthrew Batista. I couldn't believe my parents were actually two of the original rebels who hid in the Sierra Maestra Mountains with Castro and Che Guevara. They recruited supporters and fought in a guerrilla warfare campaign that was responsible for toppling the corrupt Cuban dictatorship."

"And replacing it with another," I said.

He nodded and took a sip of coffee. "Anyway, soon after Castro came to power he began nationalizing industry, collectivizing agriculture, confiscating foreign-owned property, and relying on Russia's economic assistance. My parents fled to the United States after becoming disillusioned with his totalitarian government that benefitted the working class at the expense of the middle class. Uncle Estrada said my father never would have risked his life and that of his family for socialism."

"Whew," I said, burning my lips on the coffee and setting it down, "I'm envious. Maybe you *should* write a book."

He shook his head. "I'm very proud of my parents because they believed so strongly in democracy that they risked their lives for it, and then lost them trying to get to it. Whether or not they succeeded isn't as important to me as the fact that they tried; they gave me life and their stories gave me belief in the ability to achieve. But I really owe who I am to Aunt Mimi and Uncle Estrada and Dr. Scarborough. Without their encouragement and support I never would have become a doctor or have this practice. And although my aunt and uncle didn't have the financial means to put me through medical school, they didn't discourage me, either."

"That's what I mean," I said. "You obviously benefitted from knowing about your parents and the great things they did. I didn't even know mine existed."

"Maybe there's a good reason," he said.

"Yeah, my adoptive father didn't want me to know because he said my real father was a drunken lunatic. I think he was afraid he'd lose my love if I ever found out that I wasn't his son."

"How do you know that?"

"From a letter he wrote to his wife that I found after she died."

"Sounds like he might have been right — I hear a lot of anger. It's not healthy carrying it around for so long."

I nodded. "I know, but it's only because they lied to me and..." I couldn't finish without getting emotional again. I wasn't about to let my emotions get in the way of finding my parents. "Maybe the hospital still has records?"

"I'm sure they do, but I won't be able to look for them today," he said, reaching in his shirt pocket and pulling out a gold Cross pen and small leather notebook. "In fact, I'm not very good at that sort of thing anyway, so I'm going to send my administrative assistant over and I'm not sure what her schedule is this week. I'll check with her tomorrow and get back to you. What's your number?"

THIRTY

It didn't take long to learn which areas to avoid as I toured the city looking for a place to stay. When billboards and street names went from English to Spanish, or graffiti began covering the fences, lampposts, and sidewalks, I turned around. At one point I drove past the shell of a car sitting on concrete blocks with the doors and wheels missing and all the remaining windows broken out. It struck me almost as funny that the hoodlums on this side of the country had actually left it sitting on cinder blocks. I was thankful it wasn't dark yet.

I crossed Broad Causeway with a big yellow sun glaring in the rearview mirror. Multi-million dollar estates hugged the shores of Biscayne Bay. Tidal currents lapping the Bay Harbor Islands gently rocked yachts and sailboats moored to private docks extending from the bright-white seawalls surrounding them. Turning south on A1A, I passed the pricey-looking Bal Harbour Shops and made my way through a maze of high-rise hotels and motels lining Collins Avenue. As I passed Indian Beach Park, whiffs of the briny ocean drifted in through my open windows, a familiar scent I recalled from driving down the Silver Strand in San Diego. Farther on, a behemoth pastel wall of hotels, motels, and Shangri-Las obscured my view of the ocean and I continued driving until reaching South Beach where I turned around just as the sun set.

As far as I was concerned, it seemed ass backwards. On the West Coast the sun always came up over the mountains and set over the ocean. In Miami it was the other way around, except without the mountains. Driving in the amber glare of sodium-vapor streetlights and colorful neon resort marquees soon pushed that thought aside and I couldn't recall ever seeing so many hotels and motels in any one place before. I'd heard of the Fontainebleau, which I supposed was probably to Miami Beach what the Hotel Del Coronado was to San Diego, and decided to spend the night there.

A valet parking attendant took my bag out of the trunk and set it on a clothes dolly before chirping the rental car tires in front of the entrance as he sped away. Personally, I would rather spend three nights in a luxury hotel than ten in a cheap one. However, without knowing exactly how long I would have to spend in South Florida, I decided to register for just one night. That way, after hearing from Dr. Diaz, if it appeared my stay would exceed three nights I could always move to a less expensive hotel. Regardless, I would always be able to say about Miami, "Why, yes, I stayed at the Fontainebleau, doesn't everyone?" I chuckled to myself as a bellman grabbed the dolly and led me to the registration desk.

The resort hotel wasn't nearly as old as the Hotel Del Coronado, but had a fascinating Art Deco lobby with bowtie marble floor and a two-story *staircase to nowhere*. I tried to imagine what it must have been like in those bygone days before air conditioning as the bellhop showed me to my room on the fourth floor and opened the glass doors opposite the entry. Wealthy patrons would probably stop in on hot days just for a cold bath and a seat on the breezy balconies overlooking the ocean.

Party sounds from the elevated pool deck below floated in on the evening zephyrs. After tipping the bellhop, I poured a non-alcoholic drink from the mini self-service bar and headed back down. With club soda in hand, I crossed through the opulent lobby, strolled around the pool deck, and walked down a sandy staircase to the golden-sand beach below. Ocean waves surged up on the shore, erasing the thousands of tourists' footprints left throughout the day, just as they had erased the lives of Dr. Diaz's parents and uncounted others attempting to grasp hold of the American dream. Yet the doctor had seen their footprints through his uncle's eyes. I was more than envious as I removed my shoes and socks, rolled up my pant legs, and waded into the retreating surf. The water was surprisingly warm as it tickled my ankles and I suddenly felt very alone.

THIRTY-ONE

Sunlight flooded through the open windows I'd forgotten to close the night before. I was surprised it was 7:00 a.m. already and that I'd missed my writing time as I switched on the TV and listened to Matt Lauer interview a Hollywood screenwriter. The *Today Show* seemed to come on much earlier on the East Coast than it did back home. But then, my biological clock was still three hours behind.

"It's a dog-eat-dog world in Tinsel Town," the screenwriter was saying, "and writing contracts are fast becoming a thing of the past. Studios are buying more and more spec scripts and bidding wars are being stoked by greedy young agents touting their clients' hot properties, trying to make producers feel they may be missing out on the next *Star Wars* or *Titanic* if they don't buy them immediately, which is precisely why everyone wants to be a screenwriter like me."

Well, not everyone, I thought, hitting the mute button. Gone were the days when editors maintained a close working relationship with authors such as the legendary Maxwell Perkins had with F. Scott Fitzgerald, Marjorie Kinnan Rawlings, and Thomas Wolfe. In those days a respectable editor could take a good manuscript and hone it to perfection. Today they were nothing more than author advocates in giant publishing conglomerates where writers competed to be published based solely on a potential sales number. New writers were nothing more than word farmers harvesting their crops into books and selling futures on them. Publishers took a small risk investing in the futures market. Publishing new writers, to them, was like speculating on a few penny stocks in an otherwise well-diversified securities portfolio.

So why was I beating my head against the wall trying to

get my manuscripts into their hands? The answer was so simple it amazed me: I couldn't not write, and any publication other than *self* was the only verification that I could. Family and friends all could say they loved it, but if a traditional publishing house bought it my writing would instantaneously have validity — at least to me.

Norman Mailer may have been right about the money, but my dream was to ride the trolley or bus and discover someone reading one of my books, perhaps missing their stop because they were so engrossed in the story. Maybe I'd ask them how they liked it and, if they did, offer to sign the book. But if they didn't, ask why not and get a real reader's viewpoint. I'd also like to take my grandchildren to a movie and have them read in the beginning credits: *Based on the novel by H. Morgan Hamilton.* Now, that would really be something!

It was still too early for Dr. Diaz's call, or even to phone Gloria with the three-hour time difference. I'd left a message on our answering machine after returning from my walk on the beach the night before, letting her know that I'd arrived safely and where I'd gone. I also told her how much I loved and missed her. Heat and humidity poured into my room through the open windows as the sun rose over the Atlantic Ocean below. I squinted at the deep blue streak just below the horizon where the Gulf Stream swept northward past the coast. A few people were already on the beach gathering tiny shells left behind by the last high tide. I had two hours to kill and began with a long refreshing shower before heading out for breakfast.

Wolfie's was an oversized Jewish delicatessen with exceptional food where I read the *Miami Herald* over a bottomless cup of coffee while waiting for 9:00 o'clock to arrive. Nothing changes but the names and the places, I thought as I finished the paper. Miami had as many rapes, murders, muggings, and drive-by shootings as San Diego, but they seemed to have a different slant on reporting them. Something I might need to know if I ever wrote a story set in the Sunshine State's tourist Mecca.

One minute after nine my cell phone rang and Dr. Diaz's receptionist, a soft-spoken woman named Louise, informed me the doctor's administrative assistant would begin looking for my birth record later in the afternoon and that she'd call me back at the same time tomorrow. I thanked her, hung up, and called Gloria, who was still in bed.

"You're unbelievable," she said, sounding more perturbed than groggy. "You know that?"

"You knew I might have to come down here."

"I didn't think it would be the morning after we returned. Or that you'd leave without so much as a good-bye."

"You were sleeping so peacefully I didn't want to wake you."

"Morgan, please. Give me a little more credit than that."

"Well, you didn't want to come."

"Stop it!"

"I'm sorry," I said, feeling like I was caught in the middle of a conversation between Gloria and Jenny instead of me and my wife. "But you know how important this is to me."

"Yes. And *so's* your writing, and *so's* your job, and *so's* your booze, all of which have taken you away from *me*!"

"You know I've stopped drinking."

"But for how long this time? And what's going to knock you off the wagon again?"

"Nothing, I swear... except maybe losing you."

"*Maybe*? It seems like you already have. We never spend time together any more."

"That's not true. We just got back from Sedona."

"It is, Morgan. And I'm real tired of living by myself. That's not why I married you. Even when you're here you're not."

"We spend time together every Thursday evening."

"I think we've been through this before."

"Well, we're together, aren't we?"

She sighed. "You really know how to impress a girl. And speaking of impressing people, Ralph Larson called yesterday wondering where you were. He said you missed an important meeting with him and your buyers. I guess I'm not the only one who doesn't matter to you."

"That's not true and you know it."

"I know no such thing."

Sweat trickled down my back. There wasn't any meeting scheduled; Ralph was just checking up on me.

"I hope you find what you're looking for, Morgan, because you could be paying a very high price for it."

"I just got here," I said, feeling a knot forming in the pit of my stomach. "But I'm sure I will and then I'll be home. I promise."

"I also hope you still have a job when you return."

"I will," I said, with more confidence than I felt.

"I'm not so sure, Morgan," Gloria said, her voice softening. "Maybe we should start this conversation over. Why don't you call me back in five minutes?"

"Are you sure?"

"Uh-huh… I really missed you last night. I didn't realize our bed was so big without you."

We chatted awhile without hanging up and Gloria read the mail she thought would interest me, including another rejection letter, one from an editor at Putnam.

"Dear Mr. Hamilton:

"Thank you for sending me the chapters and outline for Syzygetic Journey. The concept is appealing and will definitely get attention, and your writing seemed strong enough to carry the book. Unfortunately, as original as the premise is, I'm afraid it is not quite right for our list at this time.

"Once again, though, thank you for thinking of me. I wish you the best of luck with your work.

"Best regards,—"

"Yeah, *best regards*," I said, "who's he kidding?"

"*She,*" Gloria said. "And she sounds very encouraging."

I scoffed. "Yeah, right; he, she; who gives a damn? They're all a bunch of jerks who wouldn't recognize good writing if it bit them in the ass."

"Take it easy, Morgan. You know how subjective writing is. Forget about the rejection for the time being and concentrate on why you went to Miami."

"It's not enough to write well any more," I said, railing on, "you also have to be marketable. Which means being either famous, or infamous. What I need is to have an affair with Nancy Pelosi, Barbara Boxer, or Diane Feinstein and get it in the tabloids. Maybe even all three — then they'd buy my book!"

"Harry Morgan Hamilton! If I thought for one minute that you were serious—"

"Okay, okay, okay. I can't picture it myself," I said, taking a deep breath before telling her about my conversation with Dr. Diaz and how he was sending his administrative assistant over to the hospital later that afternoon to look for my birth record.

"That's wonderful, I hope she finds it, and I hope it's what you're looking for because I really don't know how much more of this I can take."

"Me either. I'm going stir-crazy waiting. I wish you would have come with me."

She laughed softly. "That we did discuss and you'll do much better there without me. So, try to relax. Go lay on the beach and write, or take a drive. I'll be here when you get home, but we're going to have to have a few changes around here if you want me to stay."

THIRTY-TWO

I was too keyed up to lie on the beach or write after finishing the next conversation with Ralph Larson. An hour after checking out of the Fontainebleau I was tooling down US 1; Homestead and Florida City were fading in the rearview mirror as sunshine glared off the white coral shoulders of the roadbed and windshields of oncoming traffic. The tires sang on the smooth asphalt, which I'm sure had once been black as tar but was bleached a pale gray. I opened the windows, filling the car with a salty fragrance that seemed to clear my head, and followed the numerically diminishing highway markers down the Overseas Highway until they reached zero at the corner of Whitehead and Fleming in Key West.

After finding a place to park, it felt good just to walk. I replayed the conversations with Gloria and Ralph over in my head for the umpteenth time. Gloria was right that I was being a complete shit all over again — even without the booze. I was neglecting her in pursuit of my own selfish goals, risking not only our relationship in the process but my job as well. Fortunately, as it turned out, Justin had covered for me. But if "I didn't get my head out of my ass," as Larson phrased it, I would indeed be looking for a new job.

The sun radiating through my slacks as I strolled up Duval Street past several of the open-air shops and bars made me wish I'd thought to bring a pair of shorts. At Front Street I turned left and stopped about three blocks later in front of the Little White House where President Truman used to vacation. I thought of Jenny's letter and speculated that life in those early post WWII and Korean War years had been far better for returning veterans than it was during Vietnam, when I'd enrolled in USC in an attempt to avoid the draft. As I turned back toward Whitehead on Southard, thankful that I hadn't had to go and Duke, who'd actually enlisted, made it back safely, I noticed a sign directing tourists toward another museum. It caught my interest immediately and my pace quickened as I put Gloria and Ralph's troubling conversations out of my mind.

I could almost visualize Ernest Hemingway sitting in the padded wicker chair on his front porch in khakis cut off at the ankles, belt outside the loops, and barefoot inside a comfortable pair of bedroom slippers, with *The New York Times* and a glass of whiskey as he squinted in annoyance at me traipsing through his house. Then, unbelievably, I imagined his loud voice, the one he always used when he had to force himself to be sociable, telling me "The best experience a man can have for writing fiction is a war. Wars have made many great writers," and I found myself wondering if avoiding the draft had been such a good idea after all.

The afternoon passed with the magic speed of dreams as I lost myself on the tropical island and capped off the day checking out the sunset over the sea — just as it should. Not that the Gulf of Mexico looks any different to me than the Pacific Ocean. The crowd at Mallory Square included jugglers, mimes, and musicians who collected there every evening doing their thing and panhandling the tourists. It was a festive atmosphere as everyone waited to catch a glimpse of the enigmatic green flash and, at the precise moment that the sun blinked out below the horizon, they stopped whatever they were doing and applauded as if expecting the big yellow ball to reappear for an encore performance. But when that didn't happen, the throngs dispersed through the tropical twilight into town.

I made my way past the open bars on Duval Street, which had magically come to life in the glow of Tiki torches and live music, and was somehow drawn into a place called Sloppy Joe's. I took a seat at the bar beside a barefoot blonde with teal blue eyes. She looked up from the yellow legal pad she was writing on with a smile. Against my better judgment I ordered us each a Scotch on the rocks. Then the Scotch ordered one and ultimately took over.

I remember her telling me she'd come to Key West to research her thesis on Hemingway and that Sloppy Joe's had been one of his favorite haunts. We drank to that and she began quoting him. "Something he said that I particularly like is, 'Never compete with living writers. You don't know whether they're good or not. Compete with the dead ones you know are good.' Have you read *A Farewell to Arms*? He said he wrote it at least fifty times and felt good when he finished because he knew that he'd left the rest of us something to shoot at."

"Like I even have a shot," I said, shaking my head at the muse coming between us. "Competing with dead writers is different now because you're not just competing with them on a literary basis, you're competing with them for limited publication dollars as well."

"The first draft of anything is shit," the muse said from somewhere beyond the din of music and disjointed conversations. "The most important thing I've learned about writing is never write too much at a time. Never pump yourself dry. Leave a little for the next day. The main thing is to know when to stop. If you know a good story, go ahead and write it. That's the kind you write in one sitting, but the best ones are made up as you go along from day to day. They're a hell of a lot harder to write, but it'll be more interesting for you and it's more interesting to the reader. If you don't know how a story is going to turn out, how can the reader tell?"

The smoky whiskey flavor lured me further down the path of no return as the Muse's teal blue eyes danced. "Another thing, the first crap you write doesn't mean a thing. Everybody has to learn. You don't have a thing to worry about. I never had anybody to teach me about writing, and it took me years to find out for myself what I'm telling you now. If you sell your first story, that's the most unfortunate thing that can happen, because if you can sell shit, you might keep on writing shit. And even if you do get better, the readers will always remember you by their first impression."

I stared without blinking.

"The way to tell whether it's good or not is by what you can throw away; if you can throw away stuff that would make a high point of interest in somebody else's story, you know it's good."

I raised the tumbler to my lips and the Muse smiled.

I have never known how to drink sensibly and my head was hurting like hell as I opened my eyes in another strange place. A barefoot blond in flowered bikini bottom and white cotton tee, with enough bare midriff to make me uncomfortable, was brushing her hair in front of a vanity mirror across the room. She turned to me and smiled when I stirred.

"How are you feeling?" she asked.

"Where am I?"

"You were pretty drunk last night. I brought you to my place."

I rolled my head back and closed my eyes. "Oh, shit!"

"Don't worry. Nothing happened."

"What do you mean, nothing happened? I'm here, aren't I?"

"Would you rather it was jail... or maybe even the morgue?"

"How could this happen?"

She flung her hair back and strode over to the bed. "You were in no condition to drive... or do anything else for that matter. Would you like to try now?"

My eyes focused on her ruby red toenails. "Are you crazy?" I asked, glancing up her golden brown legs and under the hem of her tee. She wasn't wearing a bra.

"I don't think so; how about a cup of coffee instead?"

I felt myself twitching and quickly closed my eyes. "That sounds like a good idea."

"I'll be right back."

The sound of her bare feet padding across the terrazzo floor pounded in my head as I rolled out of bed, somewhat relieved to discover that I was still completely dressed. Nevertheless, Gloria was going to leave me for sure if she didn't kill me first. I quickly checked my voicemail for a message from Dr. Diaz's receptionist, and my hand began to sweat as she said their administrative assistant had found my record.

The Muse, whose name was Marsha Filbert, and I had bonded over a common interest in writing, discussing some of the greats including Hemingway over way too many drinks. While working on her thesis, she'd also finished her first novel. And of all things, she wanted me to read it. But that was last night and, after gulping down the coffee, I was more than anxious to get to Dr. Diaz's office. Her teal blue eyes flashed when I tried to explain, but she said she understood and drove me to find my car, where I put on sunglasses and flipped down the visor before starting the engine.

THIRTY-THREE

Four and a half hours later my hands trembled as I stared at the copy of my birth record that Dr. Diaz had given me. All my life I thought I'd been Harry Morgan Hamilton, secretly loathing the first name my parents had given me and hadn't used since grammar school. In an instant everything I'd longed for was gone and I was holding a document stating that I had been born Harry Morgan Tesch to an unwed mother named Rosa Marie, which was damn painful after spending the past fifteen months, and probably more than Jenny and Leon originally paid to adopt me, to find this single piece of paper and only one parent.

Father: UNKNOWN it said, in capital letters for the whole world to see; all the world, that is, but me. A stain on my life like it was *my* fault. Not only didn't I know; the realization suddenly hit me that unless I found this Rosa Marie Tesch I'd probably never find out. Why had she given me away? Was she still alive and, if so, why had she listed my father as unknown? Had she been raped? My adoptive parents seemed to know who my father was because they'd written about him in their letters to each other. Unless I found her the chances of learning anything about him were zilch. And even if I did, would she tell me? After what happened with the Simmons, should I even try? The fact that I'd come this far meant nothing because half a play was still only half a play, and I didn't have a total resolution to my quest.

"I don't know how to thank you, Doctor," I said, rising to my feet.

"I'm sorry it isn't better news," he said, standing also. "I imagine sometimes it would be better not knowing."

I shook my head. "Never; I might not know anything other

than my mother's name, but it's more than I knew five minutes ago. Why do you suppose that clerk gave me Dr. Scarborough's name? Did he know something about Rosa Marie Tesch that he thought I should know?"

Dr. Diaz shrugged. "Nothing that I can see medically."

I sighed. "I guess that's good. Now, all I have to do is find her."

"Well, best of luck," he said, patting me on the back. "I'd be interested in a follow-up report after you do... if you wouldn't mind?"

I smiled at him, still feeling hollow inside. "You bet."

I was getting closer, but finding Rosa Marie Tesch could take as long, or longer, than finding the Simmons, and I was painfully aware of the consequences of showing up unannounced. Nevertheless, if she was still alive, I was determined to confront her and ask why she'd abandoned me. Unless she lived out of the country, it might be easier to add a stopover on my return ticket to San Diego than cross the country yet again. Thus, before heading for the airport I decided to call Peterson and have him browse the Internet on the outside chance he could locate her before I set foot on another plane.

"I told you before," he said, "most of the people I find are through contacts and I ain't got no contacts down there. If all you want me to do is search the Net you can do that yourself."

I hated surfing the Net same as I hated using the telephone, particularly a pay telephone outside of a noisy gas station after the battery on my cell phone died. It was much easier to hire someone else to do it, and most of the time they could find what I was looking for in half the time. "I left my laptop at home," I said.

"Listen, Hamilton, save your money. Just stop into one of them office places like Kinko's and rent time on one. Or get your ass over to the public library and use theirs for free. Either case, it's gonna cost a whole lot less than I'm going to charge you. Besides, you already owe me big time for finding out how you got Simmons' birth certificate issued to you."

My mind raced as everything seemed to be coming together. Had Leon and Jenny done something illegal to keep me from finding out that I'd been born a bastard? I swatted at a sweat bee reentering an orbit above the puddle of spilled soda in the kiosk. "Okay, so what's the skinny?" I asked, trying to talk over a pneumatic lug wrench the mechanic was using.

"Where the hell are you, Hamilton?"

"You're the detective, you tell me."

He laughed. "Sounds like a garage."

"Very good, now what about that birth certificate?"

I heard him take a drag on his cigarette and exhale. "It's like this: because birth and death records were recorded on different sides of the same office and not married up in a single file, some enterprising clerk back then saw an opportunity to make a little extra money on the side. Obviously he was very good at it, too, because, until I showed up to dispute the authenticity of your certificate, there had never been an investigation on any other, or so they said."

"Yeah," I said, "I'll bet."

"Well, my guess is that when an infant's death certificate arrived in the Office of Vital Statistics, the first thing that clerk did was look up the birth certificate and pass the information on to an accomplice working with a black market adoption agency. Since adoption records were sealed, it was unlikely that anyone would ever question the authenticity of the amended certificate. Simply by transferring the original data on baby Simmons' birth certificate to a blank form, they were able to give you an identity with enough credibility to pass even a military background check. Your case was just one molecule in a complicated chemical compound of corruption."

"Huh?"

"The tip of the iceberg, Hamilton; you're a smart guy, figure it out. Not only were dead baby birth certificates being used to conceal black market adoptions, but also to falsify natural citizenship for illegal aliens. Been goin' on for decades and I would guess the number is somewhere in the tens of thousands. You should have seen them bastards' faces when I showed up with some of my buds from the fraud squad."

I cringed at Peterson's cavalier use of the vulgar term. *Bastard* was much more personal now. Mrs. Simmons would probably become embroiled in the story and I wasn't dealing well with the aftermath myself. In my haste to confront the Simmons, I hadn't considered every possible outcome. Now

Dixie had two headstones to adorn with flowers and Peterson had discovered how the information on my fake birth certificate matched that of her dead baby's. Why should she have to suffer any more just because some corrupt clerk had given me her child's identity almost a half century ago? If she had to find out, I should be the one to tell her. Next time, however, I'd make sure to take Gloria with me to ease the tension. And maybe, just maybe, it would give us both the closure we needed.

"Of course the scam wouldn't work as efficiently today, because the Social Security Administration developed an enumeration-at-birth process back in 1987 where parents can get a Social Security number assigned to their newborn child. And anyone checking would immediately become suspicious if they got a different name back. Ain't big brother wonderful?"

I shrugged, not caring that he couldn't see me.

THIRTY-FOUR

Rosa Marie Tesch was the name of the woman who gave birth to me, but was that still her name? What was the possibility in 48 years that she could have married and changed it one or more times? People did get divorced. The lawyer Manzoni was married to his sixth wife when he died. Why not Rosa Marie?

I couldn't dwell on it; I had to start somewhere. In a country with about 275 million people, I might find dozens named Rosa Marie Tesch. How would I know which one was my mother? Finding the right Rosa Marie Tesch could have been more difficult if my birth certificate didn't also include her date and place of birth. I remember Peterson told me they were the clearest identifying statistics separating people from one another with the same name.

"Not even the homeless can escape being on file somewhere in the endless miles of red tape," he'd said with a snicker. "It keeps millions of government bureaucrats employed — full-time. Every charitable organization that provides shelter for such people has a file on 'em. Unless your biological mother is some obscure bag lady who never worked a day in her life or sought charity handouts anywhere, she's on file somewhere. Even if she's dead there's gonna be a record."

I wanted to know who I was and where I came from, simple as that. Rosa Marie Tesch couldn't be dead. She just couldn't, not when I was this close. I had to know why she'd abandoned me. I had a right to know and I remember telling him, "That isn't going to do me any good."

"No, probably not," he said.

I leafed through the Yellow Pages and quickly found that the Miami Shores Branch Library on NE Second Avenue was closest. Fortunately, school was still in session and, after explaining my plight to the librarian, I was able to get a computer terminal and use it much longer than the posted half-hour restriction.

I stared at the screen, attempting to make sense of the categorized list of website listings on Yahoo!'s busy page, wondering what to check first. Somewhere in the haze a small voice cautioned me that no matter what I found, I wasn't the only one who would be affected. Did Rosa Tesch have a husband who didn't know about me, or other adult children? At the moment it really didn't matter how many lives would be changed or shattered when I finally confronted her. The blame rested solely with her. She was the one who'd gotten pregnant and abandoned me. Whatever the repercussions in her present family, they couldn't possibly be any more devastating than finding out after 47 years that everything I'd believed in was a lie. And to cap it off, I was now a bastard! The hair on the back of my neck bristled.

Jenny Hamilton had kept the truth hidden for more than 47 years... and I thought I had known her. She and I had always been able to talk about anything, so why not this? Why hadn't she told me I was adopted when I was old enough to understand? Or given me the book someone named Rosa had sent for my tenth birthday? Had that Rosa been Rosa Marie Tesch? It now appeared that although my biological mother had abandoned me, she hadn't tried to prevent my finding out about her. Otherwise, she never would have sent the book. And out of the blue it hit me that maybe Jenny had kept in touch with her also. How else would she have known about my personal library filled with autographed books?

Was I becoming paranoid, or just being selfish? Another voice, much stronger than the first, propelled me forward and overcame what little concern I had about how my existence would affect the lives of Rosa Marie Tesch and her family. While I could almost understand why she might not want me to find her, I couldn't understand why Jenny had kept the whole business a secret. It was the worst thing she'd ever done. Regardless of how much Jenny had said she loved me, she'd loved Leon more. He was the one who wanted my adoption kept from me and she had acquiesced. So, what was the dark family secret an anonymous clerk would risk losing his job to tell me? It certainly wasn't my illegitimate birth, because thousands of adoptions were spawned from similar situations. It had to be something more.

I felt a twinge of excitement as I typed Rosa's name into the space provided and clicked on *People Search*. It gave me a small rush every time another piece of information fell into place. I couldn't help but think that if Rosa didn't want me to know about her, then why had she sent the book? Glancing over the information on the screen, I felt lucky. I'd come a long way over the past fifteen months, with moral support from my wife, legal advice from Duke, and technical support from Tommy Peterson. But only because of an anonymous phone call and a sympathetic Cuban refugee was I able to get Rosa's name. For all its faults, the United States really was a great country. I'd gotten so used to my Logitech Trackball I seldom used a regular mouse any more and my right wrist was cramped after the first half-hour.

My illegitimacy rapidly faded into the background as a list of women named Rosa Marie Tesch and their current addresses scrolled across the screen. It wouldn't do any good to speculate who my father might be until I found the right Rosa Marie Tesch. She was the only one who knew. I typed in St. Paul, Minnesota and February 13, 1927 and waited for the computer to spit out the correct name. When it did, I wasn't a happy camper. The Rosa Marie Tesch culled from the list by matching place and date of birth was a patient at Everglades Regional Medical Center, which I soon discovered was a mental institution for the legally insane. Was that the reason for the anonymous clerk's phone call?

I printed out the page listing her address and rubbed my aching wrist, wondering why she was institutionalized and if I would be allowed to visit her. If so, would she remember me? At 71 Alzheimer's was a definite possibility and depending on its advancement, I could very well have hit the ultimate dead end.

It was mid-afternoon when I left the library. But before driving all the way up to Broward County, I phoned the hospital to check visiting hours and whether Rosa Marie Tesch was allowed to have visitors. I didn't see how they could refuse her son, although they might wonder why I'd never visited before. The nurse on the other end of the line informed me that Miss Tesch was indeed allowed to have visitors, but that it would be better if I came in the morning because she was usually less withdrawn earlier in the day. When I asked why, the nurse told me that she'd only been working there a little over a week and I'd have to discuss that with one of the nurses who'd just finished their shift and they wouldn't return until the next day.

Of course, waiting for Friday morning was like waiting for summer vacation in high school. It seemed a month away, yet was less than 17 hours. The dominoes were falling into place and I couldn't wait to see my mother for the first time in more than 48 years. I tried to picture her but couldn't get past the image of Jenny. What did she really look like? My memory didn't go back that far.

At the hotel I called Gloria. "I'm going to visit her tomorrow," I said, after filling her in on my progress, "but I'm not sure if I really want to."

"Of course you do, Morgan. No matter what happens, I want you to come away from there feeling good about it. It's haunted you ever since Jenny died — and that's long enough. You need to move forward; your family needs you... I need you!"

"What about Rosa? Isn't she family?"

"Get a grip, Morgan. She may be your biological mother, but I'd hardly call her family."

"Wasn't that the name of the woman who sent me the Hemingway book for my tenth birthday? Sounds like something a family member would do for me."

"That was one time and thirty-eight years ago. It hardly qualifies."

"So we're a little estranged. I'm trying to fix that."

Gloria scoffed. "That's the understatement of the century, Morgan. You never knew she existed until Jenny died. As far as estrangements go, you and Bobby are becoming estranged. You'd better work on fixing *that* while you still can. He wants to see you, by the way."

"He'll see us our next visit, whenever that is."

"No, I mean he called and wants to see *you* when you get back from Florida."

Too restless to sleep, I tried to capture my feelings of anticipation on paper for a new character, Frank Johnson, a Navy commander forced to retire from the service for alcoholism and sexually harassing his subordinates. I was familiar with the alcoholism, not so much the sexual harassment, as I wrote about the time he spent waiting for a donor to replace his failing cirrhotic liver and how he felt. No matter how many different ways I constructed the sentences the words didn't seem to match the feeling, and I became even more frustrated. It didn't help to recall the Muse's foggy advice from the night before that the first draft of anything was shit.

Somehow I needed to be able to captivate the readers and make them feel the same emotions as my characters, or at least as I imagined my characters would feel. By midnight I gave up trying, found the remote, and flipped through the channels. Depending on my mood, the idiot box could provide either video research or escapism. The infomercials in the wee hours of the morning provided neither. I switched it off and glanced at the hotel mini bar. A drink beckoned, but I knew it was out of the question.

THIRTY-FIVE

Exiting the Palmetto Expressway, I drove north on 27th Avenue through some very rough-looking neighborhoods before entering Miami Gardens and passing the entrances to Pro Player Stadium, which I still thought of as Joe Robbie Stadium, and Calder Race Course. After crossing into Broward County, I turned west at Pembroke Road to SW 86th, then north again for a few blocks until finding the hospital's visitor lot. A yellow Cessna flew overhead, its engine thrumming as it descended over the pines barely high enough to make it into North Perry Airport on the other side of State Road 817.

It felt more like I was visiting a prison than a hospital. The administration nurse's name tag said Nola Lockridge. She listened to my story and seemed a bit skeptical, but then agreed to let me visit Mrs. Tesch, who had been a patient there for as long as anyone could remember.

"I think you're going to be disappointed, Mr. Hamilton," Nurse Gay said, after Nola Lockridge turned me over to her. She led me down a plain white hallway to a set of double doors and inserted a key, which was attached to her belt by a nylon cord. "No one here has ever heard her speak a word. Whatever traumatic event caused the selective mutism, I can tell you, it has no neurological basis."

"Selective mutism?"

She turned and looked at me as she held the door open. "It's when people elect to shut themselves off from the world and withdraw into themselves. Some catastrophe in their lives has caused them to stop communicating and we can't always ascertain why."

"She doesn't have Alzheimer's, does she?"

"Not as far as we know, but with her not communicating

it's hard to tell. She gets regular medical checks including an annual EEG, which shows us her brain activity is still normal. Somewhere in the past she just stopped taking care of herself. As far as I'm aware you're only the second visitor she's ever had."

"Really?" I said, following her down another plain white hallway to a brown Formica-topped counter at the intersection of a perpendicular hallway that widened to form a work station. The two nurses sitting behind it were busy filling out paperwork.

"Opal Betz," Nurse Gay said, "visits her every Tuesday without fail. I wish I had a friend like that."

"So she's just a friend?"

"I assume. Could be her sister for all I know; they're about the same age." Nurse Gay turned to one of the nurses on the other side of the counter. "Clare, this is Mr. Hamilton. He thinks Rosa Tesch might be his mother and would like to visit with her. I told him not to expect much. Would you please show him to her room? I've got to get back to my station."

"Certainly," Nurse Clare said, and continued writing. "Just let me finish my thought."

I chuckled. How many times had I been interrupted and had a great line of dialogue or plot twist lost forever because I'd stopped writing — just for a moment. "Take your time," I said.

She had beautiful penmanship and I watched Nurse Clare's pen glide over the lined report, forming cursive characters so perfectly that I could read them from across the counter and upside down. Unfortunately, they didn't concern Rosa Marie.

I started with the questions as soon as she looked up. "How long has Mrs. Tesch been here?" I asked.

"I don't believe she's married, Mr. Hamilton," Nurse Clare said. "At least we've never referred to her as Mrs., as I recall. And I really don't know how long she's been here, but a lot longer than I have, and that will be twenty-nine years next month."

"Twenty-nine years! My word, who's been paying for all this?"

"I have no idea. All billing is handled by our accounting department."

"What about this Opal Betz who visits her every week?"

"As far as I know she's just a friend," Nurse Clare said, rising from her chair and walking around the counter. "Now, if you'll follow me, I'll take you to see Miss Tesch."

She led me down the perpendicular hallway past a dozen solid doors with small square windows. At the next intersecting hallway she turned left and walked past another three doors before stopping and pulling a key from a patch pocket on the front of her white uniform, which remained attached to her belt by a heavy nylon cord. She looked through the thick glass window as she inserted the key into the lock. "You're in luck, Mr. Hamilton. It looks like Miss Tesch is still up."

"Is all this security really necessary?" I asked as she unlocked the door.

"It's more for the patients' protection than ours," she said. "We can't have them wandering out into the street and getting hit by a car. Most of them don't have any concept of time and little or no idea of where they are. If we didn't lock their doors... well, we just have to lock them, that's all there is to it. Our violent patients are in another wing. You wouldn't be allowed in there."

Nurse Clare held the door open and I walked past her into a plain white rectangular room. It measured about 12x15 feet and had an open ceramic shower stall and toilet basin in the corner with just enough privacy from the door window for use, yet none from within the room. At the barred window on the outside wall, a slight, white-haired woman stood holding pleated mauve curtains back with one bony hand and looking out. From where I stood, a large paper-barked Melaleuca tree with spiked white flowers, similar to the red bottlebrush variety I was used to seeing in California, took up most of the view.

"You have a visitor," Nurse Clare said, walking up behind Rosa and placing a hand on her shoulder.

Rosa Tesch didn't budge.

The nurse leaned over and spoke softly into her ear. "He says he's your son."

She still didn't budge and Nurse Clare looked back at me. "Whenever she's up, she stands here looking out. It doesn't matter if it's day or night. Even when Mrs. Betz comes she just stands here, unless it's mealtime. Then she sits at the table and eats, while Mrs. Betz tells her about her week and all the fun they used to have — anything to get through. But it's never done any good." Nurse Clare shook her head. "That Betz woman has the patience of a saint. If it were me, I would have quit coming a long time ago. I don't imagine it will be too many more years before she stops coming anyway. Poor old Miss Tesch probably won't even notice. Who knows, maybe something you say will get through and snap her out of it?"

"I don't know about that. I wasn't around when she lost *it*, whatever *it* was."

"Too bad," Nurse Clare said, leaving Rosa Tesch's side and walking around the room inspecting it for I didn't know what. "If you'd like, I'll leave you two alone and you can get acquainted."

"Are you sure it will be all right?"

"Of course," she said, closing the door and locking the deadbolt.

I shuddered as the lock tumbled into place, recalling that Bobby experienced a similar fate every day when prison guards locked him in a cell much smaller than Rosa's room. The thought quickly flashed through my mind and I wondered why he wanted me to visit him without Gloria.

I stood and hyperventilated for about three minutes, then another twenty watching my mother stare out the window, wondering what she was seeing before taking a seat at the table, where I continued observing her in silence. She didn't look anything like I had imagined, but then I really didn't have any idea what to expect. The sound of a key turning in the lock finally interrupted my thoughts and an attendant dressed in pale ochre scrubs entered, carrying a covered tray.

"It's time for our lunch, Miss Tesch," he said, smiling at me as he placed it on the table and lifted the lid. "I see we have a visitor today. Someone new, I believe."

"Yes," I said, "I'm her son."

"Would you like something to drink while your mother eats? They don't make extra meals, but I do carry pitchers of coffee and water on the cart."

"Coffee would be great, thanks. Black's fine," I said, and then waited while he left the room and reentered with a small paper cup with fold-out handles. Rosa Tesch never budged until the savory aroma from the open-faced roast beef sandwich, mashed potatoes, and green beans reached her. Then she turned and studied the table, unsure, it seemed, about coming over with a stranger sitting there. Obviously more hungry than intimidated, she slowly walked across the room and seated herself in the chair across the table from me. A blank expression graced her striking face as her brown eyes darted over the food tray. Jenny might have been attractive, but Rosa must have been beautiful. She still was and carried all the aging of her 71 years like a royal mantle.

"Hello, Mother," I said as she picked up a fork, contemplating what to eat first.

Maybe it was the strange sound of my voice or maybe the familial greeting that made her look up and gape. She stared at me for the longest time with an expression of distant recognition, as if she recalled the face but not the name or where she'd seen that face.

All of a sudden, she shoved the tray off the table and screamed, "You bastard!"

THIRTY-SIX

A pang shot through my heart as the tray and its contents splattered across the floor. Rosa Marie Tesch pushed away from the table with a malevolent look and retreated to the window, where she stood staring out and muttering to herself. Almost before I realized it, Nurse Clare was standing beside the table with her hands on her hips, glaring down at me. "What's going on here, Mr. Hamilton? Do I need to call security?"

"Uh, no," I said, still shaken.

"I think you'd better leave," she said, pointing toward the door with her brow furrowed. Then suddenly she cocked her head to the side at the sound of Rosa Marie Tesch's utterances. "Is she talking?"

I nodded and stood, ready to leave. "You asked me to snap her out of it but, honestly, I didn't do anything."

"What did you say, then?"

"All I said was, 'Hello, Mother.'"

Nurse Clare pointed at the mess on the floor. "And she did that?"

I nodded. "That and she called me a, ah... a bastard."

"I want you to tell the doctor what happened. Everything, you understand?"

We left the room and Nurse Clare put in a call to the doctor's pager before requesting an orderly to clean up the food spill. I went over everything that happened with Nurse Clare in more detail it seemed than I recalled having taken place, and then went over it again when the doctor arrived. Yet neither of them could or would answer my questions. Like, how long my mother had been institutionalized and who'd had her committed. While it was obvious that she needed to be there, the doctor expressed a glimmer of hope that she just might have taken her first step toward recovery. Nevertheless, I realized, I didn't have time to wait for her to complete the journey. After all, she'd been there more than 29 years already. Who knew how many more it would take before she either could or would talk rationally? Or perhaps recall the period of her life that involved me? And I wanted answers now.

"How about this Opal Betz?" I asked, "Maybe I should talk with her. Do you have her phone number, or address?"

"Yes, but we can't give it out," the doctor said.

I scowled. "Is there some sort of doctor/patient privilege here I don't know about? Because the last I heard Mrs. Betz was just a visitor."

"She left her number for us to call if anything happened to her friend."

"Well, obviously something has. Now, I suggest that you either phone her and let her know, or give me the number and I'll do it for you."

THIRTY-SEVEN

The Haulover Shark and Tarpon Club appeared to be catering to a younger crowd than either Mrs. Betz or myself. However, she lived in North Miami Beach, "God's little waiting room" as she referred to it with a mild Yiddish accent, and suggested the cocktail lounge as a place to meet. While I waited for her to arrive I nibbled on a platter of steak tidbits and washed them down with ginger ale, just for appearance.

"Shalom, Harry," said a voice that I recognized from our earlier telephone conversation. A small but stately woman in a gray suit and white blouse with pearl necklace and matching earrings extended her gloved hand across the table. "How very nice to meet you. I'm so glad you called."

I thought it odd that she found me without having to ask, and used my first name with such apparent familiarity. "Mrs. Betz?" I asked.

She chuckled. "Someone else you are expecting?"

I shook her hand and started to stand.

"Don't get up, dear boy," she said, sliding into the padded booth across the table from me. "You said Rosa spoke with you today?"

I chugged the remainder of my ginger ale. "She called me a bastard."

Mrs. Betz laughed. "Your papa used to say that humanity could be divided into two classes: the bastards and the sons of bitches. Rosa was probably just throwing his words back at him."

My pulse jumped. "You know my father?"

"Dear boy, it's perfectly obvious. Except for his moustache you look just like him."

I gasped with anticipation. "Do you know where he is?"

She smiled and looked at her watch. "All in good time, Harry, all in good time; it's been happy hour for nearly half an hour and I haven't yet had a drink. If it weren't for the rush-hour traffic I would be well into my second martini." She removed a glove and waved it overhead at a passing server, "The usual, Armando."

He nodded. "*Si, Senora* Betz, vodka martini rocks with a twist," he said, and scurried off.

"It's a very long story, I hope you don't mind?"

"Not at all," I lied. Mrs. Betz had the answers I'd sought for the past fifteen months and traveled thousands of miles to get. Now she expected me to wait until her drink arrived? Fortunately, the service was fast.

"Bring me another, please," she said, seizing the cocktail almost before Armando's hand cleared the table. "*L'Chaim,*" she said, drank about half, and set the iconic conical-stemmed glass down. "Mmmm. I love martinis, don't you? They just relax my legs."

"I'll bet."

She sighed. "So, what is it you are asking?"

"Is my father still alive?"

She took another swallow of her martini. "I always think it's important to start at the beginning, don't you?"

I smiled and tried to keep from grinding my teeth. "Of course."

"You have no way of knowing this, dear boy, but your momma and I met in kindergarten and were best friends growing up. Although there was a short time in high school when we didn't speak after becoming infatuated with the same *boichik*, by the time we got to college it was all forgotten and so was Walter."

"Was he my father?"

"Heavens, no," she said, waving one hand and picking up her drink with the other. "Walter was a track star who ran like the wind. He used to run around the track every day after school without a shirt and Rosa and I would stop to watch him practice. Rosa dubbed him *the bronze god* and *oy* I'm telling you we couldn't take our eyes off that magnificent tan body and flashing golden hair."

She took another drink, rolled her eyes at the ceiling, and then closed them — lost in the reverie of days gone by.

"Mmmm, mmmm, mmmm."

"But he wasn't my father?"

"No..." she said, opening her eyes and looking at me as if for the first time, "just a passing fancy."

"So, tell me about my father."

"Dear boy," she said, setting the empty glass down, "you just met your momma for the first time and don't know anything about her other than her name. Him you can read about any time. I know far more about her and what I'm going to tell you, you won't find in any book."

Armando appeared and quietly set a second martini on the table along with another ginger ale, which I needed but hadn't ordered. He picked up the empty glasses and then left to get the next dispatch. At her current rate of consumption I began to worry that whatever secrets Opal Betz was about to unlock, they wouldn't be coherent much longer.

"And speaking of books, dear boy," she said, raising her glass, "Rosa always wanted to write one. In college she saw herself as the next Edith Wharton, Margaret Mitchell, or Marjorie Kinnan Rawlings. So much time she spent trying to perfect the first chapter that I doubt she ever finished the darn thing. However, she did write a lot of short stories and even submitted some to the *Saturday Evening Post* and *Atlantic Monthly*. Unfortunately, when they were rejected, she stopped writing for a long time... until way after we graduated and took our trip to Cuba, which, by the way, is where she became pregnant with you."

Well, that caught me by surprise, especially after hearing Dr. Diaz's account about arriving in this country without his parents. I recalled Rosa Tesch's incoherent and almost inaudible mumbling from beside the window and wondered if perhaps she hadn't been speaking Spanish. Although "You bastard" had certainly been clear enough.

"Cuba?" I said. "My father is Cuban?"

She took a more reasonable sip and set her drink down. "Mmmm, mmmm, mmmm. Oh my goodness, I think I'm getting ahead of myself. Did you know your momma was a beautiful woman? Strikingly beautiful and smart as a whip, too. Rosa was a little pixie with naturally curly strawberry-blonde hair, and big brown eyes that fired men's fantasies. Jenny and I were both jealous but didn't dare tell her because she never would have believed it. Oh, don't get me wrong, dear boy, she knew she was pretty from all the wolf whistles she got; however, she never really thought of herself as beautiful. But my goodness — heads would turn whenever she passed. Her porcelain-white skin sent out electric signals that men old enough to be her father quite clearly appreciated. We never could understand why she didn't date because she had all the *boichiks* asking her out."

I swallowed as another piece of the puzzle began taking shape. "You said Jenny. Did you mean Jenny Hamilton?"

She blinked and reached for the stemmed glass just as Armando returned with the third. "Will that be all, *Senora* Betz?" he asked, holding the check until she nodded and dismissed him with three $10 bills.

"Keep the change, Armando. And keep those grades up."

"*Si, senora,*" he said. "*Mucho gracias.*"

My eyes followed him as he walked away from the table. "You must come here often," I said.

She nodded and chuckled. "In 1970 my husband, Saul, paid two dollars for a lifetime membership. We've been coming here and spreading a little of the wealth ever since."

I tried to smile politely. "Just can't get a deal like that any more," I said. "Now, about Jenny; you were saying?"

Opal was still working on her second martini and I was thankful that she appeared to be slowing down. She hadn't started slurring her words yet, but I knew from experience it was only a matter of time. "Rosa and I met Jenny Oberman at Barry College, which today is Barry University and coeducational. Back then it was affiliated with the Roman Catholic Church and strictly a religious college for women. It offered degrees in education, the fine arts, and theology."

She picked up the martini and looked across the top at me. "As I said before, dear boy, Rosa wanted to be a writer. I thought I might be able to learn to teach and didn't want to lose my best friend when she went off to college, even though she wasn't actually going away. But I just knew that once she started running around with those smarter college kids she wouldn't want to have anything more to do with me. So, although I was a Protestant, I talked my parents into letting me attend. Silly, considering the way things turned out, wasn't it?"

THIRTY-EIGHT

Opal's eyes glazed over as she finished her second martini and held the empty glass in her hand. She seemed caught in the reverie a moment or two longer than the last time, as if waiting for me to answer the rhetorical question. "Anyway, on registration day when Rosa and I were wandering around the campus trying to figure out where to sign up for classes, we met Jenny, who seemed just as lost as we were. Only Jenny didn't have anyone to be lost with, so we let her be lost with us." Opal laughed. "From then on we were like a Charlie's Angels version of the Three Musketeers — *Unus pro omnibus, omnes pro uno.*"

I looked at her askance.

She smiled, waving the empty glass like an imaginary sword. "One for all, all for one... well, that is until after the first semester, when we discovered Jenny had secretly married the most handsome man either of us had ever seen."

"You mean other than Walter?"

Mrs. Betz set the glass down with a recollective smile and nodded. "As I recall, that made me extremely jealous, but it didn't seem to faze your momma. Well, maybe jealous is too strong," she said, glancing at the third martini. "Envious would be more like it. Randy Hamilton was quite a hunk, as they say these days. It was easy to see how they got together — Jenny with her lovely figure and bubbly personality. She was quite a looker — tan skin, clear blue eyes, and glossy brown hair. But nothing like your momma. Jenny was pretty, but your momma... your momma was beautiful."

I guess I'd never really thought about my adoptive father as being particularly handsome one way or the other. However, looking back through Opal's eyes, I could see that he really

181

was. And so was Jenny, though neither one of them ever photographed well.

"Jenny also wanted to teach," Opal said. "She and I wound up in quite a few classes together and became close friends. Even closer than she and Rosa, and it was only natural that just before graduation we decided to have one last fling together before entering the job market and taking off in what we feared would be separate directions. Rosa suggested we sail to Havana for a week, but Jenny didn't know if Randy would let her go."

She eyed the third martini again. "I can't believe he did and, the week after graduation, he actually drove the three of us down to Key West, where we caught the P&O Ferry. It was a marvelous trip and one of the best weeks of our lives. I don't think I ever saw Rosa as excited about anything before or since."

"Really?"

"Oh, dear boy," she said, picking it up, "I thought she was going to have kittens. When the long flat line of the Cuban coastline came into view, and the tiny round tops of the mountains began rising above the sea, she jumped up on the rail and had tears running down her cheeks. She said it was from the wind in her eyes, but I'm not so sure.

"As we entered Havana Harbor, one of the other passengers who'd been there before pointed out the top of Morro Castle, a turret above an immense stone wall of the old fortress. Jenny and I found it exhilarating and I remember that the harbor was filled with passenger boats and freightliners from all over the world. I fancied meeting a wealthy American businessman or French tourist and living happily ever after, but all Rosa wanted was the experience to write about. Jenny just came along to be with us."

Opel swirled her martini and gazed through the frosty stemmed glass. "It was as if we'd died and come to life in a different world, dear boy. We quickly forgot everything we knew in Miami because all the sights and sounds were so strange. Back then you didn't hear Spanish everywhere like you do now, so it was just so very exciting."

"I know what you mean," I said, thinking about growing up in San Diego. However, judging from what I'd seen thus far, it was nothing like Miami. Back home there were pockets of Hispanics. In Miami, the situation seemed reversed.

She took a sip and set the glass down. "I remember as we got off the ferry a hungry-looking Cuban boy with high cheekbones and hollow cheeks was wearing shoes that were cracked open. He came up to us and pointed in his basket, which was filled with pineapples, grapefruit, bananas, and mangos, saying something to us in Spanish. But Jenny told him that we didn't speak his language.

"'Ho kay. Me speak Inglish,' he said, waving the basket in front of her.

"She pointed at a pineapple. 'How much?'

"'One, five cent; two, ten cent.'

"She handed him a nickel and picked up the pineapple, probably thinking he'd then leave us alone, but he just smiled showing a mouthful of rotting teeth and pulled a brown bottle out from under the fruit. 'Want wine?'

"Now he had *my* attention. 'How much?' I asked.

"'Opal!' my friends said in unison, 'what do you think you're doing?'

"'Forty cent,' said the boy.

"'I'll give you twenty.'

"He looked scorned at the offer but quickly countered. 'You have American cigarette, no?'

"'*Si*,' I said, using the only Spanish word I knew.

"'Trade,' he said, holding up the bottle with one hand and one finger of the other. 'Wine, one pack American cigarette.'

"'Okay,' I said, reaching into my purse and handing him a pack of Pall Malls. But the little beggar didn't give me the bottle. He just scampered off with my cigarettes.

"Rosa and Jenny laughed hysterically.

"'What did you expect?' Jenny asked when they finally caught their breath. 'It's illegal to sell American cigarettes down here.'

"From Waterfront Boulevard, the rolling foothills of the mountain range we'd seen from the ferry were no longer visible. On the dock men in tattered clothes tossed baited handlines into the harbor that, as I recall, smelled to high heaven.

"Well, Rosa flagged down an old Packard convertible taxi with no top that drove us past the luxurious mansions of Embassy Row with their gorgeous gardens, then through the back streets where I can't begin to describe the poverty. It took about twenty minutes to reach the hotel and I'm sure the driver took advantage of us because we were Americans and had no idea where we were going." Opal laughed and reached for her drink again. "The next day we discovered that the Hotel Ambos Mundos where we stayed was only a block from the waterfront and that we really *had* been taken for a ride."

She smiled, musing to herself again as she took another sip. "I still remember the name of that hotel to this day. You see, it was quite an adventure for three young women in those days, exploring a foreign country without a chaperone. Well, dear boy, I tell you as we walked the shaded streets, Cubans stepped off the narrow sidewalk to let us pass. They stopped and stared as we went by single file with Rosa always in the lead. We saw many policemen and soldiers with rifles, but they didn't bother us. I think because we were Americans and not concerned with their revolution. Besides, we were also spending American dollars and spreading the wealth."

Opal set the glass down and opened her purse. She pulled out an old black and white photograph and handed it to me. "One day while we were in a café across from the *Capitolio de La Habana* drinking *cerveza* and eating Cuban bread, a street photographer took our picture. Your momma is in the middle."

I stared at the faded, dog-eared picture of three young women sitting at a sidewalk table in the shade of an enormous Banyan tree with roots growing down from its branches into the ground. All three of them were beautiful to me, but Rosa's beauty stood out like a brilliant glowing ember from the flame. Unlike the woman I'd met earlier, her eyes sparkled with mischief.

"It was Rosa's idea to go to Cuba. She was the adventurous one, as I'm sure you can tell by the photo."

I knew if I lived to be a hundred, I couldn't begin to know this woman and why she had abandoned me. Even if she fully recovered tomorrow, the years were gone — blanked out in her mind, never to be shared with me or anyone else.

"Your momma loved the big chunks of Cuban bread and bottles of Hatuey beer that came with every meal. How she could eat and drink them without gaining weight was sinful. She also loved the strong black coffee and cigars that came after, and missed being able to have them here in this country."

I looked quizzically at Opal.

"Cigars, dear boy... in the South women had a difficult enough time smoking cigarettes in public, let alone a cigar. Rosa never did smoke cigarettes, but she loved cigars and said there weren't any as good as the Cubans made. Jenny and I just took her word for it."

"Cigars?" I said.

Opal closed her eyes and chuckled. "Oh, my gosh, we had such a marvelous time... shopping in the elegant small shops and bustling big department stores." She opened her eyes and looked at me. "I remember one of them had been around since the 1800s and was filled with stuff from all over the world, which was much less expensive there than you could buy it here. We all spent more than our budgets and almost had to starve ourselves the next three days before heading home."

I looked back at the photograph as Opal took another drink.

"Your momma bought that stunning black dress and red straw hat and they made her look like a movie star. Take my word for it, dear boy, clothes mean a great deal in Cuba and I imagine that's how she caught your papa's eye."

My throat was parched and I gulped at the ginger ale without taking my eyes from the woman in the center of the photograph. Opal was still an attractive woman, the same as Jenny had been before she died. But of the three of them, it was Rosa Marie Tesch who'd aged more gracefully, probably due to the regimented institutional lifestyle, the same as with the inmates imprisoned with Bobby.

"The next day," Opal continued, "we hired a guide named Pablo who was hanging around in the lobby. We didn't have much money left but thought if he was with us the locals might not try to take advantage of us. And he did speak English fairly well. However, after we hired him he told us he was from Spain and talked like a Spaniard, not like a Cuban. For some reason he seemed proud of that, not that we could tell the difference. But we were sure the Cubans could and wondered if maybe we'd made another mistake. Even so, Pablo knew his way around Havana.

"The first place he took us was *La Bodeguita del Medio*, or as he translated for us, 'The Little Storehouse in the Middle of the Block.' If Pablo hadn't taken us there, I'm sure we never would have gone in, but he said it was where all the locals ate. It was so crowded that the three of us had to sit on swivel stools at the counter and eat our lunch off heavy clay plates that were thick as stove lids. Rosa ordered wine and a tray of oysters with limes, which we all sampled as a trio of wonderfully talented musicians strolled through the little café serenading the customers who were packed in like sardines in a can."

Opal Betz was talking slower, concentrating on every word. "I 'member every inch of the walls, counters, and tabletops were covered with layers of graffiti. It looked like every customer since the place had opened found somewhere to leave his or her mark." She tossed her head back and laughed. "An' we did, too. It was a very popular dive, which is all I can think to call it, but it turned out to be your momma's favorite place... maybe because that's where she met your papa."

I couldn't believe my ears and found myself hanging on every word waiting for the next. Opal was beginning to truncate a few, but thus far hadn't begun slurring any. Over the years she must have developed a very high tolerance for alcohol. "My papa... what was he like?" I asked, hoping she would remain sober enough to remember every detail.

"He was a big man. Husky... and you just knew from looking that he'd won several rough-and-tumble fights and 'spected a few more. He was tall with narrow hips and wide shoulders that looked even wider in the 'maculate cream-colored suit he was wearing. He had a heavy jaw and bushy black mustache, and his dark eyes spotted Rosa the moment he came into the café. I thought your poor momma was going to have a stroke when she r'cognized him."

"What do you mean, recognized him?" I asked as Opal finished her martini and continued with her story.

"Instead of hitting the oysters, your momma squeezed lime juice all over that brand new black dress and your papa just laughed. He had a confident, good-natured laugh and ordered the owner to bring her a damp towel." Opal tipped up the empty martini glass again, getting only a drop or two. She licked her lips. "Mmmm, mmmm, mmmm."

"Well?" I asked, as her mind seemed to wander away again.

She looked at me a moment, caught again in the reverie. "Well, dear boy, after lunch he 'vited us to La Vigia, which is what he called his country home in the foothills, about fifteen miles southeast of Havana. I never forgot it 'cause, after all, how many people have exotic-sounding names for their homes? Jenny and I refused to change our plans, so Rosa went by herself, and we didn't see her again until we caught the ferry for home three days later. Neither of us thought she would make it back in time. But she did.

"I 'member the harbor was covered with launches filled with tourists on sightseeing trips. Others were taking soldiers who had spent the night ashore back to their bunks in the fortress, and the ferry moved very slowly to keep from hitting them. The three of us stood on the fantail watching Havana's waterfront grow smaller and smaller until we heard a big marine Chrysler engine rumbling in the ferry's wake. Well, it turned out to be the pointed prow of your papa's boat."

She set the empty glass down and closed her eyes, as if seeing it again. "He had a big boat... big and shiny. It had a black hull and green roof with a varnished mahogany cockpit. I 'member Rosa jumped up on the railing and made a spec'acle of herself... blowing kisses when he passed between us and Morro Tower's stone wall. I 'member, too, the swell behind his boat rocked many of the smaller boats in the harbor for several minutes.

"Jenny and I stayed with Rosa as we all watched your papa turn that big, beautiful cabin cruiser north, cutting sideways into the running waves. In no time at all it was nothing more than a little black dot on the horizon. When it finally blinked out of sight... well, that's when Rosa told us that she could be pregnant.

"Of course, Jenny and I hugged her as tears streamed down her cheeks. And Jenny, the only one of us with any sexual 'sperience, told your momma that it was much too soon to tell. Unfortunately, as we later found out, Rosa's worries were well founded."

Opal Betz waved Armando back and, to my surprise, ordered a cup of black coffee. "I still have to drive home."

I tried to ignore the interruption and leaned forward, waiting to hear what happened next. It struck me strange that for someone who didn't want to read his adoptive parents' mail, I now wanted to know everything I could about my biological parents. Nothing was personal or sacred any more. "Obviously, she didn't marry him," I said, "or my birth certificate wouldn't have listed him as unknown."

"It was all very traumatic, dear boy," Opal said, daubing at her mouth with a napkin and slightly missing. "Rosa's parents tried to do what any good parents would with a daughter in trouble back then — they sent her away to have the baby and put it up for adoption. But after you were born she couldn't go through with it and came back holding you in her arms. She wanted to confront your papa, but his lawyers insisted that you be put up for adoption. Rosa fought it, but as a single mother back then she just couldn't handle it and neither could her parents."

"But Jenny and Leon? How—"

"They wanted children in the worst way, but couldn't seem to have any. Now, I don't know all the particulars 'cause your momma never told me, but I 'spect your papa handled the legal and financial arrangements. None of our families ever had that kind of money, particularly Randy and Jenny after paying for her tuition and a trip to Cuba. Nevertheless, they somehow found a way to adopt you, and I'm here to tell you that it sure eased your momma's mind. That is, until she found out that part of the 'doption agreement the Hamiltons signed had them moving away from Miami. I do recall, though, that before everything was finalized Randy went off to war and Jenny stayed behind until getting full legal custody. Then her momma took you both out to California and we eventually lost contact."

I shrugged. "Time and distance seems to have that effect on relationships." It was little consolation that Rosa didn't want to give me up; the fact was she had.

"Maybe so, but even after the letters stopped, Rosa never stopped talking 'bout you. She spent eleven years *kvetching* and waiting for your papa to leave his wife. When he finally did... well, she just fell apart."

"I don't understand."

"It's very simple, dear boy. All stories if continued far enough end in death."

It suddenly struck me. "You mean my father's dead?"

She nodded. "I'm sorry, Harry."

"When?"

"A long time ago; you were still a boy."
I swallowed hard. "How?"
"Suicide."

THIRTY-NINE

"Suicide!" The word caught in my throat. Not that I had much sympathy for the man who apparently forced my mother to put me up for adoption, but maybe he'd done it to avoid a worse fate — a compelling medical reason that I had a right to know about. "How? Why? You haven't even told me who he was and now you're telling me he committed suicide?"

Opal closed her eyes and rocked her head. "Precisely, dear boy, but if I'm to continue, another martini couldn't hurt. Would you drive me home?"

How lucid she'd be after a fourth martini I didn't know, but I couldn't let her stop then. I had to know and driving her home was little enough to ask. "Yes, certainly."

She pushed the coffee away and waved a glove in the air at Armando. "Well, shortly after Jenny took you to California, Rosa sold a 'motional story of unrequited love to the *Women's Home Companion* and spent the money on another trip to Cuba. She was so excited an' wanted to share her success with your papa, an' she took a copy of the magazine down to show him. From what I gather, he told her it was most unfortunate that she had sold the story in the first place 'cause it was shit. And because she was able to sell shit, she would keep on writing shit. It also didn't matter whether or not she ever learned to write any better 'cause readers would always 'member her by that first shitty impression."

I swallowed hard as the Muse's familiar words echoed in my mind.

"Rosa was devastated, but for some reason it didn't stop her from loving the arrogant putz. After that trip she never submitted another story. I don't really think it was 'cause she couldn't — she just wouldn't do it and give your papa the opportunity to criticize her work an' say 'I told you so.' Rosa got so hung up on finishing that darn book she started back in college that she'd lock herself away for months at a time. She literally spent years working on the first few chapters until the day after your papa committed suicide. Then she wrote him a note calling him a son of a bitch an' took an overdose of sleeping pills. When she recovered, her parents put her in that dreadful hospital and she hasn't spoken to anyone since."

I wondered how a court clerk could possibly have ever found out about my father's suicide, being that he was listed as unknown on my birth certificate. More than likely it was my mother's 37 years in a mental institution that triggered his concern. Nevertheless... "How did he kill himself?" I asked, not really wanting to know, yet fascinated with a morbid curiosity I couldn't keep in check.

"Stuck a shotgun in his mouth an' blew the back of his head off. 'Magine his poor wife waking up and finding him like that. I don't know why Rosa took it so hard, and I really don't know if that's what sent her off the deep end, but it was all we could surmise given the note. I know I should have tried to stay in touch with her after we returned from Cuba. But our lives went in different directions. I met Saul, changed my religion, and immersed myself in the Jewish community after marrying him. Then when Jenny moved to California with you and your papa criticized Rosa's story, your momma became a total recluse. So, I guess being institutionalized was just the next step in a long chain of events that should never have happened."

"The nurse said that other than you, I was the only visitor she's ever had; how come?"

"That's not zactly true, Harry, her parents and I went every day... at first. Then, after the first year when she still wasn't speaking, I started skipping days. By the end of the second year when her parents were killed in an automobile accident I had almost stopped going altogether 'til I realized she had nobody else. So I started visiting her every other day.

"Well, talking to Rosa was like talking to a fence post and it took a lot out of me, but it was something I just had to do. Saul suggested I visit her once a week and Tuesdays worked out best for me. All these years I kept hoping I might say something she'd respond to and that I'd get my friend back, but it looks like the only thing she 'sponded to was your papa's face. I guess in her mind he was a son of a bitch for killing himself and a bastard for coming back."

FORTY

Monday morning, after having the weekend to digest all that Opal told me and having a long talk with Gloria, I stopped by the florist en route to the hospital and picked up a dozen roses. My mother was staring out the window and never looked around as I entered her room, so I set the flowers on the table, took a seat, and waited. I suppose it was their perfumed scent that ultimately reached her and she glanced back, the wisp of a smile touching her lips as her eyes locked onto the brilliant red petals.

"Hello, Mother," I said, feeling terribly awkward, but her eyes never left the flowers. After several moments she turned and strode over to the table and pulled the vase towards her, closed her eyes, and inhaled their magnificent scent.

"I wish I could say something that would make you want to speak again," I said, trying to fill the silence between us. "Opal has filled in many of the blanks and I have some idea what you've been through... Lord knows I've wanted to drop out of this rat race several times myself, even tried drinking myself out of it more than once. The alcohol helped for a while; however, I didn't like myself very much when I was drunk. I think it was the being out of control more than anything that did it for me the first time. Quit cold turkey, in case you're wondering; now I think I understand where the willpower came from." I laughed softly at the irony, hoping not to wind up in a similar institution, or maybe sticking a shotgun barrel into my mouth.

She glanced up from the flowers, but only momentarily.

I tried to keep quiet and give her time to comment without pressuring her, but the words came tumbling out. "The flowers aren't much — a small token of thanks for giving me life...

I used to give Jenny roses every year on my birthday for the same reason," I said, with a somewhat bitter laugh.

Her big brown eyes sparkled and I wondered what was going on behind them as she continued to stare at the flowers.

"Actually, I should also thank you for Leon, ah... I mean Randy and Jenny. They gave me all the love and support I could ever have wanted while growing up. It just came as quite a shock after all these years that they weren't my biological parents. Anyway, I don't believe it was ever your intent to hide that fact and I don't think you could have made a better selection for adoptive parents."

She inhaled deeply and another smile curled the corners of her mouth ever so slightly.

I had to clear my throat before allowing myself to speak again. "Deep down, I'm beginning to understand that you did the best you could — under the circumstances, that is." I felt my eyes grow moist. "My only regret is not having known you... or my biological father. While I have admired his talent since I was a little boy, I guess he really was a son of a bitch. He treated you very badly, but not nearly as badly as his wife. When he pulled the trigger he gave no thought to anyone besides himself."

I blinked several times.

"Talk to me, Mother!"

Rosa sighed, having smelled the roses long enough, I suppose.

A tear spilled from my eye with the realization that that moment was the end of my search. There weren't going to be any family reunions or shocked reactions. It was time to go home and mend my own fences.

Rosa returned to the window and stood looking out. After half an hour of silently staring at her back, I left.

FORTY-ONE

My flight touched down at Lindbergh Field at 5:23 p.m. and Gloria met me as I exited the concourse into the main terminal. I wanted to hug and hold onto her, feeling as if one huge weight had been lifted off my shoulders and another added. We'd talked some, long distance, but we still had a long way to go. No way could I ever tell her about the Muse. That would be like handing my wife a portfolio of Polaroid photographs and I couldn't begin to imagine what pictures she'd find in there. Assuaging my conscience at Gloria's expense was not an option. It was just something I would have to live with, trusting in myself and believing that nothing had happened. Besides, then I'd have to tell her about getting drunk again and no way was I going to do that. On the bright side, though, I did finally have the one thing I needed that could bring me enough notoriety to get published. "We have lots to talk about, sweetheart," I said, wrapping my arms around her.

"Later," she said, kissing my cheek before taking my hand and leading the way down the terminal toward the baggage claim area. "Duke and Susan are waiting for us and they're dying to hear about your trip. I left Susan watching the oven so dinner doesn't burn. Duke is watching the news and sends his apologies for not coming because he hates the downtown traffic."

"It's not nearly as bad as where I've been."

"I'm sure he'll get some satisfaction from that."

My bag didn't make it, which was more of an irritant than inconvenience because I was returning home. I'd packed some of the notes about my parents that I'd written in the hotel after driving Opal Betz home. She'd gone through another three martinis at the Shark and Tarpon Club and was quite drunk, but then so was Saul when he answered the door and greeted her with another drink. I left them together in alcoholic bliss; however, I'll never forget Opal's unbelievable story even without the notes.

After notifying the airline about my lost luggage, which they promised to deliver after they found it, Gloria led me to our car in short-term parking and we began a frustratingly slow ride out of the airport and headed for home. Flying to San Diego from Dallas seemed faster than driving from the airport to Mission Hills during rush hour traffic and I breathed a sigh of relief as we pulled into our detached garage. The electric garage door whined closed as I followed my wife across the concrete pavers landscaping our back yard and through the French doors into the kitchen. Susan leaned one of her crutches against the sink counter and hugged me with her free arm. "I'm so happy for you, Harry," she said as I glanced over her shoulder at Gloria.

Duke stood in the doorway leading to the den. "I thought I heard you come in. I understand you had an eventful trip."

I disentangled myself from Susan's embrace and pushed past him. "I'll fill you in in a minute," I said, heading for my office and kneeling in front of the bookcase beside my desk. I scanned the dust jackets, which were shelved in alphabetical order by author's last name, and found the one I was looking for. Inside the front cover I reread the personalized autograph:

Rosa, et al.,
   The only thing I can advise you is to keep on writing, but it's a damned tough racket. Remember, it's not who you are but what you do that counts.
                              Ernest Hemingway

I stared at the muscular short sentences and bold script. Was the et al. meant to include me? Was he recognizing the fact that he and Rosa had a child together and, in his own detached way, was passing down a piece of fatherly advice? I really didn't care because I was planning on using him just as he'd used my mother. I carried the book back into the kitchen and laid it on the counter. "This is my ticket," I said.

Duke glanced at the page with a blank expression before making the connection. "No shit?" he said.

196

"Duke Taulbert!" Susan said as she bent over to open the oven door.

"It's the break I've been waiting for," I said.

"I don't believe it," he said.

"Try picturing me with a moustache."

Gloria's eyes darted across my face, the same way they had on our wedding day when the preacher said, "Do you, Gloria, take Morgan… " as if searching to find the real me beneath the skin and bones.

Susan glanced over at me as she removed a large pork roast from the oven that seemed to slip from her hands in slow motion, clatter on the oven door, turn upside down, and splatter across the kitchen floor.

Gloria was beside her in an instant. "Are you all right? You didn't burn yourself, did you?"

"Damnation!" Susan said, starting to weep. "I just ruined everybody's dinner."

"Twenty-second rule," Duke said, grabbing the hot pads from his wife's hands and flipping the tray over. He grabbed the meat with his bare hand, quickly tossed it into the pan, and lifted it back on top of the stove. "Might not have any gravy, but there's nothing wrong with the rest of it."

Gloria squinted at him with her hands on her hips. "I got your twenty-second rule."

For some reason, this struck Susan as funny and she began to laugh and cry at the same time. The next minute we were all laughing.

"Ernest Hemingway?" Duke said, still chuckling as he wiped up the au jus puddle on the floor with a handful of paper towels. "Can you prove it?"

"That's the tough part," I said. "His name doesn't appear anywhere in the adoption papers. Nor is he listed on my birth certificate. The attorney who handled my adoption is dead and his records were lost in a fire. My mother is in a mental institution and hasn't spoken to anyone in almost forty years — until calling me a bastard. And the only other woman who knows anything about the affair is a full-blown alcoholic who never actually saw them together after they left the Cuban café where they'd met. However, and for what it's worth, she did say that Rosa named me after my father's protagonist in *To Have and to Have Not*. It was her little *coup de grace,* so to speak, because she knew that although I had Hemingway's blood I would never have his name, and my mother wanted there to be a connection however tenuous."

"Let's think about this for a minute," Duke said. "If I hear you right, you want to use Hemingway's name to help you get published. Is that really going to help?"

"There's no such thing as bad publicity," I said, as Gloria and Susan took seats on our kitchen counter bar stools.

"Well, legally you can't slander the dead," Duke said, tossing the greasy brown wad of paper towels into the garbage pail beneath the sink, "but you can damn sure look pretty foolish trying to prove it. And what if his heirs sue? Defending yourself could get very expensive."

"I thought you said you couldn't slander the dead?"

"Anybody can sue anybody for anything. You piss off his relatives and they just might."

"More publicity," I said with a shrug. "And what about DNA, wouldn't that prove it?"

"Yes, but first you have to get a court order to dig him up and if you think cutting through the bureaucratic red tape to find your parents was difficult, you ain't seen nothing yet. Besides, I thought some of the stuff you've written is far better than what's out there. Wouldn't you want to know it was good enough to compete on its own merit without some cheap publicity stunt?"

"It's not a cheap publicity stunt," I said, taking offense. "He's my father!"

"Duke is right, Morgan," Gloria said. "That's how it would appear. Regardless of how well the book sold, you would always be standing in his shadow. You know how you loathe those who use celebrity status instead of talent to get published. If nothing else, think what Hemingway himself would have to say."

Duke patted me on the shoulder. "Listen to her, pal. Instead of wishing you're someone else, be happy with who you are. Who knows, maybe some of your father's writing talent was also passed along with his proclivity for alcohol abuse. I think it would be much better for you to use that talent without diluting it trying to cash in on his name."

"Barbara Bush got a seven-figure book deal writing about a dog just because she was the president's wife."

"What's your point?" Duke asked.

"Give me a seven-figure book deal because I'm the illegitimate son of Ernest Hemingway and I won't care if I ever write again."

"That's a bunch of crap and you know it, Morgan Hamilton." Gloria sounded just like Jenny as she admonished me. "You know how when you're writing time gets away from you. I think you need it more than you realize. I also think you need to start writing for yourself instead of Jenny."

I looked at Gloria like she was crazy.

"It's true. You're always writing with her approval in mind. You have a wonderful voice, Morgan. Stop trying to write like... well, like your father. And get over the notion that publication is the only proof positive your work is any good. Look at all the trash that's out there. You want to have other wannabe writers criticizing your work saying, 'The only reason Hamilton got published was because he's Hemingway's bastard son'? Please don't tell me you don't think any more of your writing than that. Go on, Morgan, tell me."

I closed the cover of *The Old Man and the Sea* and shook my head.

"One day your writing will attract an editor's attention. When it does, I don't want it to be because of some cheap publicity stunt that no one will believe anyway. So, finish your book and we'll see how you feel about it then." She stood and opened her arms. "Now, why don't I drive us all up to Café Eleven and we can have a dinner that hasn't been scraped off the floor?"

FORTY-TWO

Bobby had gained ten or fifteen pounds since entering the prison system and it was all muscle. His shoulders were broader and his waist slimmer as he sauntered into the visiting area the following weekend. I really didn't want to be there, but Gloria had insisted. I stood to shake his hand and my palm felt sweaty as he grabbed my right hand in a vise-like grip and firmly squeezed my shoulder with his left.

"Hello, Dad," he said. "I'm glad you came."

I relaxed my non-competitive grip. "Your mom would have liked to come."

He let go of my hand but not my shoulder as he looked me squarely in the eyes. "I know, but I told her I needed to have a *de hombre a hombre* conversation with you."

I stepped away from him and sat back down. "You mean, *mano e mano*?"

He chuckled and took a seat across the table from me. "No. That would mean 'from hand to hand.' This isn't a competition where we're trying to outdo one another. I said what I meant."

"So, you've taken up Spanish?"

"Among other things, but that's not why I wanted to see you."

"And not your mother?"

He pursed his lips and shook his head. "I couldn't deal with the emotions she would have brought to the chat. Of course, I didn't tell her that."

"Of course," I said, glancing at the row of vending machines against the far wall. "You want to get something to eat?"

"Maybe later; I don't want to get sidetracked. I've been

talking to Mr. Taulbert and—"

"What do you mean, you've been talking to Duke?" I interrupted.

"Will you let me finish?"

"What's to talk about? You're here, aren't you?"

"Attorney/client privilege, Dad."

"If I'm paying for it, that would make me the client."

"Chill, Dad, he's doing it pro bono."

"Doing what pro bono? He never mentioned—"

"I asked him not to," he interrupted, "until I had a chance to talk with you. He agreed."

"Agreed to what?" I asked, standing abruptly and cramming my hands into my pockets.

"What I need to discuss with you."

"Discuss what?"

"The plea deal he's worked out for me. I wanted to discuss it with you before I signed it."

"What are you talking about? Does it get you out of here any sooner?"

"It has nothing to do with my sentence here, Dad. It has to do with, ah..." he cleared his throat and wiped the corners of his eyes on his shirtsleeves, "with me taking responsibility for Gran's death. Mr. Taulbert has worked out a plea deal for me in Arizona."

✖ ✖

For the next several months I kept my nose clean at Nordy's and worked at finishing the book I'd come to call *Precious Gifts*. I couldn't believe Gloria was encouraging me to write, considering how much we'd bickered over it in the past. But who was I to argue. Perhaps now she secretly believed that I had inherited my father's writing genes. Nevertheless, we worked out a schedule amenable to us both that included visits to Bobby once a month, a date night once a week, and quality time together in addition to grocery shopping Thursday evenings.

Writing became much more enjoyable in the sense that Jenny no longer looked over my shoulder as I wrote from the heart. Nevertheless, the closer I came to the end, the more nothing seemed to fit. At one point the Herculean effort it was taking to pull the story line together seemed more work than it was worth. Writing at that point was 10 percent inspiration and 90 percent perspiration. And to be honest, at times all I wanted to do was let the world in on my secret, sell the manuscript, and quit. However, with the exception of drinking, quitting was something I'd never been able to do. Even when reading a bad book I had to persevere to the end. I felt I owed the author at least that much, knowing all the hard work he or she had put into it.

I sent Rosa flowers every month and Nurse Clare would return thank-you notes, briefly describing how they made my mother smile. Red roses brought the biggest smiles, but she hadn't spoken again.

Then suddenly one day the book righted itself and I finished it without another hitch. I gave it to Gloria to read and edit while I drove up to San Luis Obispo to visit Bobby all by myself again. As we sat in the outside yard and gazed through the dual thirty-foot chain-link fences topped with razor wire, I asked him what he'd written lately.

He laughed. "What do you know about poetry, Dad?"

"Not much, but I liked the last one you sent me. Have you ever gotten it into the form you wanted?"

"Haiku, Dad. And, no, I haven't."

"Well, I suppose you have time," I said, immediately regretting my choice of words.

He snorted. "Yeah!"

"Look. I'm sorry," I said, trying to make an excuse. "After Jenny died and before my trip to Florida, I really struggled with... well, I just really struggled. I guess time passes about the same for us all: too slow when we're young, and too fast as we age. But finding my biological mother in an insane asylum and learning that my biological father committed suicide didn't help get my head on straight, either."

"It's okay, Dad."

"I suppose," I said, suddenly feeling more like the child than the parent. "But I really did like your poem about peace and flowers. It triggered some fond memories."

"About?"

I smiled. "A few youthful indiscretions you don't need to hear about."

"Aw, come on, Dad."

"I'll tell you this, though. I never had to make that trip to Florida, or anywhere else, for that matter. Duke told me from the beginning he didn't care who my parents were. They could have been Jacqueline and Aristotle Onassis, but it wouldn't change who I was. I was still his friend because we'd built a relationship based on performance, not pedigrees."

"So why are you telling me all this?"

"I guess I'm trying to, ah, um… well, apologize for my shortcomings as a father."

"Nobody's perfect," Bobby said with a wry smile. "And while you may not be Grandma Jen's son, you're still my dad."

I nodded. There was nothing I could do to change the past and Bobby wouldn't be in prison forever. After finishing his sentence here, he'd be transferred to the Lewis Corrections Department in Buckeye, Arizona where he'd serve between ten and 22 years for the second-degree murder charge of accidently killing his grandmother. He'd been drunk out of his mind looking for money to pay for his next drug fix when he'd broken into her townhouse. Unfortunately, she'd come home and caught him stealing her jewelry and he'd shoved her trying to get away.

He could have gotten a death sentence or even life without parole if Duke hadn't worked the plea deal with Detective Meadows and the Sedona City attorney. I was upset with my friend for not clueing me in, but extremely proud of Bobby for calling him to do the right thing. My son realized that he would have to serve at least 85 percent of the minimum sentence requirement if he kept his nose clean, and possibly a lot more if he didn't. But he wanted to take responsibility for what he'd done and have a fresh start without having to look over his shoulder the rest of his life.

"I'd really like it if you would send me your poems," I said, feeling more comfortable with my son than I had in the past few years and looking forward to future *de hombre a hombre* conversations with him. Besides, the drive to Buckeye won't be much farther than it is to San Luis Obispo. "I promise I'll learn the difference between a haiku and a sonnet."

He laughed and it actually sounded cheerful. "That's a no-brainer, Dad. Tell me the difference between a tanka and a haiku and I'll think you mean business."

"I will!" I said, tousling his hair.

He ducked away and threw a pulled punch that tapped me lightly on the jaw. "Or check out Ezra Pound's *Fan-Piece, for Her Imperial Lord*, and tell me what you think."

I flinched backward, knowing I could have never blocked it. "He's a little radical for me," I said, realizing my son had become a man and taken responsibility for his actions, "as is Allen Ginsberg. But Shelley, Byron, and Whitman don't do anything for me, either. However, that little poem of yours said something to me, Bobby. I could understand it and, as I said, it struck a chord. Which I suppose is the essence of poetry — how it makes you feel."

He jammed his hands in his pockets and kicked his foot against the ground as he looked nervously around at the guards. "There's hope for you yet, Dad," he said with a smile, apparently relieved they either hadn't seen, or had interpreted the punch as nonaggressive. "I promise I'll work on it this week."

I drove home feeling good about our visit and better about myself than I had in a long time. It was a five- to six-hour drive depending on traffic and I had plenty of time to think. I realized there was nothing I could do or say that would make Bobby's life any easier, or Barbara quit drinking. My son had to serve his sentences; I couldn't do it for him. And my sister had to find her own personal bottom just as I had. Most people couldn't just quit; they needed help. Although Mom would have hated seeing Bobby in prison and Barbara inebriated, I'm sure she wouldn't have been as judgmental. Nevertheless, I loved them all. En route I also thought about writing that compelling memoir with definite marketability and even fictionalizing it, but decided against it. My writing would have to stand on its own merits finding a traditional publisher, because, for me, there was no validation in self-publication.

It was well after midnight when I arrived home. Nevertheless, I went straight to the mantel, wound the old family clock, and set the time before going to my office. I began typing a template for upcoming query letters to editors and agents about my recently finished novel, *Precious Gifts*.

Date

Editor/Literary Agent

c/o Publisher/Agency
Street Address
City, State & Zip code

Dear Mr./Ms. Last Name:
She gave him her kidney; he took her life.
They sent her eyes to a secretary in San Diego, her pancreas to a convict in Atlanta, her liver to a fighter pilot in Norfolk, and her heart to an Olympian in Milwaukee. She healed the shattered lives of five strangers and brought them to Memphis for a ten million dollar payoff on the anniversary of her death. Not everyone walked away.
"Precious Gifts" unites the recipients of a donor's organs in retribution against the man who murdered her.
Today's headlines are filled with stories of organ donors and transplant recipients. Peter Jennings, Dan Rather, and Tom Brokaw have all run health and human-interest stories about the tragedies of lives cut short and the miracles of life passed on. Transplant surgery has gained national attention along with black-marketing organs, but fiction on the subject is scarce. "Precious Gifts" is contemporary commercial fiction snatched from the headlines with an impelling twist. Complete at 100,000 words, I believe it will have a strong appeal to women. May I send you the manuscript?
Thank you for your time.

Sincerely,
H. Morgan Hamilton

Then as an afterthought I quickly typed another letter to Dr. Diaz thanking him for helping me to find my roots and apologizing for taking so long in getting back to him. Without giving the precise details, I told him how ironic it was that they'd led to a little storehouse in the middle of the block of his hometown. But nowhere in either letter did I mention the new family secret. I was grateful for being Harry Morgan Hamilton: husband, father, department store manager, student, son, and writer. Then, as I was sealing the envelope, the old mantel clock chimed.

As I listened to the nostalgic peals, I realized that the initial sadness of losing Mom, and subsequent anger with her for not telling me I'd been adopted, had been replaced with a joyful peace that she'd made me a part of her life. I'd forgiven her and Dad, forgiven Rosa and Papa, and forgiven Bobby, which was surprisingly easier than accepting what he'd done. And I was extremely proud of the way he'd taken responsibility. I'd also forgiven Debby for not telling us about her brother's heroin habit, forgiven Barbara's alcoholism, and also forgiven myself for too many things to numerate. I said a prayer of thanks for having Gloria in my life, which was moving forward again, and knew that there were no shortcuts to success whether in writing or family relationships.

The End

ACKNOWLDEGEMENTS

Sometimes authors can write for years before getting published which, in my case, is exactly what happened before Dingbat Publishing picked up my Chip Hale mystery series. And no matter how fast I write now, I just can't keep up with my readers. One actually posted a review on Amazon the very day *Cinderella Evidence* was released.

So, it is with a great deal of gratitude that I thank my publisher, Gunnar Grey, for giving me time to finish *Champagne Wishes and Caviar Nightmares*, the next exciting Chip Hale mystery, by publishing *The Little Storehouse in the Middle of the Block* and for her dynamite cover design. Hopefully, you will enjoy reading it as much as I enjoyed writing it.

The feedback from my life partner, Cora; my mentor, Don Donaldson; and close friends Steve Wilhoit, Cheryl Ried, Bill Rutledge, Michele Hanson, and Gunnar herself, has been instrumental in getting it into its present shape. Any mistakes you may find are purely my own.

If you've enjoyed this little fictional memoir please leave a review, and tell your family and friends. I appreciate each review, whether you bought it, borrowed it, or checked it out from the library. At this point in my life, good reviews are more precious to me than royalties. So, thank you for your support.

Bruce Rolfe
Anacortes 2024

ALSO BY BRUCE ROLFE

THE CHIP HALE MYSTERIES
Cold Case in the Hot Desert
Trademark of Murder
White Collar Crime, Blue Collar Justice
Cinderella Evidence

OTHER WORKS
Noël Noir (stage play co-authored with Billy Hendrix)
The Little Storehouse in the Middle of the Block

MEET CHIP HALE,

a blue-collar working stiff who's hard as a titanium pop-rivet, a Purple Heart recipient from a war he has tried to forget.

Cold Case in the Hot Desert

originally published as Tools of the Trade, a Chip Hale Handyman Mystery

When the remains of Chip Hale's daughter are uprooted by a summer storm nine years after she went missing, he vows to find her killer. Cold case detectives from The Biggest Little City in the World have investigated her disappearance without success. But when another young woman goes missing, it becomes too much for the blue-collar handyman to handle by himself.

Hard as a titanium pop-rivet, except when it comes to raising his two tech-savvy, wise-cracking teenage granddaughters, Chip relies on the girls' computer skills and his coworkers' military and law enforcement backgrounds when looking for the dirtbag who murdered his daughter. Meanwhile the clock is ticking as his vigilante team risks everything by taking the law into their own hands. But will their old-school sleuthing tools of the trade be enough?

Trademark of Murder

Life is good for handyman Chip Hale until he begins working on a house where the owner died from carbon monoxide poisoning. He soon learns that there have been an above average number of similar deaths in the Reno area and as he investigates, life becomes more complicated. His youngest granddaughter is arrested after being expelled from school, the Handyman Inc. office is destroyed by fire, and one of his colleagues winds up murdered.

Chip's primary concern is for his seventeen-year-old granddaughter and keeping her from going to prison as criminal charges against her escalate from simple assault to first-degree murder. But as the clues to a possible murder conspiracy become more apparent and the police refuse to investigate, Chip and his coworkers once again have to break the law to bring the killers to justice.

White-Collar Crime, Blue-Collar Justice

New title, new look, same great story as found before in Trade Secrets

They say Gitmo is lovely…

After finding and spending a scorched fifty-dollar bill, Chip is arrested by the Secret Service and charged with violating the Patriot Act. Unfortunately, when an anonymous benefactor posts his five million dollar bail, there are strings attached. Chip and his co-workers must find his benefactor's missing son and uncover enough evidence to keep Chip from being sent to Guantanamo Bay for the rest of his life.

Cinderella Evidence

More skeletons in the closet than shoes...

Is Chip's nemesis, Stanford Quick, even in the country let alone Reno, looking for revenge? After a woman he worked for is murdered, and another two women he knows go missing, Chip, his granddaughters, and his coworkers struggle with an increasingly perplexing case that reminds him of hunting for his daughter's killer. What secrets do the dead and missing women harbor that could possibly link them together? As those secrets unfold and he begins to connect the dots, it becomes a race against time to keep a grisly history from repeating itself.

"This one cooks on all burners... engrossing plot, meticulous character deployment, perfect pace, and clever prose... a literary feast." Don Donaldson *author of the Andy Broussard/Kit Franklyn forensic mysteries.*

PRAISE FOR
THE CHIP HALE NOVELS

"Some mystery writers endow their hero with almost supernatural intuitive powers. In the Chip Hale Mysteries, Chip is a down to earth, working man who employs his native intelligence, true grit, deductive reasoning, and some "brothers-in-arms" connections to solve mysteries in Reno, Nevada. Bruce Rolfe has created a character grounded in reality who can not only solve mysteries which baffle the authorities but can also fix your back deck!"
John Brierley, Publisher
Fidalgo Living Magazine

WHITE-COLLAR CRIME, BLUE-COLLAR JUSTICE
(originally published as Trade Secrets)
"Another outstanding entry in a splendid new series."
D. J. Donaldson, author of the Andy Broussard & Kit
Franklyn forensic mysteries.

TRADEMARK OF MURDER
"A Reno thriller with a courtroom finale. Chip knows how to swing a hammer—and a shotgun."
William Dietrich, author of the Ethan Gage series of historical thrillers.

COLD CASE IN THE HOT DESERT
(originally published as Tools of the Trade)
An Amazon best seller
"If you like reading Harlan Coben you'll love this book."
Kathleen Kaska, author of the Sydney Lockhart mysteries.

Thanks for reading! Dingbat Publishing strives to bring you quality entertainment that doesn't take itself too seriously. I mean honestly, with a name like that, our books have to be good or we're going to be laughed at. Or maybe both.

If you enjoyed this book, the best thing you can do is buy a million more copies and give them to all your friends... erm, leave a review on the readers' website of your preference. All authors love feedback and we take reviews from readers like you seriously.

Oh, and c'mon over to our website:

www.DingbatPublishing.ninja

Who knows what other books you'll find there?

Cheers,

Gunnar Grey,

publisher, author, and Chief Dingbat

δ

Made in the USA
Columbia, SC
11 July 2024

38221258R00131